CODE 47
to
BREV FORCE

QuizMaster · MixMatcher

F.Barish-Stern

Code 47 to BREV Force

By

F. Barish-Stern

Published by Golden Quill Press Troutville, VA
a division of Barish-Stern Ltd.

Copyright © 2018

F. Barish-Stern

Interior Design Golden Quill Press
Editing- Bobbi Madry & Kenneth Bray

DEDICATION

Thanks to Bobbi Madry my mentor, editor and friend, without you BREV would still be in a drawer.

To my husband, who lived this book with me for eight years, plus, plus …and helped me every step of the way, this book wouldn't be what it is without your advice and suggestions.

For my sons who didn't want to read – thirty years later this one's for you.

QUIZMASTER and MIXMATCHER

PROLOGUE

"Frederick, where were you the last few days? I needed to reach you and…?"

"I had some things I needed to take care of, Ori, nothing for you to be concerned about."

"Where were you?" his brother demanded.

Frederick turned toward his brother and for the first time in his life raised his voice, "I told you it was nothing. I have a right to my own life! Whenever you call I am here. Did you just want to cross examine me, or do you need me for something?"

Ori was shocked at his brother's tone but did not have the time to pursue the issue. I have to go out of town in a few weeks and we need to prepare this facility for my absence."

"How long will you be gone?"

"I am not sure yet but the jackals are starting to breathe down my neck, so I have to stay one step ahead of them!"

"What if they catch you?"

"They will never catch me…those fools! They all think they are better than I am; greater than I am but they are just children. I am the teacher and now I am the father!"

Frederick was becoming concerned for his brother's state of mind. Looking toward the other room he asked, "And what about him?"

In a quiet voice, he responded, "I am so close...I know I can break him...and when I get his information," he rubbed his hands together and smiled, "oh, Frederick, what a glorious day! They will all bow down to me and I will finally be acknowledged as the greatest scientist that ever lived!"

"Ori," his brother pleaded, "what if he won't talk? What if you kill him trying to get his answers?

"He will talk..., he has to...it is my destiny!"

The BREV Force then turned their attention back to Controller who was alerted that the chemicals hadn't had the desired effect. Controller re-activated Cracko. The hologram headed toward the computer banks. Sheila got new instructions and went into action. She threw off the mask and took two hypodermics that were filled with a sleep-inducing drug, out of her bag. Unbeknownst to her the hypos were actually filled with the deadly, mind disintegrating drug, called Xnoophine. Sheila walked toward Cracko with one of the lethal hypos and then turned the hypo toward Dove. The look on Sheila's face was one of extreme pleasure.

Dove saw her approaching with the hypodermic and easily knocked it from Sheila's hand. Believing she had outsmarted Dove, Sheila reached for the second hypo but Dove was faster and grabbed Sheila's arm. They didn't struggle for long when the hypo went flying through the air. Sheila tried to get loose but Dove held her arm firm.

Raven was still trying to sever the ties to Controller when Brian saw the path of the hypo; it was headed straight for Raven. Brian alerted him, "Get out of the way!"

Raven dove to the side of the console, which left Cracko in the weapon's direct trajectory. When the hypodermic hit the hologram, it smashed on the floor and the Xnoophine flowed into Cracko. The drug merged with the electricity in its body and caused an immediate shorting out. The hologram's blood curdling screams pierced the air as its body parts disintegrated.

The students coming out of their mind trance state were able to resume breathing normally. They were groggy but due to the efforts of The BREV Force, the students did not have sufficient exposure to the drug to have the desired effect. They cheered the actions of The BREV Force.

Cracko was definitely gone but a raving Sheila stood alone ready to continue the battle with The BREV Force. She directed her anger especially at Dove, who still held her. "I'll destroy you, you, you! Controller and I are unbeatable! How dare you challenge him? Controller Controlle...Contro...," her voice diminished to a whine as Sheila realized Controller wasn't coming to her rescue; she was all on her own.

The BREV Force looked over the students to make sure everyone was all right. To everyone's amazement, Mr. Stonehouse had returned to the room with the Dean and some security guards. He explained that during the ruckus, he had regained consciousness and was able to crawl out of the room, unnoticed, to go for help.

As Mr. Stonehouse gathered the students, in the front of the room, Brian used the opportunity to slip away. Raven and Dove remained in the classroom with the security guards and tried to provide them with the facts of what had occurred. They also handed Sheila over with her bag, which was still filled with candy and some other types of chemical bombs and hypo's. Security handcuffed her and escorted out of the room.

Dean Farrell thanked The BREV Force and asked Mr. Stonehouse to take his class to the infirmary, where they could all get checked out. Dove waited for the class to start out, then changed back to Evie and fell in line with the others.

Brian watched from a safe distance until the last student left the classroom and then doubled back to help Raven who once again became Brad. He locked the door behind Brian and shouted, "We did it! We destroyed Controller!"

"I don't agree," Brian replied. "I believe we only did away with the holographic messenger, not Controller itself. However, why should we guess? Let us see if Controller will respond?"

Brad disconnected the shattered monitor and after setting up a new one, keyed in a message to Controller, "We Beat You!"

The screen began flashing thunderous screams in response: "CONTROLLER CANNOT BE BEATEN. BE WARNED. SOON THERE WILL BE ANOTHER HOLOGRAM TO TAKE CRACKO'S PLACE, ONE EVEN MORE DANGEROUS!!! THIS TIME YOU WILL BE DESTROYED! DESTROYED! DESTROYED!"

As the message faded from the screen The BREV Force knew there would surely be a next encounter with Controller.

CHAPTER 1

After the successful destruction of the hologram Cracko, the Kane family used their time to prepare for their next encounter with Controller. Not knowing how long it would be, they also used the time to try to get back to some type of normalcy.

Martin and Vivian were working solely on the formula they believed would put an end to Controller's threat. Martin used the data he'd gotten from the stranger in the high school parking lot, about how Controller was created but even with that edge, there were still missing pieces that needed to be found.

Brad and Evie spent more time studying, working and being with friends. Brian, on the other hand, did not have a former life, so he had nothing to return to. Whenever the twins tried to get him involved in "normal" teenage stuff, he declined, insisting, he wanted to spend his time gathering as much data as possible about Controller. He worked in the lab at home, scanning computer files and trying to find the keys to Controller's existence.

Brian still believed Brad had the right idea when he tried to create the Controller simulation. The program he created on his laptop, using their parent's cloning research was brilliant. It was unfortunate that Brad's mind meld with the simulation, went terribly wrong. Brian had been studying the idea and concluded, If I can create the perfect environment for Controller, I might be able to lure the virus in and integrate its system at the source. Brian also spent enormous amounts of time researching the molecular structures of inanimate objects and their relationships to humans. He believed this concept would prove useful in their battle against Controller.

"Rosie," he interfaced.

"Yes, my son, how can I help you?"

"Please examine the following hypothesis, analyze and report. Can a molecular structure, such as mine, be manipulated to match an object, molecule for molecule, such as a table? And, what would be the limitations and safety procedures required. Also, can the same procedure be used to break down the essence of thought patterns to move through the computer circuits?"

Rosie's response was almost immediate. "Theoretically, it is possible but, if that person is you, it is more than possible. Based on your exceptional abilities, I believe you could have a ninety-three point four-three... percent success rate, however, the one point five-seven percent factor, involves considerable safety issues. As I do not have any further data, and, as you are so dear to me, I would advise against any further speculation until more information is available."

"Thanks Rosie."

"Brian Vincent, I sincerely hope that answer means you will abide by my directive."

"I derive from your response, at least for the moment, that you have given me an order, so yes, I will keep you informed."

Brian heeded her warning and went about gathering as much additional data as he could. The amount of research required was overwhelming and exhausting. When he needed a break to get his thoughts together, he would first be sure he was alone in the house and then sit down at the piano to play; he never told anyone. This particular morning, he stayed in the lab since Evie was still home.

Evie didn't have classes until late in the afternoon and wasn't scheduled to work that day. For her, it was a lazy morning. Brad had already left for school and Brian was in the lab, so after breakfast she went up to her room and logged onto the net.

Evie started to search her favorite holo-modeling sites. After logging onto one of the news pages she found an ad that mesmerized her: "MODELS WANTED FOR NATIONAL AD CAMPAIGN, NO EXPERIENCE NECESSARY," the graphics filled her room, floating all around her were young, slender, long haired girls. The flashing banner read: "If this is you—we want to offer you the opportunity of a lifetime."

Evie was sure the casting would be out of Los Angeles, or New York. She couldn't believe her eyes when she scrolled down the list of audition sites and found Island Falls. Her heart really started to pound when she saw the scheduled times for that day were from 12:00 P.M. – 6:00 P.M. There was no number to call; just an address. Evie scanned the list of requirements: Digital Headshots: submitted by 11:00.

"Shit, it's eleven-fifteen. She started to panic until she saw the site clock generate a statement," Time has expired for headshot submissions. If you wish to continue with the audition process, remove all security barriers and data blockers from your computer."

Evie anxiously, did so.

A computer scan was in progress and as soon as it finished she was alerted, "Evie Kane, please sit very still for the next phase of the audition process." Lights flashed from her computer and then an h-mail was delivered. "We have now completed your headshots. You have passed the first phase of the audition. If you wish to continue, attend the audition at a location near you, please bring three on-site outfit changes: casual, formal and swimsuit."

Evie quickly gathered the outfits she needed; fixed her hair and make-up and ran out the door.

Martin and Vivian worked diligently trying to find the key to neutralizing Controller. After their children's battle with Controller and Cracko, it became even more imperative to find a permanent solution. They experimented with different chemical and plant combinations as they raced against the day their children would ultimately face Controller, again.

For the most part, Dr. Schmidt had left them to work on their own, as he was still finishing up some important work at the Institute but, he did make sure to touch base with them every day. Both Martin and Vivian knew Dr. Schmidt well enough to know he was less than pleased with their progress.

Martin also wanted to find ways to speed up their work and finally decided to try a new plant that they'd never worked with before. He went to the hothouse behind the Cottage, to retrieve the sample. The nursery was now full of plants they'd requested the I.A.S. to specially ship in from different parts of South America. Martin and Vivian had replanted many of the samples with a new soil mixture they had created in hopes of finding the right mix. Martin snipped the top part of a leaf and watched as the liquid flowed from the opening. He collected it on a slide to take back to the lab, for analysis. He also took some cuttings and put them in a special bag he designed that had a wet mesh lining filled with the life-generating soil.

When Martin finished in the hothouse he picked up the slide and cuttings' bag and headed back to the lab.

When he walked in, Vivian was seated at her station, cross-checking the previous day's records against their hand-written notes. As he approached her, he marveled at how her hair sparkled from the artificial light source he'd created. She looked so beautiful but before he could tell her so, the security alarm sounded.

"Dr. Kane, sorry to bother you but there's a gentleman here who says he's, 'Dr. Schmidt,' but he doesn't have his 'oneness' I.D. card," Captain Edderly signaled from the security post. "Please turn on your scanning camera and verify his physical identity, while we wait for his fingerprints and retina scan to be processed."

Martin and Vivian turned to each other in astonishment. They'd spoken with Schmidt just yesterday and he never mentioned coming to Island Falls. Before Martin could respond Rosie had turned on the camera and directed the scanner towards the guard house. The figure on the screen appeared to be Dr. Gregore Schmidt. "Do you have positive verification yet?" Martin asked Jack.

"Dr. Kane, the satellite connections are slow today, requests must be heavy. It may take a few minutes to get verification. As soon as the clearance check is complete, I'll contact you back, Edderly out!"

Martin walked over to where Vivian was seated. He touched the back of her neck to ease her tension and fears. "He's old Viv. He probably just forgot to let us know he was coming. Don't worry. I'll handle him."

She reached for her husband's hand and turned to look up at him. "I know you'll handle him but I also know you're not as okay with all this, as you pretend."

"You know me so well," he said, smiling as he put his arms around her. "I'm just concerned that Schmidt will find out too much about things we don't want anyone to know, namely Brian and the twins. I'm sure there's nothing here, in the Cottage, that could be a problem but, if he wants to come home with us..., I'm just trying to figure out a plan. We'll need time to set that up, if it's necessary."

Vivian thought for a moment, then had an idea. "Martin, while we're waiting for the clearance, why don't you go through our samples and make sure there really is nothing here that doesn't correspond to the computer data! In the meantime, I'll call Brian and let him know our concerns about Dr. Schmidt coming to the house. If Schmidt wants to come home with us, I'll just have an attack of morning sickness and go home first."

"Good idea! You call Brian and I'll check everything here."

Vivian pressed the intercom to connect with the house. "Brian, it's me, engage the intercom."

Within a few seconds, he responded.

"Hi." She made a bit of small talk and then explained. "We may have a visitor this evening, Dr. Schmidt, the scientist from California you've heard so much about."

Brian realized he knew more about Dr. Schmidt than even he thought; memories from a long time ago, a time before the twins. He wondered how that could be possible but he let it go as he continued to listen to his mother.

"Since Dr. Schmidt just arrived, unannounced, he may want to come home with us to see your brother and sister."

"Do not worry about me. If he does come to the house, I will stay in the lab, or my room and only use the back stairs, until he leaves. Should I tell Evie and Brad when they come home?"

Vivian listened to her son's unemotional logic and realized how much she hated having to exclude him but there was no choice. "If Dr. Schmidt is coming to the house, I will bring your dinner to you and we can spend some time talking, before he arrives."

"Mom, thank you but I can take care of my dinner but I would enjoy the opportunity to talk!"

Vivian smiled at his consideration and told him she'd call before leaving. She closed the connection just as Martin came back into the room. "What did you find?"

"So far, all the plant samples correspond to the computer records. Anything we might not want him to see has been segregated to our personal files."

Schmidt's sudden arrival reassured Martin that it was a good thing to keep a separate log of their work. He now put into the computer only what would be safe for anyone else to see. "I just have these few to finish."

"Let me help you," Vivian said, as she examined one of the samples. "Martin," she called out, "Come look at this sample. Not only doesn't it match any of the data, the accelerated growth is beyond anything we'd originally anticipated."

Martin was astonished by what he was seeing. "We better put this sample away before Schmidt gets here. Just to be on the safe side, have Rosie purge any record of the sample in the computer."

"Rosie and I can handle the files, you better find somewhere to hide it where no one would look. We can't take any chances, especially until we have some idea of what has occurred."

"I agree. After Dr. Schmidt leaves, we can try and figure out what happened."

"Rosie," Vivian called out.

"Yes, Mrs. Dr. K."

"Correlate all files with the data currently on my screen and segregate it to the home computers. Restrict access to Martin or myself.

After a few moments, the files on Vivian's screen flashed and disappeared. "Mission accomplished, as per your instructions, access home file under directory, 'private family pictures' for your eyes only."

"Thanks Rosie, what's the status on Dr. Schmidt's clearance?"

"All verifications are now being sent to Captain Edderly's station. Dr. Schmidt has level one clearance."

Unable to find a reason to keep Schmidt waiting any longer, Vivian told Jack to escort Schmidt to the Cottage.

Martin scrambled around anxiously for a place to hide the sample.

Vivian got nervous and began to feel nauseous. She went into the bathroom and a few minutes later she shouted, "Come quick."

Worried something happened to her, he ran. "Viv, are you all right?"

"Oh yes, a little nauseous but basically fine. I think I've found the perfect place to hide that sample." Vivian pointed to the eco-bidet water reservoir, "What do you think?"

"You're a genius," Martin said as he kissed her forehead. "It's perfect. The cold circulating water will keep the sample cool enough to remain unchanged and who would go looking in an eco-bidet water reservoir."

He took the sample plant and carefully draped the greenish-blue leaves in the same protective wrapper he'd created for the cuttings bag. Then he folded the wet wrappings around the leaves and put them in an air tight container.

As he did, Martin noticed how the colors had drastically changed; as had the texture and size. The leaves no longer resembled the original cuttings. It was as if they had adapted to their new environment and developed accordingly. He sealed the container; floated it in the eco-bidet's reservoir and tightly secured the maintenance access lid.

Martin instructed Rosie to key in the code to unlock the front door while he and Vivian went upstairs.

Dr. Schmidt's rental car approached as Martin and Vivian stepped out onto the front porch. They couldn't believe what they saw as Schmidt got out of the car. It had only been a little more than a year, since they'd worked together in California. As Schmidt came closer, Martin and Vivian looked at each other; shocked at how much the man had aged.

Martin never knew Schmidt's exact age but when they first started working together, the doctor had already been with the Institute for at least twenty years; that was more than twenty-five years ago. They estimated Dr. Schmidt to be in his late sixties but today he looked much, much older. His hair, what there was left of it, had become grayer and thinner. Schmidt now walked hunched over, instead of straight and tall as Martin remembered him. He looked like he was carrying the weight of the world on his back. Watching Schmidt traverse the few steps to the Cottage, they stared at each other in disbelief.

Gregore Schmidt held tightly onto the railing and looked down to watch his every step. He finally got to the landing and stopped. He steadied himself, looked up and opened his arms. Vivian went to him and gave him a long hug and a kiss on the cheek, to match the kiss he placed on her forehead. "How wonderful you look, my dear," he grinned, as they went inside. "Pregnancy agrees with you now, even more than, when you were expecting the twins. She smiled and thanked him.

Martin smiled and followed behind to his office.

"Martin! My boy!" was the excited greetings as Schmidt reached out his hand, "How are you?"

Martin was about to answer when he was pulled into the doctor's warm embrace. He was totally dumbfounded. In all their years together, at the Institute, Martin had never received more than a polite handshake. It took Martin a moment to compose himself before replying, "I'm fine, Dr. Schmidt, just fine, er, thank you."

Vivian noticed Martin's discomfort and led Schmidt to a chair in Martin's office. She took his coat, while Martin pulled the rocker out of the corner for her. He steadied it with his foot and helped her slowly sit down. Martin then walked back to his desk and sat down facing Dr. Schmidt.

Not being able to wait another moment, Martin asked, "Dr. Schmidt, why are you here? I understood you were going to call first and advise us when you would be coming!"

Vivian gave Martin a hard look hoping he would have broached the subject a little more diplomatically. She realized she hadn't offered Dr. Schmidt anything and asked, "Can I get you something, tea or coffee?"

His response was an abrupt, "No, thank you." Then he continued, "I'm here to work! I guess I should have called but I was in a hurry to get here." Then, he added, very matter-of-factly, "I came here to work, so let's get to work. We need results and we need them quickly!"

Surprised by the way Schmidt answered, Martin began to probe. "Dr. Schmidt, we didn't expect you to finish up in California for weeks and frankly, we've given you all the reports regarding our progress and fail to see the reason for this early arrival."

"Yes, yes," Dr. Schmidt said, scratching his forehead as if contemplating how to respond tactfully. "We're just not making the necessary strides, so I wrapped up what I was doing and came to provide an extra set of hands. By the way, where is the laboratory?"

Vivian immediately noticed her husband's reaction and stalled to give Martin his needed time to deal with Schmidt. Vivian said in a sympathetic tone, "You must be exhausted Dr. Schmidt, after such a long trip. Why don't you get settled in at your hotel and we can discuss all this later, perhaps over dinner? Are you staying at the Inn?"

Dr. Schmidt, sounding annoyed, replied, "I made no hotel reservations, I did not think it would be an imposition for me to stay with you."

Vivian stopped to think of a good answer while she gathered her strength and lifted her body from the rocker. She moved to get Dr. Schmidt's coat. "Oh, I'm sorry. We're in the middle of major renovations right now, you understand with the baby coming and since we didn't even know when you were arriving, well, you understand...."

And, without even giving him a chance to say another word, Vivian put the address tracking on auto display and targeted his rental car in the parking area. Then she instructed him to just turn on the auto tracker and it will drive him to the hotel.

Then she turned to her husband, "Martin, call John at the Inn and get a nice room for Dr. Schmidt." Turning back to Schmidt, to help him on with his coat, Vivian explained, "The Inn is very quiet and I'm sure you'll prefer it to our noisy house, with men banging all the time and the soot and the mess. Get some rest and we'll pick you up later and take you out for a wonderful dinner. We can talk about everything over a nice meal!"

Schmidt started to protest but Vivian played on his sympathies, "You know, I think I could use the rest as well," she told him, as she got her coat and handed it to him to assist her. "I'll see you at home later, Martin." She smiled, kissed her husband and shuffled Schmidt out the office door before he could continue to protest.

When they reached the outer door, Vivian put in the code which unlocked that door. She had Schmidt help her down the steps, then escorted him to his car. Schmidt kept looking back toward Martin, muttering to himself but Vivian put him into his car and watched as he pulled away.

Vivian walked back to Martin, who had followed them out. "Whew! That was close, what do we do now?"

"You my lady, are going home to rest so we can go out tonight. I'll stay here and try to figure out what to do about Schmidt. Rosie and I will re-set the make shift lab and make sure all the security systems are in place to restrict his access to where and what, we want.

Martin watched as she drove away, then he went back into the Cottage. Just as he closed the door, he heard the sound of a car. Wondering why she would return, he turned on the outside scanner. It wasn't Vivian's car but the car Dr. Schmidt had arrived in. He wondered why Schmidt would be returning and why the guard didn't report it.

Martin punched in the code and walked back outside. Schmidt stopped the car directly in front of the Cottage; turned off the engine and got out. "Martin, I was parked just around the other side of the house and waited for Vivian to leave. We must talk, now!"

Martin realized he didn't have any choice, "All right, Dr. Schmidt. Come in. What is it that couldn't wait until tonight?"

"I'm actually glad Vivian left," he said, managing the stairs. To Martin's surprise, he did much better this time. He came inside, removed his coat; tossed it over Vivian's rocker, then settled back in the same chair as before. "Martin, I've known you for many years and worked with you on many confidential projects but this is very different. The I.A.S. is putting a lot of pressure on me and therefore, on you. They want to find a way to 'neutralize Controller,' and they want it, yesterday. At the same time, they need to show the world that the scientific community can handle Controller, better than the computer industry did, or the law enforcement community is currently doing."

Martin got up from his chair and went around to the front of the desk. "Doctor, you know the time and effort required to achieve such a task. We're working on it day and night. I don't know what more we could do."

Schmidt could see Martin's frustration. "I'm well aware of how difficult this is, the pressure and Vivian's pregnancy, that's why I am here." Schmidt got up from his chair and put his hand on Martin's shoulder. "I'll work with you as we did in the good old days." Schmidt's voice had a fatherly quality Martin had not heard since he was the doctor's young apprentice. Then the old man added, in a very enthusiastic tone, "We can let Vivian do the data work and you and I can brainstorm this monster."

Dr. Schmidt waited a moment but Martin didn't respond. Schmidt's voice became stern and almost commanding, he looked Martin straight in the eye and stated, "Martin, let's get to work!"

Martin, didn't like the tone of Schmidt's voice and took a calming breath before speaking his mind. "Doctor, Vivian and I greatly appreciate what you want to do, however, this is not the Institute and I'm no longer your assistant." Martin realized the abruptness of what he had just said to the elderly man and decided to try again. "I don't mean to be rude but Vivian and I, we're partners, in our work, as in our life together. We not only work together, we are a team!"

Schmidt raised his hand in front of Martin's face and interrupted, "I understand my boy, after all, you mustn't forget, I've known you for a long time. I know how independent you are but, this is not a request.

Schmidt continued in a very strange tone. "The I.A.S. has instructed me to come here and expedite this research. The governments of the world are panicking."

Suddenly his voice changed; almost sounding pleased. "You see, my boy, they have never encountered anything quite like this and they are relying on us! They fear Controller will continue to get stronger every day and will eventually take over every computer system in the world." Schmidt cried out, "Martin, do you understand what this means?"

Martin started to reply but Dr. Schmidt seemed momentarily dazed, as if he was somewhere else.

Schmidt sat back down.

Martin was concerned and offered him a glass of water but he shook his head and continued. "What we have seen so far is nothing, pranks, tests of authority. Because no real damage has been done, no one has paid any real attention but recent occurrences are making everyone sit up and take notice.

Martin, was struck by Dr. Schmidt's words.

"I am now at liberty to tell you this. About a week ago, a college in New Hampshire reported that twenty-one of their students were sent for psychiatric observation after exhibiting drastic personality changes.

"The matter came to the school's administrator when their hot lines were getting calls from family and friends for information about what to do. One of the students became so violent, he had to be physically restrained.

"Normally, this would never even come to the attention of the I.A.S. but after the student was institutionalized, he kept ranting, 'you can't lock me up, Controller needs me!'

"So, you see," Schmidt sounded exhausted and slumped back in the chair, "we must find an answer before more children become like him, mindless." Schmidt could not go on. His face contorted with emotion. He looked up at his former apprentice, as one turns to a child, "Don't you see, Martin?" He pleaded, "The children, he is going after the children!" Schmidt paused, "We must protect all the children!"

Flustered, Schmidt took out his handkerchief and wiped his face, "Controller is recruiting these children to be his army and he will eventually have the resources to take over the world." Then, with an unexpected fury, Dr. Schmidt, lashed out, "These are your children that are in danger! Think man! Think of your unborn child and the twins."

Martin interrupted, "Dr. Schmidt, unfortunately we're all too aware of that. Our children and their friends have encountered Controller and its hologram and we have reason to believe some of them may have already become Controller followers. Still, we're doing the best we can." Trying not to sound annoyed Martin added, "I'm sure if you alone had been able to solve this problem, The I.A.S. would not have come to us."

Martin stopped for a moment when he saw the hurt look on the old man's face. He tried to think of what he could say that would make Schmidt understand and go back to California.

Then, it hit him and Martin pressed on, "I don't know why I didn't think of this before. If you really feel you need to work hands-on with us, we can use the teleportation system, the same way we do when Vivian works from home. That way you'll have all the samples and all the computer files and you can work from the comfort and convenience of your lab in California."

Before Martin could continue, Schmidt broke in, "Thank you for thinking about my welfare, however it was decided before I left California that I would work here with you. I will not intrude on your privacy, I will stay at the Inn but I will be here every day to work until we have a solution."

Then, as if that was all there was to say, Dr. Schmidt picked up his coat from the rocker; put it on and moved toward the exit quicker than Martin had seen him move that day.

Schmidt turned around almost as an afterthought, "You and Vivian were right I should get some rest. It was a long trip. I am going to the Inn now," he said, as he handed Martin his hand-com. "Please imprint the directions, so I don't have to use the car's GPS and then, call the Inn, if you haven't already. Tell them I want a quiet but comfortable room, ready when I arrive."

Schmidt waited while Martin finished the direction mapping and then cleared the security code. "I will see you tonight. Call me about the time. Oh, on second thought, just leave a message with the desk, in case I am resting!"

Seeing the solemn look on the face of his former assistant, Dr. Schmidt added, "Don't worry. I'm here to help you. Together we'll do this, just like old times." Then, Schmidt turned walked easily and quickly down the stairs to his car and was gone.

Martin was glad Vivian wasn't there because his thoughts were not fit to be heard. He cursed Controller, The I.A.S. and even, Dr. Schmidt. How was Vivian going to deal with this? How did everything all of a sudden, get so out of control?

Martin knew if he were in this alone right now, he would just disappear... but Vivian, the kids.... "All right!" Martin screamed, annoyed and completely frustrated. He slammed his fist down. You must forget your feelings. You must deal with this...for Vivian, for the family!

He decided to proceed in a very cautious manner. He would move all the experiments to the house lab, including all the logs. Only the materials that pertained directly to finding a solution to the Controller problem would be left at the Cottage. Martin made a mental note to get the sample he and Vivian had hidden in the bidet reservoir and to re-classify the notes he'd taken from the stranger in the parking lot; that he'd given to Rosie.

Turning his thoughts to other details, Martin noted, I must warn the twins to be careful when they're around

Schmidt. Almost as an afterthought, he added, unfortunately, Brian will have to stay well-hidden until Schmidt goes back to California.

Thinking of his new son, Martin hoped that if everything worked out, as planned, the day would come when he could proudly introduce Brian to Schmidt and the world. That thought gave him a real feeling of comfort.

Martin went down to the lab and gathered the most recent samples and carried them out to his car. He went back into the Cottage and retrieved his personal notes and his briefcase. Then Martin gave Rosie instructions to re-classify the notes regarding the stranger in the parking lot. He then headed back to the lab to get the other samples.

Rosie interrupted him.

"The fake lab is ready to be re-set?"

"Thanks Rosie. Engage!"

As the thunderous sounds of doors sealing and walls coming down started, Martin thought back to when he first witnessed this scene. This system was installed as an extra security measure to conceal the real lab and its projects. If an intruder ever tried to enter the lab, the entire room would in effect, disappear and a lab, like any other college research facility would take its place.

The greenhouse had the same system; walls were sealed and replaced with a small growing area without all the bells and whistles and of course, without the special plants they were cultivating.

Martin was amazed, how, within seconds, the space age facilities were transformed and the actual lab and greenhouse were sealed behind concrete structures.

He walked into the new lab area and pulled out some papers from one of the file cabinets and placed them on the desk to make it look as if they had been working there. He commanded the lights to go to "night mode" and then keyed in the security codes.

Next, he proceeded upstairs and gave Rosie's additional instructions through the intercom, before he headed to the outer door. He cleared the code and as the door opened he turned back toward the inner office and then hesitated. He had a strange feeling that he'd forgotten something but he couldn't put his finger on it. It couldn't have been very important, he decided. All he could think of was getting home.

CHAPTER 2

Evie was so excited about the modeling, call she drove faster than normal. She had had some minor modeling jobs in California but since coming to "Booneyville," Island Falls, there hadn't been any opportunities. She hadn't thought about how much it really bothered her. She mentioned it to Jonathan once but didn't really talk about it...not even with Brad. She just felt that she was in a hopeless situation. All the things she loved were in California but Island Falls was where her family lived now and where she agreed to get her education. So, here she was, still hating Island Falls, after more than a year; except for school.

She loved her classes but she still stayed pretty much to herself. Evie hadn't tried to make friends, or have a social life and except for work, she still spent most of her time communicating with her friends in California. Occasionally she would attend some school function with someone from school like Ginger, from the Hot Spot Shoppe.

By the time Evie found the address for the modeling call and a place to park, she was really psyched. She checked her make-up in the mirror, for first impression sake and went into the building that corresponded to the address.

A young college age guy was sitting at a desk in the office marked, "AUDITIONS TODAY." Evie checked the time: 12:00 exactly. She went up to him and gave her name and he handed her a form board without saying a word. "I filled all the paper work out on-line," she told him but he just ignored her. She thought it odd but found a seat in a quiet corner and began speaking the answers required on the form.

There were five other girls there. *Darn, why did it take me so long to park? I could've been here, first.* She noticed these girls were all around her age and older: some texting, some just waiting but all were definitely beautiful.

Evie started to feel stupid and berated herself. What am I doing here? These girls look like they've had a lot of experience. But, she mustered her determination and courage and decided to stay. After all, she asked herself, what's the worst that can happen? She hesitated for a moment and then, thought, they could laugh at me and send me home.

She finished the form and handed it back to the still non-communicative guy. When she asked if there was anything else she needed to do, he just pointed for her to sit. She moved to a seat away from the other girls and observed what was going on in the room.

The office had only the one desk and a few chairs, that was it. The girls that were waiting didn't seem nervous or anxious or even excited, they just sat or stood more like mannequins than models. Of course, there was "Silent Sam," as Evie thought of the guy at the desk. He just seemed to have a blank look on his face and moved in a mime like fashion.

By 12:30 a few more girls had arrived; each more beautiful than the last group and finally a door opened and her name was called. Evie jumped up, then gained her composure and picked up her make-up case, portfolio and change bag.

She looked around wondering why the original five girls weren't protesting, after all, they were there before her. She decided that if they didn't want to object, she was just going to accept her good fortune and hope it continued.

Evie followed the guy who had called her name through a set of doors and down a corridor to a small room. He escorted her inside, then turned around and left. He closed the door and never said another word.

Evie felt very confused but chalked it up to the way they did things in "hokey," Island Falls.

Suddenly, the room darkened and a projection appeared on the wall. This whole thing was really freaking her out. Evie was getting ready to get out of there when a kind looking face appeared on the screen.

"Welcome Beautiful Lady. You have been chosen above all the other applicants. In order for our company to award you this modeling contract you must go through the following steps: the interview process - during which you must remain seated and answer all the questions without stopping. Next, the photo shoot. You must have the three changes required and finally, the contract stage. Now, that you understand the conditions signify your acceptance by saying, yes! However, if for any reason, you do not agree, please stand and an escort will appear to take you back to the reception room and you can leave."

Evie tried to shield her eyes from the strange light that was shining at her. She thought this was the strangest way to get a modeling job but after all, she beat all those other girls, so what the heck. "Yes," she responded.

"We will now continue." A brighter light was shone directly at her face and she winced but then Evie realized bright lights were a part of modeling; she just never knew they were that bright.

The questions started and were being fired in rapid succession. At the same time the lights were strobing her. She barely had time to think of her answers and the flashing lights were really hurting her eyes. Evie remembered the instructions and just continued.

After what seemed like an eternity the lights finally went off and the face and voice disappeared.

Sitting there waiting for the next segment, Evie felt really strange; almost as if something was trying to control her thoughts but she laughed at herself and just waited for the next part to begin.

The same young man that had led her to the room returned and adjusted the surround screens and then left, again without ever saying a word.

He closed the door and the face and voice returned. "Now, for the photo shoot. Proceed to change number one, the casual. Mirrors are now being lowered to assist you."

Evie asked about a private dressing room but the only reply was, "Three minutes." She remembered that some shoots didn't have a big budget and time was important, so she proceeded to quickly get herself ready.

The room darkened and the light came on again. She had no idea where the camera was but the voice came on to tell her positions to take and she followed all the instructions without hesitation. At the end of the casual shooting, she was given the same instructions for shoot two, the formal.

When that was finished, a voice told her "The casual and formal shoots went fine."

I can't believe this! I am one-third done and on my way to a modeling career. Evie was so excited. It hasn't been that bad, she thought, a little weird, no, make that a lot weird but if that's the new modeling audition, hey, as long as I get the job!

Next, she was instructed to change into her bathing suit. This time she insisted on a private change area.

There was no response.

Very reluctantly, she began to undress. For some reason, Evie felt like the whole world was watching. She put the bikini bottom on over her panties but when she picked up the top, she decided to keep her shirt on and maneuver from underneath. She took her arms out of the sleeves and started to remove her bra. Even though she was totally covered, she still turned away from where the face had appeared.

She pulled down the straps; and stood there for a moment with her hands covering her chest.

The door opened and a guy she hadn't seen before came in. He was clad in a tight swim suit, with a towel slung around his neck.

Evie immediately turned her back.

"Hey pretty lady," he said, in a very come on, sexy voice, "don't be afraid, I'm here to help you."

"I don't need your help, thanks." she stated in a frightened but firm voice.

The guy was very sexy; dark hair and eyes and it was hard to concentrate as he moved closer. "Time is money and you need to do as you are told! He reached out his hand, "Here let me help you lift the shirt off, then I can undo your bra and we can get down to the shoot."

"What do you mean? I don't need help and besides, you need to wait outside while I get my bathing suit on!"

"First of all, you were taking too long, it was just assumed you needed help removing that bra thing," he picked up her bikini top, "and as for this little thing…"

Evie was mortified.

"Your arms are covering more than this will and that bikini bottom, wow! That is definitely a turn on!"

Horrified, Evie just stood there. She wanted to move but something seemed to be holding her against her will.

He paused for a moment and said, "Okay, have it your way. Here's an idea, why don't you just lift the shirt over your head and leave the bra on, it could be a real teaser shot. I'm sure you will get warmed up to the camera and then you'll be happy to shed it and the rest.…"

"Is that what the job is? Nude shots and teasers?" she said, forcing her mind to get control.

"Hell no! Calm down sweetie. These are just the private shots, you know, for the interview, everyone needs to do them. This job is for a new magazine internet site; real high profile and you, baby, will be the new star! It and you, will be making a debut in about a month."

"Oh, what site."

"www.fashiontoday.CON."

"Well, I never heard of that but it sounds cool, I guess." Evie said feeling a bit better but still with a lot of apprehension.

"I will tell you what you are so incredibly gorgeous and so right for this shoot, so, to make you feel more at ease, I will go back out and wait on the other side of the door. I will give you exactly one-minute to put on that bikini top…at the end of the time I will come back in."

Evie nodded and the boy walked to the door. She stood so her back was to the door. She used the mirror to hide her while she changed as quickly as possible. Evie put the bikini top around her waist and fastened the clips; then shifted it around and pulled it up. She reluctantly unhooked her bra and set it with the rest of her clothes.

While he was waiting out the time the boy called out through the door, "We may have gotten off to a bad start, so let's try again. I'm Paul and when I come back in, all you have to do is whatever I tell you, without questions or discussion, agreed?"

"All right, let's do it," Evie said feeling more secure now that she had her bathing suit on.

Paul programmed the lights in the room to low and indicated the spotlights to position on Evie. The camera was nowhere to be seen but the lights again were flashing before her eyes.

Paul told her they would start with some standing shots. "You are very seductive!" Then, he moved closer to her and instructed her to place one arm behind her back. Next, he asked her to lean forward toward him. He never touched her but the positioning caused her stomach to flip flop with nerves. She was hard pressed to do anything but smile for the camera. Evie felt like she wanted to stop but something was exerting pressure on her to keep doing whatever he said. She knew she was only posing in a bathing suit but something made it feel wrong.

On top of that, she hadn't been this close to a guy in a bathing suit since Eddy. Paul stood directly in front of her and as much as she couldn't explain the stirring she felt, it was very arousing. Evie wanted to run but she couldn't force herself to move.

She could hear a clicking but still didn't see any camera.

Next, Paul had her sit on the floor with her legs bent to one side; one on top of another. He told her to put her hand underneath her hair and the other on her hip.

More lights flashing! Paul lowered himself to the floor and this time he told her he would position her body for the camera.

The shivers of excitement ran through her being. He touched her face gently and it was very exciting. He didn't touch her in a sexual way but his closeness, was very provocative.

Suddenly the door opened. One of the girls from the waiting room and the "Silent Sam" came in. They were both clad in very sexual attire. Evie didn't want to wait to see what was going to happen.

She drew on every bit of strength she had and tried to get up but something was making it hard for her to move. The girl came over and lay on the floor next to her and the boy walked over to them.

Evie cleared her mind and reached deep inside for her inner powers but she knew her emotions were raw. She continued to struggle against whatever was holding her against her will and this time, exerted force of her own. The girl put her hand on Evie's arm and that was all she needed.

She catapulted up and grabbed her clothes. Strangely, no one tried to stop her. "I'm so outta here," Evie said as she threw on her blouse and pants over the bikini, then she grabbed the rest of her stuff and left. Surprisingly no one even said a word.

Evie got to her car and locked herself inside. She sat with her head pressed against the steering wheel crying, shaking; embarrassed at the pictures she permitted to be taken and ashamed that she had allowed things to go so far. She couldn't believe that she had let her desire for a job drive her to do things without even thinking. She berated herself for allowing sexual desires to be awakened, so easily. What's wrong with me? Dumb, dumb, dumb—how could I have let that happen?

In between sobs Evie tried to get control of her mind. Oh, Evie, what's wrong with you? She asked herself. And, why the hell, when I really wanted to leave, couldn't I just go? What was holding me?

Dammit Evie! She yelled at herself out loud and then she remembered all her training. Being alone would hamper my abilities and extreme emotions block my powers but that would only have to do with my super powers, what happened to my own will? I am Evie Kane! Strong, confident and I know right from wrong, so what just happened to me? She had so many questions and just couldn't seem to get control.

Suddenly there was a tap on the glass window. She jumped and her heart raced. She was trapped. She raised her head and couldn't believe her eyes.

CHAPTER 3

Brad caught a break with a cancelled class and returned home early to get in some Internet chat time before he had to go to work. He felt Brian's presence in the house and yelled out, "Hey Brian. I'm here for a while. Be up in my room if you need me. Then he realized, Gee I could've just thought that instead of shouting. Yeah, I've got to get used to this telepathic stuff.

Brad started up the stairs and heard the garage door closing. He glanced at his watch and knew it was early for anyone else to be home. Starting back downstairs, he heard his mother, "Brad is that you," she called out from the kitchen." Suddenly, the door off the kitchen area that led directly from the garage opened and his father appeared.

"What are you two doing home so early?" Brad asked, as he greeted his parents.

"Your mother came home earlier to rest and I just arrived."

Brad nodded and started toward the stairs, when his father stopped him. "Oh, Brad, Dr. Schmidt is here from California and your mother and I are going to dinner with him tonight."

Brad noticed how on edge his father seemed to be, "That's great Dad, isn't it?"

"Well, of course it's good to see him but we're right in the middle of an important project and, well, you get the idea."

Brad only half believed his father and he didn't know why. In all his life Brad never felt his father deliberately misled him.

"Viv, why don't you go up and start getting ready, I'll join you in a moment!"

"I'm just putting together a snack for Brian and then I will."

"How about, I'll wait while you finish and then we can take it downstairs so I can also have a moment with Brian." As if a second thought entered his mind Martin turned to his son, "Oh and Brad, when I get some time, we need to discuss school."

Brad watched his parents disappear into the kitchen, as if he didn't exist.

He stormed up the stairs and slammed his door. Brad plopped down on his bed and just shook his head. He wondered why he let these things bother him. All Dad cares about is whether I am acing my classes. Nothing else about me is important to him! Brad got frustrated every time these topics came up. Forget it dude, he told himself. You came home to have a break, so chill.

Brad checked his messages. It looked like Evie had tried to reach him and then cancelled the call. That's strange, he thought but let it go.

The rest of the messages were nothing special that couldn't wait.

Brad knew what he was hoping for. He opened his connection and started to search for Patti. He flung himself down in the chair and began surfing, "Bingo!" he almost flew out of his chair....

"< Where ya been? >"

"< Hey Be raD, how are you? >"

"<I'm great now that I've found you, again.>"

Brad couldn't believe what he saw on the screen. Silhouetted images of Patti.

He re-read his words, "Jeez, I sound desperate!" Brad never let his emotions get out of hand for any girl; so why now and with some unknown chick in cyberspace.

"< I've really missed our meetings. >"

"< Do you have time to do some virtual? >"

Brad read Patti's invitation and felt an immediate rush. He didn't even bother to look at the time.

"< Yeah, I'm here to please! >"

"< I've recently been introduced to a new type of virtual, Be raD do you want to give it a try? >"

"< Hey, Patti, I'm game for anything, with you! >"

"< You've got to wear a mask and be blind folded but that's when the fun will start. >"

"< Let's go! >"

Brad was panting to begin. He and Patti met in virtual at the address she gave him and he forgot all about work; his sister's message, his father's comment and anything that wasn't Patti.

Brad was totally wiped out when he finally signed off. He emerged from cyberspace to realize he'd better get his act in gear or he would be later than he just realized he already was. He grabbed his stuff, shouted goodbye to whoever was in earshot and left knowing his head was still spinning and his knees were still weak; but he had to go.

On the way to work Brad couldn't help reliving his virtual trip. And, what a trip it was...Patti had taken him to new heights. Even he wasn't aware such things were possible. When he arrived in the virtual room, there was romantic music playing and the atmosphere seemed warm and cozy.

Patti removed the blind fold and there were three of her. Each one was dressed in a different outfit but it was her; all at the same time. She was in a short skirt and tight blouse, covered by a long vest and boots up to the bottom of her hemline. The second Patti had on a bikini that was hidden under an off the shoulder netted wrapper and the third; a very elegant black and red negligee, that was fitted from her neck to the floor. Her hairdos matched her outfits: straight, curly and wavy and silky long; each one seemed to enhance the outfit.

Once again, she wore a mask of different design for each outfit. He didn't see her facial features and she never saw his. Brad was goin' crazy. Oh baby, how I'd love to see your face!

The three of her danced around him mercilessly and when he couldn't take anymore, each different version approached him, as if she were three different people. First, one at a time, then two then…. Just the thought was getting to him all over again. You'd better calm down, man. You gotta go to work, he kept reminding himself. Brad stopped the car at a red light and just sat there. He was really hooked; he wanted to meet her so bad and see what it would be like to hold her in his arms for real! What's wrong with me? I'm hot for a girl I know only in virtual, who's face I've never seen!"

But Brad felt like it was more than a physical attraction. He liked being with her, as if she completed him; made him feel special. "Oh Patti, damn, I gotta get control of myself!"

CHAPTER 4

"Hey, you in there…"

Evie was terrified someone from the modeling job must have followed her.

"Hey, open the window."

She turned away to wipe the still flowing tears from her face and decided to ignore whoever was banging in hopes they'd go away.

"Hey, com'on, are you okay?"

Finally, she decided to look at the window. Through her tears, Evie saw the guy she came to know as Rick, Sheila's friend and her car's rescuer. He was standing there with the neatest smile, tapping on her car window. Evie was in shock and wiped away some more tears, before she commanded the window to open.

She took a deep breath and couldn't believe her bad luck. Of all times; her make-up was running down her face, her eyes were swollen, this could only happen to her. Why now? she thought. "Oh, hi! It's you," is all she said.

"Is your car actin' up again? Is that why you're so upset?"

Oh shit, he can see that I'm really upset. Well, duh, Evie he doesn't have to be a rocket scientist to figure that out!

Evie realized Rick must think she's upset over car trouble again. That must be why he's knocking on the car window. "Oh, uh, thanks, no, no, you did a really good job when you fixed it. It's been runnin' fine. You can go," she stammered.

"Great! Uh," he got kinda fidgety standing outside her car. He waited a moment and then added, "You know, this isn't the greatest neighborhood, are you alone?"

She didn't want to admit what she was doing there and lied. "I was meeting someone but so far he's a no-show."

"Well, do you think your friend would mind if I waited with you, just to be on the safe side?"

Flustered, Evie didn't know what to say but he didn't give her a chance.

"Good, I'm just gonna lock my rig first"

Evie engaged the unlock button but not before she grabbed a fresh tissue and her lipstick to do a quick repair job.

"Rick Armitage," he said, opening the passenger side door and smoothly sliding into the seat next to her and extending his hand. "I guess we were never formally introduced."

Evie's blood was boiling as his aroma filtered through her nostrils and surrounded her in the small car. "Hi, I'm E v...uh, Evie Kane," she stammered, nervously.

"Well, I'm glad to hear your car is still running."

"Yeah, thanks again. You were a real life-saver!"

"Well, not that I mind playing rescuer but this isn't a great place to meet. Why'd your friend choose it?"

"Beats me," she wanted to get him off that subject. "So, do you just ride around town looking to help girls in distress?"

"No but I'm really glad I saw your car here today."

"Oh really." Evie acted like she didn't understand and asked, "Uh, why?"

"It just looked like you might need help again."

He reached for her hand and she melted in his eyes, which she now saw were blue; piercing baby blue.

"So, why don't you tell me what's really goin' down."

She turned her body toward his and saw the concern on his face. Her heart melted in his eyes and she broke down and told him the whole story.

He put his arm around her and for the first time today she felt completely safe. She gazed up at him and then realized she's really told him everything; even about the almost...shots. She was so embarrassed, she pulled away.

"Hey Evie, it's okay," he said, stroking her hair.

"No, it's not okay, I'm such an idiot and now you must think I'm..."

He cut her off. "I'm not sure what your next word was going to be but you couldn't be more wrong."

He pulled a tissue from the box on her dash and dabbed her tears. His touch was so gentle, she started to calm down.

"Better?" He asked.

"Getting there."

"Are you okay enough to just sit here for a few minutes by yourself?"

"Why?" she started to get upset again.

"'Cause," he said, angrily, "I'm headed inside to beat the shit outta somebody! Oh, sorry!"

He wanted to kick himself. Rick knew there was something about her that made him want to be more careful about the words he used.

She turned back toward him, tears wrenching from her heart, "No, please, I just need to forget this and get away from here! Please, Rick," she pleaded.

"Okay, c'mon. Please don't cry anymore. You know nobody should treat you that way and get away with it!"

"Yeah but it's my fault. I've just been so stupid. I wanted this modeling job so badly that I..." the flood of tears began to flow again.

"You're being too hard on yourself." He cradled her to him. "We've all done things we wish we hadn't but the real you knew it was wrong and you got outta there before things went too far."

She wanted to kiss him so badly, "Thanks Rick. I guess I really needed to hear that!"

"I've been told I'm a good listener, so how about we head outta this part of town and go get a cup of coffee somewhere where we can talk. I'll take my rig and follow real close behind, just so I don't lose you."

Evie couldn't believe this was really happening to her.

CHAPTER 5

The night was clear, cold and crisp and the drive to pick up Dr. Schmidt at his hotel was the first real chance Martin and Vivian had to relax all day. Martin knew he had to tell her about Schmidt's return to the lab and their conversation. He smiled as he began, "I don't want you to be upset about Schmidt."

"I'm not but how soon do you think he'll be leaving?"

"That's what I don't want you to be upset about. He came back after you left and told me, in no uncertain terms, that he's here to work, for the duration."

She was quiet for what seemed like an eternity.

"Viv, please say something?"

"I guess he just needs to feel needed. We can just give him the simple tasks and you and I will do the real work at our lab at home."

"That's my girl. Whenever I think I know how you'll react, you always surprise me."

"After all these years of marriage, Martin, do you really think I can let you figure me out that easily? That would be boring!"

They both laughed and relaxed for the drive through town to the Inn.

They picked up Dr. Schmidt at the Island Falls Inn and drove to the Lakeview Restaurant. They showed him all the sights along the way. They pulled up to the restaurant and Schmidt could see why it was so appropriately named. The view was truly magnificent. "Lake Karmia," Vivian explained, "is the largest body of water in Island Falls. We chose this restaurant, because the water is frozen at this time of year and the reflection of the moon shining down is breathtaking."

The food and service were excellent, as usual and they spent a long time over dinner. They talked leisurely about old times; old friends in California and what it was like living in a small college town. "We've had to make a lot of adjustments since leaving the Science Institute but we've grown to love rural living. This is really a college town and the two major schools here are excellent."

Martin continued the light conversation not wanting Schmidt to change the subject. "Norton University, where Vivian and I work and where the twins attend classes, as you know, is a very highly respected school, with a good reputation for its research programs. Island Falls College, on the other hand, isn't as well-known but over the past few years, the school has specialized in the arts and is gaining a reputation for excelling in each area."

Dr. Schmidt started to interrupt but before he could get a word out, Vivian picked up the conversation.

"You know Dr. Schmidt, we were very surprised to learn that because of their diverse programs and the location of these schools, they both not only have full enrollment but there is a long waiting list of students from all over the United States, Canada and many other foreign countries."

Vivian thought about what she'd just said and wondered if that was the reason Controller had made

Island Falls its headquarters: academia and students of the arts all in the same location. Vivian and Martin kept the conversation going through dinner and by the time the check came, both Martin and Schmidt had noticed how tired Vivian looked.

"Vivian, my dear," Schmidt began, "you look so tired, child. Since I am here now, I can take over your load and you can rest more."

Martin started to respond but Vivian spoke up instead, "Thank you for the offer but this is as much my project as anyone's, so I'll carry my weight. All I need is some rest." Noticeably upset, Vivian turned to her husband, "Martin, I'd like to go now!"

Vivian didn't wait for an answer. She rose from the table; grabbed her coat from the empty chair where she had put it and then turned and walked toward the front door.

Schmidt got up and followed her.

In her haste, she never heard Schmidt mumbling under his breath.

"How am I going to get Vivian out of the picture? I can handle what I need to do so much better with just Martin."

Martin paid the check and drove Dr. Schmidt back to the Inn. The car ride was without much additional conversation.

On their way home Vivian burst into tears. Martin stopped the car on the side of the road and took her in his arms and just let her cry. After a few minutes they separated and he gently placed his fingers under her chin in an effort to have her look at him. She started to turn away, when he cupped her face in his hands, "Hey, what happened to my brave, in control girl."

"She got hit with a dose of the enemy," she said under her sobs.

"I know this is a really tense time and we certainly didn't need Schmidt to deal with, on top of everything else but I won't let anything hurt you, or our family, so please trust me."

Martin reached for his handkerchief and lovingly dabbed away her tears.

Vivian tried to calm down. In a half crying voice, she answered him, "I do believe in you but I'm so afraid with Dr. Schmidt here. You saw how he already tried to take my place."

"I know that's what you feel but I won't permit it! And, more than that Viv, I know you and you won't permit it either. We're partners and he can't get between us. He's an old man but still a very brilliant and determined one, so yes, we must be careful."

Martin's tone changed as he remembered his shock at seeing Schmidt's current physical condition. "But Vivian, he looks so very troubled and so tired, I don't think he wants this anymore than we do. Let me do the fighting for us and I promise everything will work out."

She rested her head on his shoulder and felt better than she had all day. "Can we just go home now?" He kissed her again, then started the car.

CHAPTER 6

"So, tell me more about yourself?" Rick could see Evie finally starting to relax after her harrowing experience.

"Wow, are you kiddin'. I've been talking for over an hour," Evie smiled as she took another sip of her coffee. "Rick, you know way more about me, than anyone, especially now this modeling fiasco. I wouldn't have told that to anyone!"

Rick smiled and flagged the waitress for fresh coffee. "I'm sure there's a lot I don't know but I'm glad you finally explained about this afternoon. You looked really crazed when I tapped on your car window." He stopped talking while the waitress refilled their cups. "I can understand why you went there but if I were you, I'd stick to the better side of town for jobs in the future."

"Yeah, I guess so but I really couldn't pass up the chance. If this were a real modeling job…" Evie stopped.

"It was a real modeling job but not for a nice girl like you."

"How do you know I'm a 'nice girl'?" she asked defensively.

"After a while, a guy can tell. Besides, from everything you said about the modeling job, if you weren't a 'nice girl,' you would've stayed." Stopping to think about the whole set-up Rick concluded, "You know, I'll bet that light you mentioned had some kind of hypnotic properties and from the way you described the events after the light, it sounded like you weren't acting of your own free will. And another thing, I've been around my share of girls and I know the nice ones from the, uh, not so nice!"

"Girls, you mean like your girlfriend, Sheila?" As soon as the words were out of her mouth Evie was sorry!

Rick acted kind of embarrassed. "Oh, you know about my relationship with Sheila."

He didn't correct her, "girlfriend comment." Evie now knew Brad was wrong. He'd said he thought Rick and Sheila were just friends. "Yeah, I kinda heard." Evie's heart dropped.

"We've been together for a long, long time."

When Rick had invited her for coffee today, Evie felt confident that he must be unattached, her thoughts then were, could it be that somehow this incredibly gorgeous guy doesn't have a million girls he's tight with?

But now, after all their conversation and the way he looked at her, all her thoughts screamed, how could I have been so wrong?

She couldn't believe she could be so gullible twice in one day. But, she had to admit, he just confirmed the relationship with Sheila, his "girlfriend".

Evie couldn't stand being that close to him now. "I guess I'd better be going, uh, it's getting late." She rose from the booth they were sitting in and started to put on her jacket.

Rick rose to help her, "Are you sure you gotta go?" He signaled for the check.

"Yeah!" was all she said, turning her back and fighting back the tears. Evie reached into her pocket, took out a few dollars, turned, dropped the money on the table and without looking at Rick said, "Thanks for the coffee and the rescue, bye!"

She barely got the words out. Without waiting for his response, she just ran past him.

"Wait Evie," he called after her, "I'll walk you to your car," but, by the time he took care of the check, she was gone. Rick didn't even have a chance to say goodbye. He searched outside for her but she was nowhere to be found. He put her money in his pocket and vowed to return it to her the next time they met.

When Evie got home she ran to her computer to check out that web site: www.fashiontoday.CON. She was thrilled no such site existed but there was a re-direct to an h-mail for Paul. It read, "Looking for models for the upcoming site." Evie knew she'd have to check it often to make sure her pictures never showed up.

CHAPTER 7

About nine o'clock that same evening, Sheila was sitting in her black convertible at the main entrance to Norton University, when she heard another car approaching.

She had been busy since her arrest for her part on the Cracko caper. Luckily for her, she'd been able to convince Dean Farrell and the police, that she was just an innocent dupe and that her mind had been controlled, or she'd be in jail today, instead of being here waiting for Controller's next plan to begin.

She'd been reprimanded about being careful who she associated with and now she was making sure she only associated with people who could get her what she wanted. In this case, that meant getting her hands on the exam answers and messing up the school's system. She knew that would put her back in Controller's good graces.

The approaching car was a black Foremost sporty model, which she recognized as Rick's. Sheila jumped out of her car and ran toward him as he stopped the car and the window opened. "Okay Sheila, I got your beep. What's up?" He asked impatiently. "Why'd you drag me out here tonight?"

Sheila's heart was racing. She had secretly been in love with Rick all her life. As she looked into his eyes, she found it difficult to answer. Rick was incredibly good looking. His amazing blue eyes with really long lashes added with his great dimples melted her heart. His charm only added to the overpowering effect.

When she didn't answer, he pushed, "C'mon, Sheila! What's going on? Why did you want me to meet you here?"

Feeling the warmth of his body through his open jacket was too much for her and she backed away. "You and me...we grew up on the right side of the tracks, with the wrong side of everything." Sheila added, "Controller could be our chance to change all that. We could finally get the same respect as the poor kids do."

"You're so wrong, Sheila. They don't get respect because they're poor but because they earn it. You and me, we never tried. He took her hands, "The only 'chance' here is for you to wind up in jail, or worse. You were lucky with Cracko. You talked your way out of jail and the fancy lawyer your Dad hired didn't hurt but I'm not so sure you'll be that lucky again."

He moved closer and grabbed her by the shoulders as if trying to shake some sense into her. "Controller only uses you. You're not a leader, you're just its flunky, a last resort helper. You see, you are the one who pays a very heavy price, while your beloved Controller is nowhere in sight."

His words made her very angry and she pushed his hands away. "You're so wrong. I'm important to Controller! I'm gonna help him take over and then I will rule! Controller is getting more powerful every day and he'll protect me... and you too, if you join us!"

"If you believe that, I really don't know you anymore." Rick tried to think of what else he could say, at least for the sake of their long-time friendship but Sheila kept going on and on. Finally, he responded, "Oh what's the use." He threw up his hands and rushed back to his car. Rick slammed the door and sat there for a moment before starting the engine.

"Come on Rick," he heard Sheila yell out, "just give it a try. It'll be fun and no one will be the wiser."

Totally frustrated, Rick shouted back at her, "You're wrong Sheila, I will!" He started the engine and sped out of sight.

CHAPTER 8

Shortly after 9:30 that same evening, Brad parked his car at the far end of the university. He walked toward the meeting place, where Jonathan said he'd be waiting.

"Oh, Brad! I can't tell you how glad I am you got here. I'm wasted!"

"What's going on? When I saw you this morning you said you were going to be getting the exam answers down pat?"

Jonathan seemed to be in a daze and stammered, "Er, oh I, a . . . I am er sort of ..."

"What the hell is with you?" Brad was about ready to leave but he could see Jonathan was in a really bad way.

"Look, Jon, I've had a rotten night and work sucked, so spill it, or I'm outta here!"

"Please, please, don't leave. I'm in really bad and I don't know who else to turn to."

Brad couldn't help noticing the drastic change in Jonathan from macho egomaniac to this meek, unstable personality.

"You said that when you beeped me, so I'm here, now give, or I'm leaving."

Jonathan signaled for Brad to follow him. They dodged in and out of the shadows but Brad couldn't understand why all the cloak and dagger. When they came around to the Parker Administration building, Jonathan saw Sheila and moved back into the darkening shadows and listened.

"SHH," he indicated to Brad, "this is it! Brad, please, just listen."

Brad nodded and he and Jon listened to what was going on.

"Nice of you to show up late!" Sheila said, not bothering to conceal her annoyance. She continued to bark at Jimmy and when he tried to explain, she cut him off with a biting, "Save it. If you still want to do this, QuizMaster is inside with some of the other kids. Because you got here late, now we'll have to wait until they're done screwin' things up, before we get our turn."

Jonathan, still hiding in the shadows, turned to Brad who couldn't believe what he'd just heard. "Jon," he asked in a whisper, "are you a part of this?"

Terrified by what he'd done, Jonathan broke down. Brad managed to get him away from the Parker building, so they could talk. "Okay pal, spill!"

Jon told Brad the truth about the candy and Sheila, "I had to have more candy and I knew she was the source, so I went to her house. I rang the bell and she finally answered. Just standing next to her I got really turned on. When she doesn't bark she's really attractive and tall and thin and different, somehow. That long wavy blonde hair hung down over her face and those eyes just stared at me. I stood there until she finally got impatient and really annoyed, then she screamed, "What the hell do you want?"

"Yeah, like I'm getting impatient, right now too Jon! C'mon get to the point."

"Well, you see she wasn't wearing the usual tight black pants and top, which give her that tough girl image, she almost looked 'sweet,' so I asked if I could come in and talk to her. Finally, she agreed.

"The house she lived in was totally not her. From the outside, it looked like a castle. The inside was incredible and you'd think some debutante dressed in fancy clothes would come waltzing down the long winding stairs. The hall entrance, where I stood was larger than my living room."

Brad was looking annoyed. "So?"

Jon stammered to regain his focus, "Uh, where was I…oh, yeah, I told her I needed those candies she was giving out. Brad, I pleaded, I was desperate. I had to have them, so I told her I'd do anything for them. She said she could only get them now for special circumstances, you know, with Cracko gone and all. Brad, I was so hooked, I would've done anything. I was going nuts."

Jonathan took a really long, deep breath, as if he was about to confess something really bad!

"So, she made me a proposition. If I helped her get the answers to the exams, she'd get me the candy. Brad, she was my only hope and she looked so incredible that I kissed her and believe it or not, she kissed me back and we both liked it!

"Next thing I know, I'm in her bedroom and she's kissing me hard, like she wanted to tear my clothes off. It was mind blowing, then suddenly, she stopped and it was over."

Jon swallowed his embarrassment before continuing. "She got up like we didn't even like each other and said, 'Get out!'

"I did as she said and went downstairs where she was already holding the door open for me to leave. She ordered me to be here and gave me the time and then slammed the door behind me.

"When I got here tonight it got even more intense. That QuizMaster was giving multiple choice directions for each kid, what to do and where to go. They were breaking into the school's files and stealing exams, changing scores and stuff like that."

Jonathan hung his head in shame for what he was about to say, "I went in as instructed and did what I was told. Brad, my hands were shakin' by the time I came back out, I wanted to crawl in a hole."

Jonathan began to weep. "And, when I came out, I asked Sheila for the candy and she said she only had one piece and threw it to the ground! Brad, I need that candy! Brad, I need it!

"Then I screamed, me Brad, I screamed...I needed more than that one lousy piece she threw at me! Oh Brad, this is too much for me! I didn't know what to do, so that's when I called you," he cried. "Brad please, please, you have to help me!"

Brad couldn't believe what had happened to his friend. Jonathan was on the verge of a nervous breakdown. He wasn't thinking straight; his emotions were raging and he was having trouble acting rationally. I need to do something to help Jon.

"Okay Jon. Did you eat that last candy?"

Jon nodded.

"Then, I assume it will kick in for you soon. So, just hold on. Do you want me to call someone or can you pull it together long enough to get yourself home?"

Jon nodded, "I'll get home!"

"Good. Go on and I'll take care of this."

Jon stood paralyzed as he watched his friend go. He weakly called out, "Brad, are you still my friend?"

Jon didn't know what Brad was going to do but when he saw Brad approach Sheila, took hold of all his strength and forced himself to move closer to listen. Jon tried to stand still. He finally heard Sheila say, "It's not up to me...QuizMaster will have to decide."

Oh Man! What have I gotten my friend into? Jon panicked and mustered every ounce of strength he could... then left.

CHAPTER 9

Evie was reading off the holographic screen in her room. She was so unsettled; she needed something to take her mind off Rick and the events of the day but also to bring her back to reality.

Now, sitting on her bed, she didn't even remember driving home, she just remembered the humiliations; the modeling job and then, throwing herself at Rick, who then confirmed his relationship with Sheila.

After she left Rick, she'd driven around for what seemed like hours, crying, then yelling at herself and then crying again. She wasn't even sure what time it was when she finally calmed down and decided to go home. "How could I've been such a fool! First the modeling job, then believing that Rick could be interested in a relationship with me. Duh, how dumb?"

Evie tried to take her mind off things by getting caught up on the fashion ads in the paper. Scanning the local section an article caught her eye. the headline was, **"CHEATING, THE QUIZMASTER WAY!"**

The article read:

QUIZMASTER Identity Confirmed! It has now been confirmed, that a supposed Island Falls college teacher the kids call QuizMaster, is actually Controller's latest hologram. Supposedly,

fashioned after a college professor, the hologram looks and acts like a real teacher and the holographic projection is so perfect that you wouldn't know it wasn't human. QuizMaster has gotten away with the farce, swapping exam answers for student's loyalties to Controller, the computer virus that has been plaguing Island Falls. First, there was Cracko, now it's QuizMaster. This hologram is wreaking havoc with our educational system. The administration at both colleges have been trying for weeks to figure out how failing grades were changed to passing ones, absentees to attendees, course drops to full credits and a long list of other tampering.

Since the administrations are now aware of Controller's tactics, all systems have been pass protected and both schools believe the pranks will now end.

With the end of the first semester fast approaching, officials from both colleges are instituting safety measures to prevent students from obtaining the final test answers.

But if it's a case of, 'too little too late,' and QuizMaster can succeed this semester, Controller will have amassed an army of cheaters and slackers but for what purpose? No one, seems to know.

Is Island Falls a test? If Controller succeeds here, will the rest of our country, or the world, be next? The fear continues!

###

Oh great! This is the perfect ending for this day. Not only has Controller made good on its threat to create another hologram but this one sounds more invasive than the last.

She closed the holographic paper in disgust and began to pace her room. Evie picked up her favorite little stuffed animal; a white monkey and began to tell it her story. She cradled it in her arms and said, "My monkey, I can't believe I've been so self-absorbed while all this has been going on. Where have my brains been? After all, I do work in the Administration Office. What good am I? Oh, monkey, am I just interested in my own things?" The monkey didn't have any answers.

Brian had heard his sister's tirade and raced up the stairs. He knocked and then entered her room, "Evie, are you all right?"

"Have you seen the paper? Evie said fiercely. "It's worse than we thought. Controller was responsible for the problems the colleges are having and now there is proof it is gathering an army of grateful cheaters! And, guess what, your sister, BREV Force member, was right in the midst of it and didn't pay enough attention to...."

Brian turned to her, "Evie, you must calm down. This is not going to get us anywhere. Let me see the article." She turned on the screen and he reviewed the story.

When he looked up, Evie added, "Don't they understand, Brian? Cheating and changing grades can be just as mind-controlling as drugs. I should've figured this out and stopped it."

"I have been monitoring the schools and would venture to say that the article is correct in its evaluation of QuizMaster and Controller. Therefore, I conclude, nothing you, in your capacity, as a part-time administration office worker, could have done would have stopped this. As long as these things were considered harmless pranks, Controller was able to make very good use of the system.

"I also agree that these so-called, 'pranks,' were however, a test. I believe Controller now has a strong enough foothold in the education system to begin to build an army of grateful, happy students, who will do anything to get passing grades."

"Yeah, Brian, that's what I think too. Controller's using this teacher type, QuizMaster to cripple the education system and further build its army. Not just of 'grateful, happy students,' but of devoted followers. We need to get these kids and the schools, to take QuizMaster more seriously."

"I agree."

"But how will anyone ever take a, so called hologram Quizzer, seriously? It even sounds like a joke. Maybe Mom and Dad can come up with something." Evie checked the time digitizer, "They should be home soon!"

"No, Dr. Schmidt is in town. They are taking him out to dinner and Brad has already left for work."

"Then I guess it's just you and me. What can The BREV Force do with just the two of us?"

Brian shook his head, somewhat bothered by his lack of a solution, "My only answer at this time, is to be on the alert and wait for Controller to make the next move."

"I think The BREV Force got lucky with Cracko but Controller won't be caught off guard again. We need to be ready for anything."

"I agree. QuizMaster is too likeable to cause the same concerns as Cracko did. We will need to correlate the information I have been gathering with Rosie and together we should be able to give The BREV Force some insight into Controller's future plans."

CHAPTER 10

Brad couldn't believe what had happened to his friend. Jonathan seemed on the verge of a complete breakdown. Brad knew he had to do something to stop Controller. I need to pretend to want into QuizMaster's inner circle, if I want a chance at stopping Controller. It's the only way I might be able to help Jon and the others Controller has manipulated. With that thought in mind Brad approached Sheila.

"What are you doing here Kane? You weren't invited!"

"Cool it, Sheila. I'm not here to wreck your party. I just want in on the action!"

"You? Is this a joke? What do you know about what's goin' down?"

"Jonathan Morris clued me in."

"Well, as you can see your cry baby friend isn't here, so take your business elsewhere."

"Look, I need this as bad, if not more, than the rest of you."

"Yeah, hot shot, give me a break!"

"Nah, c'mon, you give me the break. You don't know me that well but my twin sister's a whiz kid and I just don't match up. My parents are freaking out with exams coming and I know I'm not gonna make the grade but I can't even compete because I can never be as good as she is. I need this real bad or I'm gonna fail in more ways than one!"

Sheila made Brad wait while she thought about it and then said, "I'll tell you what, I'll let QuizMaster decide."

It'd been about an hour since Jonathan saw Brad talking with Sheila, in front of the Parker Administration building. His hands were still shaky when he pulled his car into the Kane driveway, not knowing quite how he got there. He looked at the timer on his dashboard, hoping it wasn't too late to ring the bell. Jonathan tried knocking first but nobody answered so he started ringing the bell until he heard, "All right already, I'm comin'," before the door opened.

"Sorry, it's so late, Evie but I..." Jonathan was stammering like he was drunk and after the day she'd had, Evie wasn't in the mood to have a go 'round with Jon.

"Jonathan," she said holding the door only slightly open, "go home and sleep it off."

Jonathan pushed his way through the door and closed it behind him.

Evie didn't want to reveal her powers, so she allowed him to push his way in the door. "What's gotten into you?" She protested as she made him think she was trying to pry loose his hold on her arm.

"I'm sorry," panted Jonathan. "We must go now! Brad's in trouble."

"Jonathan you're drunk, Brad's probably hanging out after work, so..."

"No, this is all my fault!" Jonathan broke down crying. He slumped against the hall wall and collapsed down on the floor. Looking up at Evie, he pleaded. "I know I'm in bad shape but you have to hear me out."

Something in his voice, told her he needed her help. She hoped she wasn't being as foolish now as she'd been at the modeling audition and then later with Rick. After all, hadn't Jonathan had sexual ideas where she was concerned. "Stay put, I'll get you a glass of water and then I'll try to help you up.

Evie went into the kitchen where Brian was having a cup of coffee. "I'm glad you're in here." She told Brian what Jon had said and then asked, "I haven't felt anything but you saw what my emotions have been like. Can you sense Brad in trouble?"

"No but depending on where Brad is, you know distance is still a factor. I suggest before we can proceed we must try and find out what Jonathan knows."

"I agree. I'll try and get him to make some sense."

"All right, I'll remain here for now and keep my hearing tuned to you and Jonathan.

Evie returned to the hall and tried to comfort Jon while he drank the water she handed him. "Okay Jon, let's see if we can't get you on your feet and into the living room."

Jonathan's knees were weak but he slowly got to his feet and Evie supported him into the living room, where she helped him onto the couch. The candy Jon had taken had kicked in but for some reason it was not having the usual results.

"Now Jon, tell me about Brad."

Jonathan told Evie the same story he told Brad and then added what he'd seen and heard between Brad and Sheila, outside Norton University.

CHAPTER 11

At Norton University, Sheila had finally received a message from QuizMaster to proceed to the Administration Office with Brad.

They walked through the halls, following the instructions QuizMaster had given her. Sheila proudly proclaimed that at that very moment, Controller was ingeniously setting off fire alarms; one after another, throughout the campus, to keep nighttime campus security busy while they have fun with the school's records.

Sheila had gotten a flashlight from her car, in case the back-up generators hadn't kicked in after the alarms, then she and Brad maneuvered through the corridors until they came face to face with the hologram. Brad couldn't believe his eyes. QuizMaster looked like a professor and certainly more like a person than Cracko had. The hologram had some dimension and coloring; brown hair and eyes of green that moved and blinked. Even its clothing was more conventional, including glasses, dress shirt and slacks. Controller had made so many improvements it was hard to tell this was really a hologram.

"Sheila tells me you are not afraid to break into school buildings and steal semester finals. That is very good," QuizMaster taunted, "but first let me see what you are made of, are you,

A.   Ambitious,

B.   Stupid, or,

C.   Eager to get ahead with little effort Mr. Err..."

"Kane, Brad Kane and to answer your Quiz... Master, I'm really in need of the answers, plain and simple!"

"Fine, Kane. You wait over there while I give Sheila her assignment." The hologram took a pad from its pocket and read the list to Sheila. "Now, to properly pay for the prize, you get your choice of,

A.   Filing false attendance reports,

B.   Sending out memos to all Professors about grading on a curve, or,

C.   Downloading the names and records of the entire student body."

"Don't you A, B, C Me, you HOLOGRAM!" Sheila yelled, "I am Sheila, Controller's Human Helper. Controller always...."

QuizMaster interrupted her outraged sputtering with the teacher's lesson for the day, "Sheila, you must pay the price, like everyone else."

She again started to argue but the hologram cut her off.

"This is college! The big league! Do the assignment, or fail, your choice!"

QuizMaster then walked over to where Brad was waiting. "Do you understand today's lesson is history."

"I'm not sure," Brad said going along, "this is my first time in this class."

"Well, then, come along and learn." QuizMaster moved to the large disk cabinets which housed all the DR's, digitalized records. The hologram indicated where Brad should begin, then smiled from ear, to ear. "This is,

A.   The back bone of this college,
B.   Its confidential records, and,
C.   Our target!
D.   Get it?

Here's your history lesson," the hologram boasted, "you have entered the realm of genius. Controller has masterminded the perfect situation and in order for you to benefit you must understand your role.

"First, the background. When Controller first decided to use the education system to his benefit, he lured students from all the major colleges and universities in the world with on-line ads that promised higher grades. The response was incredible but as the wise ruler that he is, Controller was very particular about who was chosen to do his bidding. The recruits had to 'pass the tests.' They had to get jobs in the administration offices of their respective college and learn the inner workings of the computer systems. They were then instructed to set up passwords that linked back to Controller.

"Before long, Controller had established an educational net that included the names of entire student bodies, faculty, courses given and research being done. Stealing exams and changing scores really got the new recruits hooked, er, indebted, as history always teaches, make your enemies your friends and be sure they owe you! Oh well, the bell is about to ring, so we are out of time for today's lesson. Now, for your assignment!"

Brad was very puzzled as he listened to what the hologram had to say. He couldn't understand why Controller would allow so much to be revealed. There were only two possibilities: first, this was just a ruse, or second, Brad would never live to tell anybody!

Brad didn't have time to question that theory as QuizMaster seemed done with him and was moving toward Sheila.

QuizMaster questioned Sheila, "What is the delay! Is it that you just cannot handle the assignment, young lady? I believe you may have to stay after school and learn a lesson about rules and how they are to be followed."

Sheila was outraged, "You are very mistaken, hologram! I told you I am Controller's special helper. Controller would never have me do this junk!"

"First of all, Sheila, you will address me properly," QuizMaster fired back. "Secondly, if you choose not to do this 'junk,' as you call it, you can be expelled!"

Sheila, was mad as hell! She wasn't quite sure what her next move should be and decided, at least for the moment, to reluctantly sit down at the computer station and follow QuizMaster's orders.

Brad was busy at another station. QuizMaster walked over to him, "Brad, you have been an obedient student and passed the quiz with flying colors. So now, your next quiz is,

A   Begin downloading the files on this list,
B.   Recode the scores from this last exam,
C.   Put this password protected encryption around this new data.

Brad was downloading the files QuizMaster had specified but when he began reading what they were, he decided to re-route the information to his home computer.

"What are you doing Kane?" the hologram's voice resounded.

CHAPTER 12

10:45

Evie told Jonathan she had to get her things and would meet him outside in his new car.

She went into the kitchen to talk with Brian who decided to follow them in Evie's car. She argued with him that he didn't have a license but Brian stated, "Since each member of the family has driven with me and I did not have an accident, or any problems, at this moment, the license is a technicality we cannot afford to be concerned about." Brian added he would leave a note for their parents stating they were all out together.

Evie went outside and slid into the passenger side of Jonathan's car and then thought better of it. "Jon, seeing how you're still a bit shaky, how 'bout I drive?"

He had no objections and she changed places with him.

On their way to Norton University, Evie kept watch in the rear-view mirror for Brian. He seemed to be keeping up okay. She was a bit tense and decided to make idle chatter, "I've never driven such a hot car, what made you get this?"

They talked about a lot of nothing until she turned the car into the campus entrance. Evie saw security police everywhere. But she got hopeful and nervous when she spotted Brad's car. Well, at least he's still here!

With campus security everywhere, Jon directed her to an out of the way parking area, near the dorms, where he knew Sheila met up with other kids.

Evie touched the emergency button on the steering wheel and the flashers came on. "Man, how'd I do that?" She said covering the fact she purposely hit them to signal Brian they'd be stopping.

Jon responded, "Emergency flashers off and then told Evie where to park. He reached into car glove compartment and got a flashlight then got out and went around to help Evie get out.

They walked toward the Administration building, being careful not to alert campus security to their presence. It was late and even Evie's position in the administration office, would cause them to question her about being there at this hour. But her working in the Administration office did give them an advantage, she had the passcode to open the doors. Evie made sure no one was around before she keyed it in.

The computer consoles in the Administration office were on and information was flashing on every screen. Looking around Evie didn't know whether she was happy or sad that her brother wasn't there. Now, however, she was beginning to doubt Jonathan.

"Oh Evie! When we saw Brad's car I was sure he'd still be here. Now I don't know what to think," it sounded like Jon also doubted himself.

"Jon, maybe this is all in your mind?"

"Well, maybe but," Jon thought for a minute, "but are these computers in my mind too, Evie?"

Trying desperately not to believe the worst she walked over to the flashing consoles and suggested, "Well, that much is true!

"Sheila and her friends were probably here, I'll give you that but maybe it wasn't Brad, or maybe if it was...

maybe, he became impatient waiting and realized it was wrong to get involved with Sheila and left."

Evie kept searching for answers. "I'll bet this is all just a big misunderstanding. Brad's probably just hanging out somewhere on campus. Or maybe he's in the Hot Spot Shoppe. That's it, he just went to get something to eat. Let's see if he's there – or if not, maybe Ginger saw him tonight....."

Jonathan didn't believe any of Evie's conclusions but for lack of a better idea, he went along. They walked around campus but Brad was nowhere to be found and nobody had seen him. When they got to the Hot Spot Shoppe it was as they both feared. Brad wasn't there and now they got Ginger worried as well. She told them campus security had been coming and going all night but they wouldn't say what was going on.

Evie was desperate to find her twin. Her mind cried out, *Code 47 to BREV Force, Brian answer, please!* Her emotions clouded the link and the silence was deafening. She knew Brian was somewhere close but her feelings were so raw, she was unable to connect, even with him.

Ginger tried to be supportive when she asked, "Maybe there's something you missed, why don't you go over it again."

Jonathan and Evie recounted the details as Ginger listened, carefully. By the time they finished, it was obvious that Jon's mind was so blurred he wasn't sure of anything, anymore. "I think when I saw Brad with Sheila going into the school building, I panicked and left. Maybe I just overreacted." Jon was certainly panicking now. He didn't know what to do and now neither did Evie.

Ginger suggested, "Since Jon knows for sure that Brad was with Sheila, why don't we give her a call? I know she's not a friend but maybe she can straighten this out."

Evie checked the time. It was almost midnight, "It's a bit late to call don't you think?"

Jonathan nodded, "Yes but I don't think we have a choice."

Evie left Ginger questioning Jon while she went to get the number from the administration records, to make the call.

Evie tried to calm down as she walked back through the corridors but she was having a very difficult time. The events of the day, each piled one on top of the other, were now flashing through her mind. She was startled when someone came up behind her.

"I heard your call but you did not respond," Evie was so happy to see her brother she hugged him, then directed him to an area where they could talk.

"Oh Brian, thank you for finding me!"

"I have been here all the time, just waiting for you. I have made several attempts to reach your mind but, the block was too strong. I have also tried to reach Brad and he also did not respond. He may of course, still be too far away." Brian stopped himself from saying what he was thinking, or Brad is unable to communicate.

"I'm not doing very well tonight! I know I've got to get hold of my emotions. I'll try and keep it together, better." Evie calmed down enough to quickly fill her brother in on what they found out so far.

"Did you try Brad's C-TEL again?"

"Yes, there's still no response. I also holo-messaged him but nothing."

"Then I suggest since he is not responding to any communication, that you should try and contact this Sheila."

Brian pulled down the brim of the cap he wore and he accompanied Evie to the administration office to look up the number. The computers were all still on, generating information but they didn't have time to deal with that now!

"Here it is," Evie said, after logging into the system's student records. 'S. Tillman, 57 Drury Lane.'" Not really knowing Sheila very well, Evie figured out this should be correct since Drury Lane was in the rich part of town. She clicked the mouse that directed the computer to connect to the number. The wait seemed forever until Evie finally heard, "Sheila's out and I really don't care if I talk to you or not, so what you do is your choice. If you must leave some message, press one for video feed, two for audio only, or who cares!"

Evie knew she had reached the right number.

"Beep…"

She pressed two and then began, "This is Evie Kane. I'm looking for my brother Brad. I know we aren't friends and you have no reason to help me but if you know where he is…please, please call me!" Evie left an immediate page request with her C-TEL number and added, "Sheila, please, this is really important!"

Evie disconnected and led Brian toward the door. "We'd better get out of here. Campus security is everywhere tonight and we can't afford to get stopped by them." She also knew she could lose her job for just being caught in the Administration Office, without permission.

She secured the door and they headed back to where she had left Jon and Ginger. Brian found a secluded spot where Evie could see him. "Since your emotions are still on the surface, use a hand signal if you need me and then make an excuse to leave the table. Just know I will be right behind you, wherever you go."

"Thanks." She kissed her sibling and watched as he disappeared down the corridor.

Evie told Ginger and Jon that Sheila wasn't home and then Ginger came up with another suggestion. "I know this guy Rick that Sheila always hangs with. They're real close and if anyone would know what's going on with her, he would."

Evie's heart fell just hearing his name.

"The only problem is," Ginger added, "I don't know his last name, or how to reach him?"

Evie sheepishly stated, "That's okay Ginger, I do."

"You do?" Jonathan questioned. "How would you know some high and mighty rich kid, jock…?"

"Forget it Jon, it's a long story."

Evie's hands were shaking. She'd looked at Rick's number so many times and could never find a good enough reason to use it. Now, after this afternoon's embarrassment over the modeling job and the realization of his relationship with Sheila, Evie couldn't help but wonder why fate was playing this horrible trick on her. Of all people, Rick might be her only hope! She knew she had no choice but to call him.

She took out her C-TEL and with each number she called out, her heart beat faster. Evie didn't want Jonathan or Ginger to see her anxiousness and turned her back as she walked away.

When Rick answered the phone, her heart began to beat faster. "Rick, this is Evie Kane. Please don't hang up. I'm sorry to bother you so late but I need help and I didn't know who else to turn to."

Afraid of what he might say, after she ran out on him earlier that day, Evie just continued talking. "My brother, Brad, somehow got involved with Sheila tonight and…now, he's missing and …."

Without letting her finish Rick said, "Where are you now?"

"The Hot Shoppe!"

"I'll be right over!"

"Thanks Rick!"

When she disconnected, Evie walked back to where her friends were and just said, "Rick's coming…he's coming right now!"

While they waited for Rick, Evie listened to the voice in her head. *Code 47 to BREV Force, remember I am here, Evie.* Brian's voice told her.

She pulled herself together and responded, *Code 47, BREV, thanks Brian.*

Evie sat in front of the window. She hadn't said another word since she told them Rick was on his way. Jonathan sensed something strange about her; something that he was sure had nothing to do with Brad. Jon just didn't know what it might be and right now he didn't even trust his own judgment.

Evie saw Rick's reflection in the window and ran to meet him, "Thanks for getting here so fast."

"Hey, pretty lady, I'm here to help anyway I can," Rick's response gave Evie hope.

Jonathan took note of the look between them.

Rick exchanged a polite greeting with Ginger and Jonathan. Not wanting to waste time, he pushed on. "Let's get down to it. Fill me in."

Evie tried to keep her eyes off Rick while Jonathan again relayed what he'd seen and heard. Once he explained about Sheila's involvement, Evie was certain Rick wouldn't help.

Much to her surprise Rick turned to her and said, "I'm really sorry Brad got involved. Let me see what I can do to find him."

Rick then told them about his meeting with Sheila earlier that evening." After I left her at the college parking lot, I headed to the mall and saw some of the other kids Sheila had said were involved, so, something must have gone wrong but only with Brad?"

Rick thought for a moment and then said, "I know some places Sheila hangs. I'll see what I can find out. I'll be back as soon as I know anything."

"Shouldn't we go with you?" Jonathan asked.

"No. It's better if I go alone. If I run into Sheila, I can find out what's going on without arousing her suspicions. I'll be back as soon as I can."

He turned back to Evie and gently took her hand. "Evie, I know this is difficult but trust me!" He didn't wait a response.

Rick pushed through the double swinging doors at the entrance to the Hot Spot Shoppe but swung back around one more time to face Evie. Their eyes locked for a moment, "Try not to worry," he shouted, "I'll find him!" The doors closed and he was gone.

Jonathan used the opportunity to go to the men's room, while Ginger went to get another round of coffee for everyone.

In her mind, Evie could hear Brian saying, "I have continued my attempts to connect with Brad. Although they have been futile, my last two tries produced very strange feelings. Are you up to trying with me?"

Evie concentrated on the link and their thoughts melded successfully and together they reached out to Brad. But again, they were unsuccessful. "Oh Brian," she telepathically communicated, "this is really strange. It feels like we are in front of a wall. I know that Brad is out there somewhere but I can't get to him."

"Yes, although it is very basic, I believe your assessment describes the feeling accurately. Brian hesitated a moment, trying to decide what other options they had and then transmitted his thoughts to his sibling. "Evie, we have no choice for the moment but to see if your friends can help us."

"Do you think we should call mom and dad?"

"No, I would like to wait until we can assess the situation better."

"All right, Brian, just stay close, please!"

"I am right here, Evie." She terminated the link, just as Jonathan came back to the table. He tried to calm her fears and reached for her hand. "I'm sure Rick will be back soon with Brad."

It was after two o'clock in the morning and The Hot Spot Shoppe staff was beginning to prepare for the breakfast meal. The Shoppe was open and served 24 hours a day, seven days a week. Evie was so glad for the fresh hot coffee and the just baked cookies. Her nerves were raw and she kept eating and drinking coffee waiting for Rick to return. She knew if she was a nail biter, her finger nails would be down to the bone. She got up and began pacing. Evie was glad the only other customers, a group of students hitting the books before exams, weren't interested in her erratic behavior.

Finally, Rick returned. "Hurry!" he said trying to move them along. "They're holding Brad! We must move fast! I'll tell you what I found out on the way. I would have called your C-TEL but the place where they have Brad is really hard to find."

As Rick ushered Jonathan and Evie out the door, she turned and said, "You two go ahead, I'll be right out, I need to, well you know."

Ginger was still on shift and couldn't leave, "Evie, please call me as soon as you know anything."

"I will. Thanks, you've been a real friend!"

Evie rushed to the corridor to connect with her brother. "Brian, Rick found Brad but he's in real danger!"

"You must try to keep calm so we can keep communicating. I will follow in your car."

"Brian, I have a feeling Rick is going to drive like a maniac, you can't do that. If you're stopped, you don't have a license, or valid identification, or... And, you haven't had experience driving at high speeds and besides, in the past, someone was always with you, and..."

"Evie, it is fine! His voice calmed her. "This is not the time to worry about my driving. Brad needs our help and this is the only way. When we find Brad, he may need The BREV Force. We have prepared together for the possibility that someday I may need to be Raven, if it was ever needed. Now, it seems it may be. So, go, hurry now, before your friends get suspicious and return to see what is keeping you."

Reluctantly, Evie agreed.

"When the time is right, Evie, we will link and rescue Brad. I will be with you the entire way. Do not worry!"

Evie half smiled at Brian's, still formal, speech pattern, then nodded, kissed and hugged her brother. She rushed outside to where Rick and Jonathan were waiting.

Jonathan had started to open the rear door for her, hoping to comfort her in the back seat during the ride but instead, she had gotten into the front seat and slid in toward Rick. Her heart pounded at being so close to him. Jonathan got in next to her and the seat adjusted to accommodate the two of them. He shut the door and then moved as close to her as possible.

"Please Rick, tell us what you found out?" her voice quivered.

"I saw Sheila with QuizMaster and Brad in one of the McNab Lobster Plants. You know the one, the deserted warehouse off McNab Boulevard and Thomas Drive. Sheila often hangs out there."

Rick was cautious about his next statement. "Evie, don't panic but Brad was tied up and QuizMaster was attaching something to his head." Swerving to avoid a bump in the road, Rick tried to concentrate more on his driving and less on Evie's feelings, as he continued. "When I saw what was going on, I didn't wait, I just raced back to get you guys."

Evie and Jonathan held their breath until Rick finally brought the speeding car to a halt. He stopped in front of the warehouse, behind some trees. They all got out and cautiously crept up toward the warehouse entrance. Rick pointed to a window which was one level above where Brad was being held. They walked quietly and positioned themselves where they could see inside.

Brad was tied up in a chair with wires connected to his body. They couldn't see much else but they knew the situation was bad.

"What on earth could Brad have done to get himself into this mess?" Jonathan whispered.

"We need a way into the warehouse without alerting QuizMaster," Rick suggested.

"It's all my fault!" Jon was moaning. "Brad did this for me, and…"

Rick looked over at Jonathan, "Look you can cry all over your new image when we're done but for now, zip it and help, or leave!"

Evie pleaded, "Stop! Stop it both of you! Then, she pretended to faint, Jon caught her. "Oh, I'm uh, all right, I'm just not feeling good!"

Rick suggested she and Jon wait in his truck but she insisted that Jon stay with him. They both decided to walk her back to the truck. "Please, both of you, I appreciate your concern for me but just help Brad and be careful!"

Evie watched as they walked back toward the entrance to the warehouse and then she signaled Brian. He had managed to follow Rick's car, even at the high speed. Evie filled him in and they decided to try again to mind link, especially now that they were in a closer proximity.

After several tries the same strange blocked sensation was echoed back at them. Evie wanted to keep trying but Brian felt it would be useless. The silence in her mind told Evie, he was right. Something was blocking Brad from responding. Their only hope now was The BREV Force. "It feels strange being two and not three. Brian, I know we prepared for just this situation but are you sure you're ready?"

"Yes, I am ready but I am more concerned about you. After all, it is your twin in danger, not some stranger?"

"Yes, Brian. I can do this for Brad. And, with you there, I know together we can get Brad out of this mess!"

"Then, let us believe your trust and our abilities alone are good enough. But first, may I suggest that we call and leave a message, just in case someone is up and concerned. The hour is very late and we do not want mom and dad worrying."

"Yes, but what can we say, Brad's been kidnapped by QuizMaster?"

"No, I believe we can, as my step-mom Rosie would say, 'Tell the truth, without telling the truth.' Just say, we have encountered QuizMaster and we are all together."

"That's easy for you to say. But, what if Dad calls my C-Tel what will I say?"

"I suppose step-mom Rosie never gave you these lessons, so make the contact and I will compose."

Evie took out her C-TEL and made the connection directly into the message center, then handed the C-Tel to Brian.

She heard him speak the message, "A situation with one of Evie's friends occurred that led straight to QuizMaster. We have followed up and wanted to inform you before we proceed. We are all together and fine. We do not know when we will return home, however, it is advisable to not wait up, or try to contact us at this time," he then quickly disconnected.

"Wow, can you get Rosie to teach me that?"

Brian and Evie joined their minds power. Moments later their clothing transformed and Dove and Raven emerged.

They quickly formulated a plan and then Dove raced around the corner to the old window Rick had shown them and flew past Jonathan and Rick. "Excuse me gentlemen," she said but all they saw was the crashing glass as she landed on the floor below and positioned herself to face off with QuizMaster.

Jonathan turned to Rick, "Did you see that? Wow!"

"For once Jon, I agree with you. She is, wow! I wish I knew who she was."

CHAPTER 13

"Oh, not you again!" Sheila shouted. But, looking around and feeling the upper hand she added, "Where's your protector, Dovey girl, or did he just realize how wimpy you are and abandon you?" She laughed and put her arm on Brad's shoulder, showing her position of superiority.

"No, I'm is right behind her." Brian in the Raven disguise stated.

Even though Dove expected Raven to come crashing in behind her, it was still a shock seeing Raven, while Brad was sitting there captive.

QuizMaster warned, "Do not come any closer or the choices will be,

A. This boy will become one of Controller's unfortunate victims,

B.   Maybe the next hologram, or even better,

C.   You'll have to wait to find out."

Dove and Raven stood very still as QuizMaster held up a finger like a pointer as it spoke. "Controller has devised the instrument you see hooked up to this student, as just another way to create his army of followers.

Just imagine," the hologram cackled, "someday it might also turn us holograms into people. After all, look how much more real I am compared to the now disintegrated Cracko. But, for now, let me give you today's lesson.

As the hologram rattled on, Dove called out in her mind to Raven. Oh, look at Brad! He's tied up in that rickety old chair with electrodes all over his body… and I'm not sure what we can do and…

First, you must get a hold on your emotions. I barely can read your thoughts, even though we are standing next to one another. Try to analyze the situation and that will help.

Still going on, QuizMaster continued, "This holographic duplicator allows the victims brain waves to respond to a signal sent out by Controller. Once all the brain waves have responded, Controller adjusts the patterns and reverses the signal. The brain waves flow back to the victim's brain but with a new pattern. Individual traits and all semblance of personality will have been removed and replaced with all new programming. All that is left is a very obedient servant. It is really quite ingenious!"

Raven started to walk around the table that was in front of Brad, when QuizMaster put up a hand to halt him. "You must raise your hand Raven, when you want to move around the room. The hologram continued sarcastically, "Now sit down on one of the lobster crates and pay attention or you will have to write one hundred times, 'I must raise my hand before leaving my seat.'"

Raven ignored QuizMaster, who kept going on about the rules of the class room. Dove was starting to panic, when she heard her brother's voice in her mind. Please try and calm down. I have analyzed Brad's condition. He is not responding in any manner but it is too soon to know if it is because his thoughts are being blocked or whether he is unable to respond. However, the good news is that his brain pattern is still normal. So, at least for now, there is no irreparable damage.

Dove began to feel stronger and questioned QuizMaster, "Tell me, why are you doing this to this boy?" she was careful not to reveal that she or Raven knew Brad.

"He was a very bad student. He disobeyed the Quiz Rules and cheated. He was given a Quiz and he failed!"

"Yeah, leave it to Brad. We were at Norton University and he pleaded for the test answers," Sheila chimed in. "He said he really needed them to compete with his sister and he was really willing to do everything he was told."

Dove was visibly upset by Sheila's remark.

Raven couldn't leave the conversation there, "So what happened?"

"Goody two shoes Brad is what happened. He said he had a change of heart...couldn't screw with the files. But you know what that rat did instead, he sent the test answers he'd downloaded straight to his personal computer. Then just for spite he destroyed the files, depriving the rest of us of the answers."

Dove couldn't believe Brad would do such a thing just to get the test answers for himself, Sheila had to be wrong.

Raven seeing her dilemma, cautioned, Dove, do not be baited by Sheila. We need to concentrate on this situation and will assume Brad is innocent for now, until he is proven otherwise.

"How did he get here in this condition?" Raven asked.

"All these questions," QuizMaster was getting annoyed. "All right I will answer just this last one and then you will both come to order in this classroom. Here are the answers,
A.   Sheila drugged him with a healthy supply of her candy,
B.   Sheila seduced a guard into helping her move him to her car, that is after she said he was drunk and somehow wondered into the Administration office,
C.   She drove her vehicle right up to these warehouse loading doors behind me and dumped him,
D.   Then the fun began, when she hooked him up and turned on the juice!

"So, pretty Miss Dove," QuizMaster instructed, "now that you have all the information about the curriculum for this class and the consequences of not obeying the rules, please take a seat. Raven, be a gentleman and fetch another crate. Bring it here for teacher's pet, so Miss Dove, can sit at the head of the class." Raven moved the crate to where the hologram pointed and returned to his seat.

"Just a few of the rules... there is no sleeping in my class. Anyone caught sleeping will be doused by this water." QuizMaster went on, pointing to a large pitcher on the table in front of Brad.

Just then, Jonathan and Rick came busting through the door. "We came to make the odds more even," Jonathan boasted.

"You are late for this exam." QuizMaster shouted at the two boys. "If you do not find your seats in one minute, you will both be marked absent and will,
A.   Fail,
B.   Fail and be made to pay
C.   Fail and cause Brad here to have a very nasty accident."

Jonathan and Rick quickly found crates and sat down.

QuizMaster then informed them, "Now, you boys did not do your homework, or you would have known that when you opened the door, you tripped an electronic devise," the hologram laughed. "The common term, for your edification, might be,

A.   Bomb,
B.   False alarm,
C.   Electrical explosive, or,
D.   Booby trap or not...

"This, of course, is multiple choice but whether you choose, A, B, C or D, the timer is counting down the destruction of this warehouse as we speak. Oh, what fun we are having!" the hologram danced around. "This is turning out to be an incredible lesson. Everything and everyone will be destroyed. That is, of course, except me!"

Raven wanted to get everyone out of the warehouse to safety but without knowing what other disasters might be triggered, he did not dare. He signaled Dove, who was keeping an eye on a very distraught Sheila.

"What about me, QuizMaster? Controller won't let anything happen to me!" Sheila moved away from Brad and positioned herself between QuizMaster and the class.

"Sorry, my dear, it is just one of the casualties of being in this class you know! You are expendable along with your other classmates. Sometimes it is necessary to make a point so everyone can learn and if you must go too...ah well!"

Dove was trying to think of her own teachers and what worked with them when suddenly, she came up with an idea!

"QuizMaster," she said. "We're all so very appreciative of the good lessons we've learned today but I know I will need a little extra help, if I'm going to pass this test. Can't you just help me," she took a deep breath and hoped the hologram would take the bait. "You wouldn't want me to fail. Maybe you can tell me something that'll help me to find the answer. After all, I just want to prove my I.Q."

QuizMaster laughed, "I believe I can help you, little lady. I will give you an oral exam, while the rest of the class takes the following quiz."

Raven nodded, as he realized what Dove was doing and motioned to Jonathan and Rick to play along with taking the test.

"Now class," QuizMaster began, "before we start, I have decided, thanks to the request of sweet little Miss Dove, to give you a clue. In order to successfully answer the quiz, you will have to list all the steps and come up with the correct answer." Writing the clue on a holographic blackboard, QuizMaster turned to the class and said, "Clue. The counter sees better in the dark!"

QuizMaster gave a hollow laugh and then decreed, "Now, you must come up with steps A through D and then arrive at the correct answer. Where is the counter?"

QuizMaster chuckled, "This is one of the hardest quizzes I have ever given. If I were you students, I would just accept a zero, that is, except for you Miss Dove. Oh, by the way, in this class, if the detonation doesn't destroy you, all failing students will happily take their place in the chair after Brad and be willingly transformed into obedient followers of Controller's army."

QuizMaster went on and on, while Raven looked for the answer. He signaled Dove. Let's turn around

QuizMaster's clue and create a blackout. He and Dove and concentrated on a light fixture overhead, until the bulb started to vibrate causing a loud noise as it shook against the fixture. The light began to flicker on and off.

"What are you doing? There must be quiet while the students are taking this quiz!" the hologram shouted. But, before QuizMaster could do anything the bulb shattered sending shards of glass flying in all directions.

Raven raised his hands to gather all the pieces of as they shattered so no one would be hurt but he didn't see the wire that had sparked and was threatening, as it danced on the ground.

Dove instinctively reached for it, before she could properly insulate herself and was jolted by the electrical current passing through her body, like a shock treatment. She fell to the ground in the darkness.

QuizMaster moved toward her but Raven moved around everyone to get to her first. "Everyone stay where you are, including you, hologram!" he shouted having adjusted his vision to the dark. Once he was sure QuizMaster was not taking advantage of the situation, he charged his hands and placed them on her temples neutralizing the electrical charge.

Dove started to move and Raven made sure she was all right before he helped her to her feet.

While all their eyes were adjusting to the dark the hologram was laughing. "Young amateurs, trying to compete with me and Controller, you are just young fools! You have not accomplished anything. The timer is attached to its own backup generator. So, you see, ha ha, it sees, better in the dark and it is still very functional." The hologram boasted, "So, I ask again, is it,

A.   Bomb,
B.   False alarm,
C.   Electrical explosive, or,
D.   The whole warehouse is just one big booby trap?"

The BREV Force fixed their night vision to search the warehouse for the timer. Finally, they located a blinking red light on the far side, behind a window shutter.

They zoned in their optical night vision and read the blinking numbers: it read: "4:23." It was the countdown to destruction but, was there really anything destructive, or, was this just another ruse by QuizMaster.

They decided to assume the danger was real and act accordingly. Dove and Raven knew they had to get to the timer before it ticked their time away…or find a way to stop it. Raven believed the only way to deactivate the device and keep everyone safe was if BREV Force was three, instead of two.

Brad was still in a trance-like state. They had to find a way to revive him. The portable computer he was hooked up to was still operating; probably off a battery backup.

Raven signaled Dove to keep QuizMaster occupied while he tried to disengage the portable computer. He recharged his hands and when he was sure Dove had QuizMaster's full attention, blew the charged particles at the battery, draining its power. Immediately the light on the computer went out, confirming a full shut down and with it, any immediate threat to Brad.

No one seemed aware of what had just happened. Raven then attempted to link with Brad.

With the lights in the warehouse still out, everyone was still afraid to move in case they might set something else off.

Jonathan and Rick were closest to the door and Sheila remained crouched in a corner.

Raven could feel a slight response from Brad as he moved toward him but QuizMaster caught him, "Teachers have eyes in the back of their heads, Raven, even in the dark." Then, QuizMaster warned, "No tricks or I will decide to, uh, destroy that one!" QuizMaster said pointing to Rick. Dove and Raven held back and waited tensely for the hologram's next move.

The count down now read: "2:04."

QuizMaster announced, "Quiz time is up. You see, my accelerated student, the computer you just shut down, oh and you thought I did not know what you were doing, well, that computer process was speeded up when the lights went out and your little scheme which I admit, was brilliant, was in fact, too late! YOU FAIL!"

QuizMaster returned to the role of the disciplining school master. "Now, even though the process was interrupted on Brad, Controller decided to re-route the energy to me, so I can still complete the process on Brad, or anyone else at my choosing!"

Glowing like an electric Christmas Tree, QuizMaster lit up the room. Pointing to its own hand that now glowed brightly, it said, "By placing this appendage, on the head of a victim, all brain cells are immediately destroyed. Now, since we have completed today's lesson plan with Brad, I believe we can work on the homework assignment, getting new victims for Controller. Let me show you method A." QuizMaster slowly passed the hand near Rick.

Sheila screamed but QuizMaster continued to bring the deadly hand closer to Rick's head.

"1:11," remained on the timer.

"No!" Sheila cried. "Controller doesn't want Rick! Take Dove! She's already a mindless idiot! Please, don't hurt Rick."

"Sorry Sheila, Controller has taken a liking to Miss Dove and wants her, not as a follower but for his own. No harm will come to her. But Rick, on the other appendage..."

"QuizMaster," Dove pleaded, "I can't let you harm Rick. If Controller wants me, I will go willingly. But, please don't harm Rick!"

Rick called out in the dark, "Dove, don't do this for me!"

QuizMaster sympathized, "Such a brave one, that Rick! He would make a good follower."

"0.45," remained.

"No," screamed Sheila, "Controller doesn't want Rick. Take Dove she'd make a great hologram! That might be her only usefulness. Controller needs me. I am his chosen helper. He would want to please me!"

"0.31"

The lights from the hologram's appendage sparkled over Rick's head. Sheila continued to argue with QuizMaster.

Raven was using the time to focus on Brad. He was positive that he had seen Brad's eyelids flutter but he was not getting any other responsive brain signals. He quickly identified the brain cells that weren't responding and telepathically repaired them.

Brad still wasn't moving.

Sheila and QuizMaster were still arguing and the timer was still ticking.

"All right, Sheila! QuizMaster gave in. "You are so loud and disruptive in class! So, I will summon an answer from Controller. But remember, that will be the Final Answer, ha...ha...!"

"0.15,"and counting!

Then at "0.14" a loud piercing noise permeated the warehouse, "0.13

0.12

0.11

0.10

0.09, then 0.08, then…"

The high-pitched sound was affecting everyone, including the hologram. "S o m e t h i n g   s t r a n g e   i s   h a p p e n i n g   t o   m e." QuizMaster's voice began vibrating. Its holographic form began to shake uncontrollably, "C o n t r o l l e r, H E L P!" As the hologram shook, the light provided by its appendage began to flash on and off.

Sheila, Jonathan and Rick were holding their ears, trying desperately to shut out the noise that had brought them to their knees in extreme pain.

Raven and Dove blocked their ear passages shutting off the sound and shielded Brad in the same way. Raven tried to help the others while Dove searched for a way to stop the counter.

She tormented the hologram, "It seems to us, QuizMaster, the sound is disrupting your matrix and unless you stop the countdown you are on your very own countdown to destruction"

"C o n t r o l l e r, I n e e d.   the   a n s w e r   or I will   F A I L   t h e   t e s t…!"

"0.07, 0.06. 0.05"

QuizMaster was having a difficult time holding its holographic form and did not notice that Brad had regained consciousness.

Raven saw the shock reflected in Brad's open eyes and quickly established a communication link, *Code 47 to BREV Force,* not waiting for a response, he signaled, *Stay calm. I have assumed your role as Raven and will give it back to you at the appropriate time. For now, just know that you are all right. We must be careful. We do not want to alert QuizMaster to your recovery. Feign a state of unconsciousness, while you attempt to loosen the ropes.*

It took a few minutes for Brad to process the message. He started to work on the ropes.

"0.04, 0.03…"

QuizMaster's image rapidly began to fade in and out. Feeling time had run out, Raven rushed toward the counter.

"Oh, oh," QuizMaster jeered.

"0.02.…"

CHAPTER 14

Everyone ducked as they waited for the anticipated explosion. Dove rushed to try to shield bodies but there was no need. There was no explosion . . . "Ha, Ha," QuizMaster laughed. "B. the answer was B. False Alarm!"

"Controller cheated! The test was rigged!" Laughing hysterically the hologram announced, "You all fail!"

They all looked up in amazement as the lights came on. QuizMaster, back to its holographic image, was flitting around the room with delight. "I told you Controller gave me all the answers." the hologram bragged. "But, we neglected to tell you this was a timed test!"

Raven looked at the timer. It had stopped at "0.01."

Sheila, Jonathan and Rick were still regaining their equilibrium when QuizMaster added, "Do not get too comfortable, Controller can start the final countdown again, whenever he chooses!"

Dove motioned to Rick and Jonathan to leave while they could but QuizMaster moved to stop them. "Sorry, Little Girl, I have established a force field to stop them from leaving. They have caused a lot of trouble. It has been decided! One of them will have to stay for detention. Controller does not care which one. Sheila seems to fancy Rick so..."

QuizMaster raised its electrified appendage and plunged toward Rick. Sheila and Dove both rushed to protect him. Raven grabbed Sheila, to prevent her from interfering, while Brad continued to struggle to loosen the ropes on his wrists.

Afraid QuizMaster might get to Rick before she could shield him, Dove reached for the water she had seen on the table and threw it at QuizMaster's appendage.

The water missed and hit the force field, stopping QuizMaster in its tracks. Sparks flew like a Fourth of July fireworks display and Dove yelled to Rick and Jonathan, "Run! Get out now!" They didn't hesitate, they just turned and ran through the warehouse until they were safely outside.

When the force field stopped sparkling, Raven was still holding Sheila. He glanced toward Dove and knew she was the one now in danger. She was too close to QuizMaster to get away before some part of the deadly arm would touch her.

"QuizMaster," Raven yelled out. "Rick and Jonathan are gone. The odds are even again. We hold your ally captive. Allow Dove to pass unharmed and you can have the advantage. Then, I'll release Sheila."

QuizMaster responded by moving closer to Dove.

"What you do, or do not do to Sheila makes no difference to me, or to Controller. The odds are always in the teacher's favor but, just to prove that point, if you do not let Sheila go, Dove will,

A.   Suffer,

B.   Be punished, or

C.   Definitely die, die, die!

And, just to give you an added clue, the results would be unfortunate, since Controller really took a liking to Miss Dove!"

Brad couldn't believe what was happening to his sibling and all because of him. He had to get the ropes untied. He worked at fingering the knots but his abilities seemed very limited. *Code 47 to BREV, it's taking me too long,* he signaled back to his brother, *my fingers aren't working too well!*

Raven replied, *Keep your fingers on the ropes and allow me to telepathically maneuver them.*

Brad remembered back to the first time Evie had used her mind power to make his finger move. He relaxed and felt his fingers manipulating the ropes. The twisted rope gave way and his hands were free. He opened his eyes slightly just to glance around and be sure he was not being watched and then reached down and untied his feet.

Free to assist The BREV Force, Brad mustered all his energy and flung himself toward Dove, driving them both down to the floor. As Dove fell QuizMaster reached to touch her with the appendage but, stretched too far, losing its footing. The hologram flayed its arms but couldn't regain its balance. Its holographic body hit the wet floor, electrocuting the deadly appendage and transposing the hologram into a glowing prism of blinding lights.

Raven shielded a stunned Sheila and watched as QuizMaster slowly faded.

With QuizMaster now destroyed, Sheila realized that she was completely on her own. Dove got up and helped Brad stand, while Raven tightened his grip on Sheila.

Dove took the lead and guided their way through the dark warehouse. Suddenly, the warehouse was lit up with a flashing red beacon and a piercing alarm. Frightened, Sheila tried to break free. "Take Sheila, I will carry Brad," Raven said, as he picked his brother up into his arms.

Grabbing Sheila's struggling arm, Dove warned her, "Fighting me now, will only delay our getting out." Sheila didn't seem to care. Dove squeezed Sheila's arm tighter, "I don't care if I drag you but we are getting out of here together. Now, just move it!"

The red light began to flash more quickly as they all raced toward the exit. Then suddenly the flashing stopped. Raven shouted, "Hurry Dove!"

CHAPTER 15

Looking at the clock on the night table Martin wondered if the twins and Brian were home yet. A few times during the night he'd been awakened with unsettling thoughts but decided to stay in bed and put his worries to rest. With Vivian sleeping so soundly beside him, he didn't want to get up and take the chance of waking her.

His thoughts wandered to the events of the evening. The dinner with Dr. Schmidt had been a disaster and no matter what he said, he knew Vivian was still worried about Schmidt being in Island Falls but so was he; he just couldn't tell her. He'd promised her he would protect them and their work.

When they arrived home from dinner, the house was empty except for a note Brian had left. "We are out together. Do not wait up!"

Vivian didn't make anything of it and she went up to bed while he checked the message center. The system signaled two messages. Message one origination: Norton University Sender; Dean Farrell. Martin pressed audio-video and the face of the dean appeared on the screen. "I hope all is well with both of you and that you'll finish the I.A.S. assignment and return to your research soon. We have authorized continued use of the Cottage and if you need anything let us know. If not, take care until then!"

The second message was from Dr. Schmidt, who thanked them for a lovely evening and reminded them he looked forward to getting an early start the next morning.

Martin hoped there would be some good news somewhere and decided to check his h-mails:

"< To... UNDISCLOSED >"

CC...

Subject:

"< R U the 1? >"

"Dammit! This has got to stop." Martin was furious and needed to calm down before going back upstairs. He checked his files for reports from Rosie. Lists began coming up, each in a separate folder highlighting her research and results. Martin scrolled down to the conclusions. In each case the words were the same: "Inconclusive."

Martin knew he needed to really read the contents but it was late and if Rosie wasn't satisfied with her own results, he knew there would be no new answers found by his re-reading the materials.

He deleted the two messages; saved the report file, closed up and started up the stairs. Martin felt weighted down, as if heavy chains were attached to his legs; making each step more difficult.

He opened the bedroom door expecting Vivian to be fast asleep but instead she was sitting up in bed. At that moment, he was sure everything else could wait.

They talked and finally Vivian fell asleep but Martin was still very much awake. The evening ended on a beautiful note but he couldn't shake the feeling something was still very wrong.

As if feeling his uneasiness, Vivian woke abruptly. "I'm here Viv," Martin said trying to comfort her. "Everything's all right. I'm sorry if I woke you."

"It wasn't you, I must have been dreaming. I feel as if something terrible has happened."

"It was just a dream." He pulled her to him and kissed her forehead. After a few minutes, he sensed her calming down.

"You know Viv, I could be insulted. After all my promises to keep you safe and protect you and our work and of course, all my tender loving care," he laughed to ease any remaining tension she might still feel, "you have a nightmare!"

Vivian smiled and said, "Martin those are just some of the reasons I love you!"

Martin decided to get her some warm milk to help her get back to sleep. He went downstairs and looked around but didn't see any sign that his children had gotten home, so he went down to the den to check for any new messages.

Martin returned to the bedroom and tried to hide his concern but Vivian saw right through him. She took the glass of milk he'd heated and pressed him for the truth. He decided, what she would suspect was probably worse so he calmly told her about the message Brian had left.

"Brian sounded positive Viv, so let's just hope tonight The BREV Force will defeat QuizMaster and Controller and all this will be over once and for all."

CHAPTER 16

"Run Dove, run! You can make it!"

The BREV Force knew that when the red light stopped flashing in the warehouse, their chances of getting out alive would end. Dove turned back toward her siblings and saw Raven carrying the still weakened Brad in his arms.

Sheila used that moment to try to break free of Dove's grip but Dove just tightened her hold. She started to move toward her brothers, when the flashing light stopped. She heard the deafening blast and with the street in sight, gave Sheila a forceful shove.

In that split-second Dove had to decide between helping her brothers or protecting Sheila. She flew through the air and landed on Sheila, shielding her body from the force of the explosion. It seemed like an eternity had passed in that split second. Dove felt Sheila squirming under her and pushing and kicking, "Get off me, you!" Sheila spat.

Dove got up and kept her grip to help Sheila.
"You could have killed me with your weight," was Sheila's only response as she tried to pull away.

Dove saw Jonathan running toward her. She was so glad he'd made it out of the warehouse unharmed. Her heart stopped, she didn't see Rick.

Jonathan told her they'd both gotten out right before the explosion. "Rick went to call the police and I was to keep watch for you. I'm glad you're safe," he said, "but where's Brad?" Jonathan asked in a tone that revealed his fear for his friend.

"I'm not sure! He and Raven were behind me. I have to go back into the warehouse right now and look for them. Do you think you can hold Sheila until the police come?" Jonathan nodded as Dove handed, a struggling Sheila, to him.

"This warehouse area is still unstable. For now, until we know the warehouse explosion has been contained, I suggest you take Sheila and get away from this entrance."

"I'll take Sheila around to Rick's car and we can wait there with him 'til the cops come."

Dove watched as Jon dragged Sheila away. She then tried to link with her brothers but all she heard were her own desperate thoughts, reverberating back at her.

She looked around the warehouse wreckage but saw nothing. Raven and Brad had been behind her in the warehouse when it exploded. Were they trapped somewhere inside…, or worse?

The debris was everywhere. Dark heavy dust and smoke filled the air impeding her "super vision." Without the help of her brothers, Dove was feeling a little hopeless. She also realized her emotions were hindering her. She knew she couldn't breathe in the smoke but she thought she might be able to focus her efforts on penetrating the thick cloud.

Dove concentrated on the layers of smoke and reduced each particle down to its smallest molecule. Soon, she was breathing easier and seeing more as she moved very cautiously through the warehouse.

She forced the ruins out of her way and ventured deeper into the wreckage. Dove spotted a piece of cloth, which she hoped was from Raven's costume. It was buried under piles of rubble. She mustered all her strength to lift the heavy beams and debris that blocked her way. They must be here! She knew she was still too emotionally wrought. Dove called out in a loud resounding voice, "Raven, Brad can you hear me…please!"

"Yes, we are here…," the weak sound was Raven's voice.

Relieved, Dove kept removing debris; deeper and deeper layers, while following the sound of his voice. His effort to speak, gave her the strength to keep going. When she finally found them; they were pinned down. Dove summoned every ounce of her abilities and dug through. She lifted away what she could, then, crouched down and used her hands to sift through the ruins. Finally, she was able to grab Raven's hand. "Oh, thank God! I'm so glad I finally found you!" She hesitated for a moment and asked, "Where is Brad?"

He tried to talk and she could see his pain. "Here," was all he said. There was a beam that had fallen across them. She had to work fast to get them out. Dove could see she wouldn't be able to just slide them out. She tried to dislodge what she could and finally reached Brad. He was lying unconscious next to Raven.

"Has Brad been unconscious the entire time?" Dove questioned as she examined the situation. Both her brothers were still completely pinned down.

"Yes. Raven responded, still, with a great deal of effort.

Dove started to move a plank aside but as she did Raven cringed.

"Yes, my leg has been injured. But, right now we cannot worry about me. You have to keep trying to clear our way. We must get Brad assistance. I am not certain of his condition."

She turned her attention to her twin. Her conclusion was that Brad must have been shielded by Raven's body in the blast. He seemed unhurt. "He's out of it but as far as I can tell, that might still be from whatever QuizMaster had done to him.

The fires are still burning all over this warehouse, so we'd better get out of here, while we still can!"

"I am still weak, so you will need to remove the rest of this rubble but I can try and assist you with a mind meld?"

Raven concentrated his thoughts on her physical attributes; muscle content and strength.

Dove began to feel her muscular structure pumping and began lifting the remaining beams that still had her brothers pinned. Raven kept his thoughts centered while Dove continued to draw on the link. She worked as fast as she could. "I feel it coming loose but I still can't move this last girder."

Because of Raven's condition and Dove's emotional state, he was having trouble giving her all the needed strength to finish freeing them.

Brad must have sensed his sibling's difficulty. He opened his eyes and saw his sister struggling to free them. He took a deep breath and drew on all his strength but he collapsed.

Dove however, felt the added push from Brad and heaved the beam, releasing Raven. She helped him up and together they lifted the remaining rubble that held Brad trapped, then slid him out from under the barriers.

Dove could feel the heat of the fires getting closer. "I'll carry Brad. You lean on me and we'll all get out together."

"No. I will only slow you down." Raven replied. "Now hurry. Take Brad, I will be right behind you."

"No, not this time!" she protested. "We'll go out together and that's final!"

Dove lifted Brad who was now unconscious into her arms and with Raven struggling with her, they headed for the exit. "We're almost out, just a little further." Her last words were muffled by an explosion and a burst of flame that threatened to engulf all of them.

Somehow Dove staggered out in time, still carrying Brad but when she turned to look for Raven all she saw a huge fire ball surging toward them; threatening to envelop them. She gently put Brad down on the ground and turned to face the danger but where was Raven? If he was still in the warehouse, she had to get back in there. Feeling the extreme heat on her face she raised her hands to repel the flames.

Dove was very grateful she'd trained to use her powers on a solitary basis. Now, she mustered all her strength and set up a shield that surrounded the fire and robbed it of its oxygen.

When it had safely died out Dove began to see what she needed to do. Even though Brad was still unconscious, she didn't detect any real danger to him but Raven, on the other hand, well, she didn't want to think of that…, certainly not yet.

She ran back into the warehouse. "Raven, Raven," she cried. "Where are you?" But there was no answer.

The smoke was thicker now and the interior of the warehouse was extremely hot. Get a grip on your emotions, she kept repeating as she concentrated on enhancing her range of vision. She knew she had to increase her acuity if she was going to see through the dense smoke molecules.

After what seemed an eternity, Dove was finally able to see into the warehouse; the sight of total destruction scared her. How was she going to find him? Acting on pure instinct, Dove used her optic nerves like a camera shutter and scanned every inch of the ruins. Tears were running down her face but these were from the smoke and not her out of control emotions. Her eyes were burning from the heat and she knew she had to get back outside to clear them but she couldn't leave. She was getting desperate. Brad was still unconscious, so he couldn't help her. Dove tried a link but again, Raven didn't respond.

She had no choice. Dove turned her attention back to Brad and the hope that if she revived him, together, they could find Raven. She went out of the warehouse to where her brother was still lying on the ground. Brad's breathing had become even more labored and he was very pale. His ordeal with QuizMaster had left him in such a weakened state that now it seemed to be hampering his ability to fight the effects of the smoke.

Dove did mouth to mouth techniques on Brad to help flush out his lungs. Within minutes, he started to cough out the effects and breathe more easily.

With Brad regaining consciousness, Dove began the process of locating and repairing the damage the fire caused him. She had to work fast. She may have lost one brother but she was determined not to lose two!

Using all her ability, Dove held her emotions in check. She worked at superhuman speed, accessing the damage and repairing each nerve, cell and organ, as needed.

Soon, Brad was coming back to himself, "Where's Raven," were his first words. The tears rolled down his sister's face and he saw everything in her eyes. "No! This is all my fault and I won't let him die because of me," he said, struggling to get up.

But Brad's expression changed as he saw Raven stagger out of the warehouse and collapse to the ground

"Raven," Brad screamed!

Dove ran to him and Brad pulled up and scooted his aching body painfully inching closer to his siblings

Raven was covered in black soot and obviously shook up but he nodded his assurance that he was all right.

"Oh, Br... oh, Raven! We're so glad to see you." Dove was having trouble remembering she must stay in character, especially since both of her brothers faced such grave danger. She held her brother tight. "But, how did you make it out? I saw the warehouse explode, everything was destroyed and I searched every inch and ...."

A labored Raven reached for her hand and drew enough strength to speak. He proceeded slowly and found with each account he grew stronger; more determined in his resolve to tell his sister and brother what happened. "I saw you carrying Brad and was sure you made it to the door but then I felt this mass of fire close behind me. I knew I would not make it out in time, so I concluded that I had to get out of its path, or be burned to death. I huddled in a corner near the door. There was an old asbestos tarp on the ground that gave me protection from the fire and a small window above me that had broken glass that seemed to be letting in just enough oxygen to help me breathe."

"No wonder I couldn't find you. You were under the tarp. Now that I can think more clearly, I guess I should have changed my optical nerve to an infra-red signal that would detect body heat."

Brad's tears were flowing, "I'm just glad you're both alive. This scheme I pulled almost got you both killed!"

"We can discuss that later," Dove told Brad, as she tried to help Raven. She knew how drained she felt and realized that Raven must have depleted all of his energy, in the warehouse just keeping Brad alive and then surviving under the tarp.

They had learned during their development training time, that when they acted alone, it took more effort and used up more energy. Even though Raven seemed to have more abilities, he also had a breaking point. Dove took his hands in hers and the energy that flowed between them helped Raven regain his strength and made them both feel better.

Dove was about to do the same for Brad, when she heard Jonathan and Rick approaching.

Jonathan saw his friend on the ground and ran to Brad. He got down next to him. "I'm so sorry I got you into this, Brad. Do you know how close that was? I'm just so glad you're safe."

In his weakened state, Brad just nodded.

Rick filled everyone in. "The paramedics, fire department are on their way. When the police got here they wouldn't let us go until they were satisfied that we didn't cause this mess." Rick turned and spoke directly to Dove, "Sorry it took us so long to come back to help you." They seemed to be locked in each other's eyes when he shifted the conversation to Sheila. "The police are questioning her now but I hate to admit it, I'm feeling a little sorry for.

"You're what!" Jon screamed! Look at Brad, for that matter, look at Raven, how can you feel sorry for Sheila, she caused this!

"I know that sounds crazy after all this but while we were waiting I took her aside and got really angry at her. I told her we could've all been killed because of her! I told her I could no longer run with her, unless her attitude changed. She seemed so devastated... and... I just wanted her to apologize to all of you for her behavior but..."

Dove could see that Rick felt responsible for Sheila's actions.

"Rick, I'm sure she would be devastated to lose your, uh, relationship but nothing that happened here is your fault, if anything you helped save Brad and .... even you can't change her."

"That may be true but I wish she could see. Controller just uses her and she winds up getting into big trouble. This time she endangered all of our lives..." Then Rick added, with regret, "I've always been there for her but, I guess that just hasn't been enough." He turned to Dove to express his gratitude, "You were just wonderful! Thanks."

Dove heard Rick's tender words regarding Sheila and felt a bit jealous. "I'm just glad we were able to defeat QuizMaster without anyone being seriously hurt," Dove said, then lightly touched Rick on the shoulder.

"All this gushing over Dove, the little sparkling twinkle girl," Sheila fired as she was being escorted to the scene by a policeman.

"I'm Officer Jackson. You must be The BREV Force. I'm so pleased to finally meet you. I've heard so much about you and well..." The officer was in awe and just kept rambling. "Uh, I'd like to ask you some questions. Sheila here is claiming she's not the culprit. She swears she's innocent and that someone named Brad Kane is the one we should be arresting. She has also made a very serious accusation against you, Miss Dove. She says you tried to kill her."

Everyone started talking at once.

"Quiet or I'll haul you all in!" The officer looked down at the ground and asked, "Are you Brad Kane?

Brad again struggled to nod.

Sheila interrupted, "Of course that's him there on the ground. Mr. Goody Turncoat Brad! He helped QuizMaster at Norton University. After all, his sister works in the administration office and when he got the answers for the final exams, he tried to turn the rest of us in."

"Well, no matter what you have to say Miss Sheila, I still need to get to the bottom of this. The boys gave me their version but it differs greatly from what you had to say."

"They are just trying to cover up and pin this on me. Jon there, is Brad's best friend. But, Rick, Rick...I don't understand...." Sheila actually had tears welling up in her eyes but turned so no one would see. She yelled, "It was Brad, just ask him, see if he'll tell the truth!

Dove attempted to come to Brad's defense but Raven cautioned her to stay in character and not say anything.

Brad, mustered all his strength to reply, "Sorry Sheila but you've got it all wrong. I never intended to help you, or QuizMaster. My plan all along was to just defeat you!"

"Liar! Liar! You wanted those test scores to get brownie points with your family over your sister...we all know she's the genius. You can't lie your way out of this!"

"Quiet both of you." Officer Jackson was getting annoyed. "You'll get your chance to tell your stories to the D.A. For now, I am investigating what happened here."

When the bickering finally stopped, Officer Jackson continued. Everyone questioned agreed that, you, Sheila, are guilty of breaking and entering and your actions resulted in the destruction of this property. There is also a charge of kidnapping. So, you're under arrest on these charges." He took the force field generator gun from his holster belt and incarcerated Sheila. Then, he read Sheila her rights.

She again started protesting but no one was listening.

The paramedics came around the corner to the door of the warehouse, where everyone was standing. They asked Officer Jackson to hold on his questioning while they checked everyone for effects from smoke inhalation.

They gave everyone an oxygen tube which expels all hazardous elements from the lungs while it adjusts the proper levels of oxygenation. The BREV Force accepted the apparatus even though it really wasn't necessary; it was easier than an explanation.

When the paramedics were satisfied that there weren't any serious problems, they began to run routine vitals. Rick and Jonathan said they were fine but Sheila wanted to have a complete examination. "After all," she said, "that Dove pushed me so hard and then landed on me."

Then, Sheila seemed to have a change of heart. "Before me, why don't you examine The BREV Force, then maybe someone will realize they're just freaks!"

She kept going on while Raven and Dove also refused any examination. They couldn't risk an examination that might reveal their body's physical enhancements.

"Well, it's obvious young man that you're not fine," one of the paramedics pointed out, speaking to Brad.

Brad thought quick and replied, "My parents are doctors and I'm sure they would rather give me the once over, you understand…"

The paramedics wrote up their reports and recommendations and had each one of them sign a release. As there was nothing further for them to do, the paramedics left the scene.

While the remaining fires were being put out, Officer Jackson was talking with The BREV Force. He knew the warehouse had been abandoned but he needed details to explain the fire and how they came to be there.

When he was finished, the officer turned back to Brad and exclaimed, "Sheila here keeps ranting about everything being your fault but everyone else here tells a different story. Let's have yours," he knelt down to question Brad, who was now sitting up.

With a lot of effort Brad attempted to explain his ordeal. "I saw my friends being lured into QuizMaster's plan and tried to get in good with them. Then, I tried to correct the school's records, that's when QuizMaster and Controller got wise and I was captured. I was brought here to this warehouse. That's about all I can tell you." Brad never implicated Jonathan or any of the others, including Sheila.

The policeman took down Brad's story and advised him, "Since The BREV Force confirmed that you were a victim in all this, you're free to go, for now. However, I am sure you will be called in to give a statement regarding the incident at Norton University, so stay available."

"I'm sure, if I know my parents, you will find me confined to my room."

Another policeman approached the scene, "How's the interrogation going?"

"Looks like we're about done here Chief. This young lady seems to be the prime suspect and I have read the girl her rights and these two gentlemen will be coming to the station to give their official statements. I have taken preliminary statements from all concerned." Jackson then filled his superior in on the details.

Apparently annoyed, he turned to Raven and Dove and stated, "While Officer Jackson feels we owe you a debt of gratitude and of course we appreciate your assistance here, just know, that in the future, it would be preferable if you would leave police work, to the police. "Oh, and by the way, next time, you should advise the authorities of your intentions, or, you might be arrested too." And, with that the Chief started to walk away but then turned back, "On second thought, I believe I would like to question you myself, so if you would accompany me to the station."

Dove said, "As the representative for The BREV Force, I'll be more than happy to, Chief." She smiled at him, "We are more than willing to cooperate in your investigations."

"Fine, let's go!"

Dove said her goodbye's and followed him.

Rick and Jonathan were asked to follow in Rick's car. Officer Jackson said there was a squad car waiting to take Brad Kane home. He un-holstered the force field generator gun, set it to moving object and escorted Sheila to his squad car.

Watching the police car drive away Jonathan turned to Rick, "Hey! What happened to Evie? She was supposed to be waiting in your truck."

To keep up the pretense Brad asked in a concerned tone, "Evie? What's she got to do with all this?"

"Oh, she was with us until we got here and then she didn't feel good and was going to wait in my truck. Sorry Jon, I forgot to tell you. When I got back to the truck there was a note that said she was still feeling really sick and was going to have a friend come and take her home. She wanted to let her parents know what was happening but I thought for sure she'd be back by now."

"Oh," Raven chimed in to cover, "when I was talking to the officer he explained that the police called her house and told the Kane's Brad was all right. Brad's parents said, Evie was going to come back with them but the officer said there was no need. He told them everything was winding down and the police would see that Brad got home."

Rick said to Jonathan. "Well then, we'd better get goin' before the police put out a warrant for us."

Jonathan bent down to Brad and whispered, "I've really been an idiot! I promise I will get my head screwed back on," he hesitated, "well, if you'll just give me another chance. I know I don't deserve your friendship but..."

"Hey, we're friends, so leave it at that. We'll talk about all this tomorrow, or today. Oh, you know what I mean."

As they started to walk away Brad stopped Rick. "I don't know what part you played in all this and I know I've never made a secret of how I feel about you but you being here tells me a lot. I hope you can accept my apology and my thanks."

Rick reached out to Brad and they shook hands. "No Brad, you don't owe me an apology, you're the real hero. I heard what you told the cops. At least you tried to help your friends and you didn't even put the blame on Sheila. You see, I now know I let Sheila and the others down, so maybe helping out here tonight was a bit of a reprieve."

Brad nodded and added, "Yeah, for both of us."

Rick turned to thank Raven and left.

Once everyone was out of sight, Brian relinquished his disguise. He checked the time, it was six o'clock in the morning. He needed to call his parents, they would be up by now and worried.

Brian got on the call and calmly explained that they were all safe and on their way home.

Brian favored his leg but was able to help Brad up and together they helped each other walk to where he had parked Evie's car. They were surprised to see a police car still waiting. Brian leaned against their car and hid his face, while Brad hobbled over to talk to the officers who said they waited to give him a ride home. "My friend just showed up. He'll take me home but thanks anyway!" Brad walked back toward the car and waved to the officer, who finally nodded, then drove away. Brian limped over to help Brad. "We had better get you home."

CHAPTER 17

It was after 6:00 in the morning and Brian had to get Brad home soon! When they arrived home their parents rushed to meet them. Brian's words helped calm their fears, "I know it looks bad but we're both just a little shaken up." Brian went on to assure his parents that Evie, still posing as Dove, was also safe and all danger had passed.

Martin and Brian helped Brad to his room. His father didn't say anything to Brad, he just walked out. Brad grabbed his brother's arm, "Thanks Bro. Oh and Brian, I know you said you can't wait for me or Evie to help you at school but I wish you would.

Brian knew what had to be done and did not understand his brother's apprehension. "Thanks for the concern but you need to rest and I am aware of what needs to be done and will see to it."

Brian smiled. He turned to leave when Brad said, "Oh, Brian, please don't forget to leave my message."

"I will be sure it is conveyed!"

Brian went downstairs to talk with his parents. Vivian was very shaken from the sight of both her son's conditions but she was trying really hard to be calm. She and Martin had so many questions but Brian asked if they could wait, "I'm sorry but I must go back to Norton University," he explained. "Evie and I were going to fix what QuizMaster and its supporters had done but we didn't get the chance. Evie gave me her administration codes and Brad told me which files QuizMaster had tampered with. Evie told me the administration personnel will be in by seven-thirty so, I will need to get there before that and finish before school opens if I am to make things right again."

His parents argued, first about his driving without a license. "I do not believe based on the 'commuter hour' that there is any real danger of my being stopped by a traffic officer."

Then, they further argued that he shouldn't go alone. But Brian convinced them, "If you are seen with me, Dad, there will be a lot of questions and problems and besides, I believe you are needed here, more."

Martin knew Brad and Vivian, needed his attention and agreed. However, he did insist on doing a quick examination of Brian, first.

The examination took only a few minutes and proved quite interesting. Martin was totally amazed at Brian's recuperative powers. From what he'd told his father, Martin expected the injuries to be severe but everything he saw was superficial. Martin bandaged Brian's leg and walked him out to the car, "Here, take my C-TEL with you and call if you need me."

"Do not worry. I will be fine!"

Brian drove to the campus, just as the sun was peaking high in the sky. He parked where Evie told him to and then used her passcode to get into the building. He went directly to the administration offices. Once Brian located the link to Controller's educational net, he could not believe the data available from major colleges and universities throughout the world.

The clock was ticking and Brian knew he had to work quickly. First, he identified where Norton University's link generated from, then severed the connection. Next, he sorted through the information and fixed the internal school records.

Following Brad's instructions, Brian purged the links that had aided Controller in stealing the college tests and then down-loaded the student-net information. They all hoped this procedure would eliminate Controller's threat to the education system of Norton University but hopefully the link was part of a network and would crash Controller's hold on the education world.

Brian followed Brad's direction to a separate computer file room. As he entered that room, Brian was startled by voices in the hall. He quickly hid behind a file cabinet. He was surprised by what he heard, "Well, thank you for all your help in this matter, Miss Dove. We'll take it from here."

"Commissioner Davis, I would like to assure you that The BREV Force will assist you in this investigation, whenever and wherever possible."

Brian heard the male voice which he knew must be the police commissioner. He continued to listen, "That's very good of you Miss Dove but this is a police matter and as I told you, as the Chief, I am the one in charge!" Then he continued very matter-of-factly, "I will handle it from here."

"Yes, Commissioner but if I might ask one more question? At the police station, I tried to find out if any action would be taken against Brad Kane but no one would give me a straight answer."

"That is for the D.A. to decide. Right now, I have evidence to uncover. So, if you'll excuse me…?" The police commissioner put his hand on the door knob of the computer room.

Brian heard the door begin to open and signaled his sister, *Code 47 to BREV Force, I am in the computer file room.*

Dove quickly responded, in her mind, *Code 47 BREV.* Then, she placed her hand on the commissioner's arm, "Uh, Commissioner Davis, I believe I heard Brad Kane mention the auxiliary computer lab, I know you said you don't need help but I know my way around computers…"

The commissioner removed his hand from the door knob and told Dove she could assist them.

Dove signaled and simultaneously, she and Brian relaxed.

Dove saw the dean of Norton University coming down the hall and he was shouting, "Sorry it took so long for me to get here," he shook hands with the police commissioner and nodded courteously to Dove.

"Glad you're here now," the commissioner responded. "Miss Dove was just about to show me to the auxiliary computer lab."

Dean Farrell directed them down the hall.

Dove followed the men until they were far enough away, then saw her chance to leave, "Gentlemen, since Dean Farrell is here, I guess now you don't need my services any longer, so if you'll excuse me!"

"We can't thank you enough for your help!" Dean Farrell, responded.

Dove turned to the police commissioner, "Thanks for the ride here."

Davis replied curtly, "Yes. Goodbye," and motioned to the dean to continue on.

Dove watched them walk down the corridor, then she dashed back to where Brian was still hiding.

He was so grateful she was there or he would have been discovered for sure. Brian told her what Brad had said about the files QuizMaster got into and what Brad had been able to do to try and fix it.

They worked quickly together to sever the last few connections and then prepared to leave.

Dove was ready to transform back to Evie but Brian being extra cautious, asked her to remain in her disguise; just in case the commissioner, or the dean returned.

With college personnel now arriving for the school day, Brian and Dove devised a plan to leave the building undetected.

Dove went first to clear the way and then telepathically instructed her brother to follow. "Leave the computer room, turn left and walk straight down the corridor for three rooms, then turn left again. You'll be in front of the stairs. When you make the turn, wait until I signal you before you continue."

Brian followed her instructions but unexpectedly bumped into the janitor coming out of a nearby utility room. "Hey..." he stammered, "what are you doin' here, boy? The school ain't even open yet, so how'd you get in?"

Startled, Brian ran down the stairs. His mind rushed with thoughts clouding his judgment and abilities. What will happen if I am caught? How will my family explain my existence?

He reached the bottom of the stairs and collided with Dove. "Brian, what happened?"

"I will tell you later. Please, we must get out of here, now!" He panted.

Dove had never seen Brian so shaken. She grabbed his arm and led the way. They raced toward the entrance and made it to the door when much to their surprise an alarm sounded, triggering a lock down which totally sealed the building. Stunned, they knew they had to find a way to escape and quickly.

They mustered their strength and pushed at the exit door together but surprisingly they couldn't budge it.

Dove couldn't understand what was happening, until she saw the fear in Brian's eyes. He was having trouble controlling his thoughts and his fears; surprisingly, they were overpowering him. Dove searched the windows and doors along that corridor for an easier way out but everything was locked and sealed.

Then, she had an idea. "Brian, you've become quite good at changing the structure of your molecules. Can you concentrate enough now to mirror those of the door and pass through it?" she asked hopefully.

Desperate to escape and running out of time, Brian was unsure, for the first time in his short life but he agreed to try. Normally, he knew he could do it with little trouble but now...

Brian placed his hand on the door's steel panel and detected the composition of the door. He tried to match the pattern but he was flustered. This was the first time he'd ever experienced an inability to do something. He was determined not to fail and tried again and again and finally was able to watch his hand dissolve into the structure.

"Hurry now Brian, before we are found," she said, as she kissed her brother. "And please be careful."

Just as Brian's entire body seemed to fade into the door, three men, Dean Farrell, Commissioner Davis and a third man, Dove didn't know, came running down the hall. The commissioner couldn't believe what he'd just seen, "What on earth was that?"

"What was what?" Dove asked innocently?

"Yes Davis, what're you talking about?" Farrell questioned. "I didn't see anything!"

"I don't even know how to describe what I saw," Davis stammered.

"Well, if you don't know, I surely don't," Dove feigned ignorance, "I can't imagine what you think you saw, I just got here and didn't see anything." She shook her head and changed the subject, "What's happened, Dean Farrell?"

"Miss Dove, this is the school janitor. He reported seeing an intruder."

"Yea," the janitor interrupted. "There's some strange kid here. I saw 'im when I came outta the storage room. I got a good look at him. Yeah, I'd know him in a minute, if I saw him again."

"Well, you know gentleman, this person, might have been one of Controller's helpers left here to finish the job," Dove suggested.

Dean Farrell explained, "He won't get away! Security set off the alarm locking all the doors and windows. No one can get out until I give security the all clear."

Dove went with the men to help them search but when the intruder wasn't found, the dean had no choice but to order the building opened for school. He concluded that if this was the work of Controller, the suspect must have been aided in his escape.

The commissioner wasn't as sure and argued that the security protocols should remain in full force until the culprit was found. They argued back and forth.

Dove decided that was a good time to leave. She made her way back to the door and rushed outside to find Brian but he wasn't there.

She looked around but the area was clear of students or other on-lookers. She signaled to Brian but the response was very weak. Dove scanned the area and finally saw him behind a clump of bushes. She raced to his side, dropped to her knees and lifted her brother into her arms, "Oh Brian, I'm sorry it took so long for me to get back for you."

"It is all right, you were protecting my identity."

"Then let's get away from here. Just tell me where the car is?"

Brian pointed to the nearest parking area. Dove made sure no one was within sight and then transformed back to Evie. "I'll bring the car as close as possible and then come back to help you. Stay here until I return."

Evie found the car and went back to where she'd left Brian and helped him get in. She was overjoyed when they drove away from the school, without any further incident. Evie called to tell her parents she was with Brian and they were on their way home.

During the drive home Evie listened while Brian explained how he managed to get through the door. "Passing through the door had been both terrifying and exhilarating. It was very different from putting my hand through a table and I had the added fear factor. At first, it seemed as if I would become a permanent part of the steel."

Stopping to take a deep breath, Brian went on reliving the experience. "Once I realized I was able to push my way through the doors layers, I thought I was going to be fine, until I encountered the next hurdle, controlling the urge to breathe...."

Just saying those words seemed to cause Brian added distress but he took a calming breath and continued, "...then, my fear caused me to grasp for air. I never would have imagined that fear could be such a powerful emotion. It truly took hold and affected me both emotionally and physically."

Evie was mesmerized as Brian continued his account of the incident. "The steel was cold but pliable, moving as I moved. At one point the structure was harder and passage became more difficult. I felt I was losing the ability to keep my molecules scrambled. Then, I stopped and gathered all my strength to analyze the situation and when I did, I realized I had come in contact with the outside surface of the door.

First, I tried to pass my hand through. When that proved successful, I proceeded to move the rest of my body in the same direction. To my amazement, I was able to feel myself emerging on the other side of the door. It took all my will to get through those stages and make it out of the door but once I did the experience was simply fascinating."

Brian stopped again to catch his breath. "Once my body had materialized outside the door, I knew I was in trouble. My head was spinning and I fell to the ground. I believe that restructuring my cells had created a need for more energy than I could muster. I then dragged myself to the secluded place where you found me. I just needed to get some fresh air."

Evie placed her hand on his and expressed her feelings, "You were great and I am so proud of you! Now, just sit back and relax, we'll be home soon."

CHAPTER 18

It was almost eight thirty in the morning and Martin and Vivian were glad to know their children were on the way home. They were relieved when they finally saw Evie pull into the driveway. They watched as their daughter got out and went around to the passenger side to help Brian. Martin ran out to assist her.

"Are you all right?" Vivian asked as she sat down on the couch next to where they had placed Brian.

Brian nodded but Martin decided to be sure. While he examined Brian, Vivian took Evie into the kitchen with her to get them some food. "How did you two find each other?"

"I'll tell you everything Mom but first I think I need a cup of coffee."

Vivian expressed in her motherly manner, "And, some food too, I'll bet." She prepared toast and eggs, while Evie sipped the hot coffee, her mother had handed her.

Martin helped Brian into the kitchen and then Evie recounted all the events leading up to that morning. Brian was still feeling drained and so he let Evie do all the talking. Several times during the story their parents expressed their astonishment at what had taken place.

"To sum up," Evie told her parents, "Sheila's been arrested for Brad's kidnapping and her involvement in the warehouse break-in."

Martin questioned in a hesitant manner, "What did the police say about Brad?"

Brian, finally was able to eat a bit and answered, "Brad told the police he had tried to foil Controller's plan and they took his statement. Other than telling him he was free to go, they did not say anything else. When I went to the administration office it was only to fix what Controller's followers had done and not to cover anything Brad might be accused of in the future."

Evie reached for a piece of toast, "Yeah and maybe that would've been the end but no! Sheila implicated Brad in the Norton University break-in and claimed he was the 'mastermind' behind his own plot to steal the upcoming exams."

"Well, they can't believe that...can they?" her mother asked.

"I'm afraid they can, Mom. You see when I went with Commissioner Davis to the university we found tracers that were in place to send the exams to Brad's laptop, which of course, corroborated Sheila's story. And, with Brad's fingerprints all over the consoles, why would they doubt anything that Sheila had said?"

Martin thought for a moment, then said, "Maybe I should call Farrell?"

"It won't do any good. It appears that because QuizMaster was involved, the crime is being treated as a security issue and a special D.A. is being called to review the case.

"As far as school, the dean didn't say what the administration will do about the stolen exams, or Brad's part, or whether he can stay in school. I guess we'll have to wait and see what they decide."

When they were finished talking Evie went to call Ginger, as she had promised.

Martin also went to make a call.

CHAPTER 19

After breakfast, Martin took off Brian's bandages and examined his leg more carefully. He made a mental note that the leg looked better than it had in the morning when he'd first bandaged it. He knew he had to put the discussion about Brian's healing abilities, away for another day. He then re-bandaged the leg and sent him off to bed.

Martin and Vivian took the opportunity to further question Evie about her condition and made sure she was also all right, before they sent her to bed for some much-needed sleep. It was fortunate neither Evie nor Brad had any classes or exams that day.

Martin called Dr. Schmidt to explain that the twins had come down with something and he and Vivian would be late. "No, no, they'll be fine, we're just monitoring them and doing some tests. We will call you when we're ready to leave home."

Schmidt started to argue about time being of the essence but Martin cut him off saying, "I agree and we'll be there as soon as humanly possible," then he hung up, not giving Schmidt a chance to respond.

Vivian cleared the dishes, while Martin went upstairs to check on Brad. As he walked up the stairs Martin couldn't believe the events of the past twenty-four hours and how much they could've lost if things had turned out differently. Brad was still asleep and Martin decided not to wake him. Instead, he went to Brian's room and gently knocked on the door.

Brian, called out, "Come in."

Martin was glad to have a chance to talk with his son alone. "Thank you, Brian, for being there and helping Evie. You both saved Brad's life and I'll always be grateful." Martin sat down on the side of the bed beside Brian. "I never told you this but when we knew our experiments had produced a life...," a lump formed in Martin's throat, well, to say the least, we weren't sure what to expect. But, as soon as you began to develop, there was an immediate bond, as if you were meant to be. That bond was not much different from what I felt when the twins were born, or even now, when this new baby moves in your Mom's body." Martin's emotions began to show. He stopped and looked around Brian's room.

He waited a moment and then composed himself to go on. "Even this room, the pictures of your mother, sister, brother and me, your shelves of books and research equipment, it shows your individuality and yet expresses you as a member of this family. But, there's something more about you. I feel a closeness to you that is very strange for me. Something I've never felt before, not even with my natural born children. Maybe it's because of the way you came to be. I'm not sure but sometimes I think it's just some connection special to only me.

Martin knew he was having a hard time converting his feelings into words and he wasn't even sure he could convey to his son the overwhelming feeling he had for him! But he tried as he continued, "What I do know for sure is, you're a part of me and, I love you…, and, I thank you for being my son." Martin wasn't further able to express his feelings and so he just put his arms around Brian and hugged him.

Brian hesitated, somewhat uncomfortable with the embrace, while his mind started recapping the warmth with which his father expressed his feelings. That emotion triggered a strange response in Brian but one that endeared him to bring his arms around his father.

Martin realized he might be pushing the boy and broke off the embrace. "Get some sleep, we'll have plenty of time to talk later." Martin got up and closed the door, still confused by this strange but powerful bond that existed between them.

Brian pulled the covers up to his chin. He didn't understand his desire to respond to his father's embrace. His emotions were teeming within him and combined with the events of that day, had totally drained his ability to comprehend what was happening. "I must get a handle on these emotions."

Turning toward the wall, Brian concentrated on his reason for being and vowed not to let these strong feelings jeopardize his mission; put an end to Controller.

Martin decided to check on Brad again. He heard the main C-TEL ring but decided to let the computer answering system pick it up. He made a mental note to check it later.

Brad, feeling very shaky but stable, bumped into his father in the hall. He had hobbled to the bathroom, holding his right side. His father's voice was gruff, "Get back in bed, I'll be back to give you a complete going over as soon as I get my medical bag."

The order from his father was in a tone of voice Brad hadn't heard since he was a little boy.

He returned to his room and sat very still on his bed waiting for his father. Brad glanced around at the shelves of science books, posters, sport memorabilia and the collections of music but felt he should be looking instead at the Sesame Street characters that adorned his room when he was a child. Not only did he feel as though he were five years old but he was about to be treated, as such.

When his father entered the room, Brad was glad that something kept his mother from coming in to examine him too. His body tensed as he watched his father assume the role of Dr. Kane.

"Brad you have some lung congestion but with rest and treatment you should be fine. Now, lie down and let's take a look at that side."

Martin moved Brad and the pain shot through him but Brad wouldn't show any weakness to his father. Instead, he just watched as his father set up the portable imaging machine he'd brought up from the lab.

"These pictures show no damage to the organs but the bruise on your side warrants you staying in bed." Without saying another word, he matter-of-factly packed up his medical bag.

Brad couldn't take the silent treatment and grabbed his father's hand. "I know you're disappointed in me but can't you at least ask me for my side of the story before judging me?"

"I have been trying hard to calm down before asking you anything, Brad. Your mother and I have always trusted you. Even when you betrayed our trust by listening to our private conversation and then used that information to break into our lab! You endangered your sister and yes, you gained your new abilities but what about Brian...?"

His father thought better and decided to not go there. "We were upset with you but we tried to give you some latitude and get over that but...but, this... this has been a shock for us. Why would you involve yourself with the one force we are all trying to defeat?" Martin turned his back.

Brad had never seen his father so hurt and upset. He started to sit up when his father turned as if reconsidering what he'd just said, "I don't want to upset your mother any further but maybe you are right... we need to hear what you have to say. I'll get her and you can tell us both what happened."

When Martin returned to Brad's room with Vivian, she sat down by Brad's side while Martin stood on the other side of the bed. Brad started by explaining how he tried to live up to their standards and his sister's abilities. "You never say it out loud but you expect everything I do to be as good as Evie and to exceed you both!"

Brad had to stop. It was so very difficult for him to finally tell his parents how he felt. Now, looking at their hurt faces, he wanted to stop and keep it all to himself but he realized, now that he had started, he had no choice but to go on.

"I just want you to be proud of me, as proud as you always are of Evie. You know, when Jon came to me, wacked out of his mind with fear about stealing tests and drugs and all, I knew if I could help him and get Controller at the same time, then maybe, I could be the family hero."

Brad turned his face away from his parent's sight to cover his overwhelming defeated feeling. "I used the 'having to live up to my genius sister' routine with Sheila. She never liked Evie and I knew that would get me in on the exam scam. Then, I convinced myself I could get to Controller if I wiped the exam answers from the network. I sent them to my laptop hoping I could defeat Controller at its own game."

Brad listened to his own words and the realization of what he had done made him feel very guilty. He realized there had been no reason good enough for what he'd done. "You have to understand, I'm not Evie and I'm not either of you...I'm...."

Vivian took her son's hands in hers. "Brad, why didn't you come to us? Why didn't you tell us how you felt? Don't you know we just want you to be you and ..."

Brad couldn't let her go on, "No, you don't want me to be me...I'm the screw up...I'm the less than.... I'm....!" Brad knew he was going too far but he couldn't turn back now.

"How could I come to you!" Brad was fighting back all the raging emotions that had filled him for so many years. "Don't you see! This is me! This is what I do. I react. I don't think things through first...," something deep inside Brad knew he had to tell them everything. "As much as I screwed up, I did believe that this was the perfect opportunity to get into Sheila's good graces and find out more about Controller. I convinced myself if I could re-route the exams and fix what the others did, that I would have foiled Controller's plans...," Brad continued reluctantly, "and shown both of you...." He just couldn't finish the statement.

Vivian turned to her husband, "Martin, why didn't we see this? How did we allow this to happen?"

He didn't answer, he just looked away; tears evident in his eyes.

Brad looked his mother straight in the eyes and told her, "How could you see what I so carefully hid? I didn't want you to see. I wanted to shine for both of you, just like Evie but all I've succeeded in doing was making you more ashamed that I'm your son." Brad grabbed his pillow in disgust and leaned against the back of the bed.

"No son, we're not ashamed of you," his father broke in. "We are disappointed and hurt that you couldn't be honest with us."

Martin's voice cracked a little as he went on, "I'm sorry that you've gotten the feeling that you need to compete with your sister. We've never wanted you to be anything other than who you are and that means you are Brad, not Evie. We love you both but differently and hopefully we thought we treated you each as who you are. But, we now know we haven't."

He looked to Vivian. She was so deeply distressed by the realization of what their son had gone through because of them. She nodded her agreement but could not make her throat utter a word.

Martin's emotions surfaced as he choked out the next words. "Brad, I make you this promise. I will try to be more aware of you, you Brad and not who I think you should be and more in tune to your needs. I also want you to know that I will try to be more open to your telling me when I am not hearing or seeing you!"

Vivian got up from the bed and stood by her husband. "Brad, I will too," were all the words that choked out.

Vivian noticed her son's eyes I tear up and she gathered her strength to go on. "Maybe we have been too busy with our own lives and didn't check in on yours enough."

Vivian glanced up at her husband, "Let's see if we can't all repair the damage and go from here." Vivian moved back to Brad's bedside extending her hands to her son.

Brad responded by hugging his mother tightly. He then slowly extended his hand to his father.

Martin feeling his own failure hesitated.

Brad withdrew his hand and broke the embrace with his mother.

Vivian turned toward her husband, who finally got the gist of what had just happened.

"No, Brad, you misunderstand, it's my... disappointment in myself, that makes me hesitate! My actions, as your father have been..."

Brad didn't let his father finish, "No Dad!"

Brad extended his whole body and Martin immediately reached for his son and they embraced.

Brad looked up, as emotions flooded his face. "This has been all my fault. I put everyone in jeopardy! I need to go to Evie and Brian and apologize for putting them in such danger."

His father ordered, "No, you need to stay put," but this time his voice indicated more concern, than command.

Vivian held Brad's hand, "Brian and Evie are sleeping now and I suspect you should be getting more sleep, too. There's plenty of time for all of us to make amends and you will have plenty of time later"

Brad had one more thing on his mind. "Have you heard yet, if I am going to be arrested?"

"No but I'm going to call George and get a head start on that now." His father said it in a concerned manner, rather than the disappointed tone Brad had expected.

Martin agreed with Vivian's prescription of rest for Brad for the remainder of the day and then left him alone with his mother.

Vivian smoothed the cover over Brad and he gripped her arm, "Mom, I know I've hurt you and Dad, and...I'm really, really, so sorry..."

Martin went downstairs and put in a call to their lawyer and friend, George Fenbrook.

Before going to the Cottage, he remembered he wanted to check the message center. There was only one message. The audio portion was garbled and the video was distorted. It was so hard to make out the facial features of the caller but something seemed familiar. Martin played the message over several times but he couldn't put his finger on it. He slowed down the audio and was able to make out a few sounds, "hel . . my fri...." The rest of the transmission was static but he thought he detected the faintest sound of music in the background.

Martin realized he'd been in the lab for quite a while, when Vivian called down that she was ready to go to the Cottage. He called to her, "Just finishing up, need a few more minutes."

Then, he gave Rosie instructions, "Analyze this message and have a report waiting for me when we arrive at the Cottage, oh and put me on a secure scrambled line to the President."

After his call, Martin walked up the stairs to get Vivian.

"What took you so long?" she asked.

"I wanted to try to do something good for Brad, for a change."

CHAPTER 20

The roads were icy from a severe drop in temperature and the light rain that had started to fall.

Martin wanted Vivian to stay home, not just because of her condition but all the emotional happenings of the day but she insisted. "Martin I'm going! Especially now with Schmidt here, you couldn't keep me home!"

Dr. Schmidt was already waiting at the college guard house when they arrived. He'd left the Inn as soon as Martin called and when Martin drove up Schmidt yelled, "Kane, I want clearance, a passkey and the security code. I shouldn't have to wait for the two of you to arrive and sit here like a prisoner!"

Martin didn't want Schmidt to have access to the Cottage when they weren't there but he wasn't sure how he'd get around that issue, except to ignore it, for now. They drove past the guardhouse with Schmidt trailing close behind.

"Good morning, Dr. Schmidt," Vivian said, as Schmidt came around to assist her getting out of the car. "Sorry we kept you waiting so long. We're usually here quite early but with the twins being sick, oh, you know. I was just being an over protective mother and Martin was indulging me."

Once inside, Schmidt said he was going straight to the lab but Martin asked him to come into his office with

Vivian first. Martin knew the wire services would've gotten the story about Controller and Brad's involvement by then and he wanted to explain the events of the preceding evening to Schmidt first.

"Yes, I saw this morning's news and figured that had something to do with the 'twins not feeling well,'" Schmidt said.

Vivian answered, "I'm sure you understand why we wanted to wait 'til we got here to discuss this."

Almost ignoring her comment, Schmidt went on, "Well, you know, boys will be boys and Brad has always been all boy!" Schmidt continued, "I'm sure Brad will never try anything like that again." Oddly enough that was Schmidt's only comment about Brad's involvement.

He was, however, interested in learning about The BREV Force. He had heard about them and the destruction of Cracko but he heard nothing since and just thought they had disappeared as mysteriously as they'd appeared!"

"Yes, I guess we all did," Martin stated, "but it seems they're still very much around."

Schmidt started firing questions at him, "When did The BREV Force first come to Island Falls and where did they come from?"

But, more than that Schmidt seemed to be most interested in the powers they possessed and their identity. Schmidt kept posing questions, "and this QuizMaster, my goodness, are you sure it is really gone?"

Martin walked around the desk to his chair. "Of all your questions, that is one I believe I can answer. Yes, from what the holo-paper said, QuizMaster has really been destroyed. As far as The BREV Force, we only know what we read in the news. They seem to come and go and no one knows very many details about them, including their real identity or why they appeared in the first place. We're all just glad they're helping with our Controller problem"

"Well, I just wish you knew more about them." Schmidt's tone sounded annoyed, as he continued, "After all, they first appeared here, in your town! Shouldn't you know something more?"

Vivian didn't like his innuendo and answered back, "Sorry, we citizens of Island Falls are no more privy to the agenda of The BREV Force than the authorities... or the Alliance."

"Yes, speaking of the Alliance, "Schmidt said, as he got up, "I better go and inform them of these recent developments."

After a long time, Schmidt returned to Martin's office; turned to Vivian, hugged her like a father and whispered, "Children can get crazy. This too will pass," then he grabbed his coat and without further explanation walked to the outer door and called, "I have to leave now."

He stood at the front door and waited for Martin to signal the security code. When the door opened, he said without further explanation, "I'm going back to California for a few days but I'll be back, so keep working." Schmidt shuffled down the stairs then turned back to Martin, "I will expect reports every day!" He then turned back and left without another word.

Confused, Martin walked back into his office and sat down in the chair next to a surprised but happy Vivian. They both wondered if his call to the Alliance revealed something about The BREV Force but finally decided not to speculate any further.

Martin's office monitor indicated a report from Rosie:

Report regarding message left on Home Message Center

Analysis:

Voice: Male-no voice print match in any current database

Transmission Point of Origin: insufficient information -- call was routed through at least 3 terminals—conclusion unknown

Background: Musical notes detected, appear to be of a classical composition but the garbled transmission prevented identification, not enough evidence presented

Report Conclusion: Transmission ended before any significant information could be obtained.

CHAPTER 21

It was late in the afternoon when Brian and Evie finally got up. They each made something to eat and then decided to check on Brad. When they knocked on his door he responded immediately. He told them he was just lying there trying to reconstruct everything that'd happened. But, there was one thing he knew for sure, "I have to tell you both," Brad struggled to stop the flow of emotion. "I…I don't even know what to say…, I'm just so sorry!" Brad tried to lift his body from the bed to reach out to his siblings but instead they went to him. He hugged them both and this time let the tears fall, "Thank you, just doesn't seem to be nearly enough to say."

Brian and Evie held their brother. They didn't need his thanks they were just glad Brad was going to be all right.

Brian was the first to break the hold. "Right now, I believe we need to look at the next step. We need to put together all that we've learned and analyze what happened. Then, we will be able to use the results to further combat Controller."

Brad still wasn't clear on all the details but the more they talked the more information surfaced.

In the middle of their conversation Jonathan called. He was concerned about Brad and wanted to thank his friend again. Jon sounded more like himself but there was a shaking quality to his voice. Brad inquired as to whether he was suffering some kind of withdrawal but Jon shooed him off, "Hey man, I'm fine! Back to the old self, ya know. It seems the shock of almost losing my best friend, kinda cleared my head."

Brad wasn't sure he completely believed him but at least the cocky Jon was gone. "Hey Man, you just get better and then maybe we can do some partying, to celebrate."

Brad disconnected the call and turned to Brian and Evie, "Jon's got it real bad! He sounds like he's about to fall apart. First, he was macho and then, fearful, now he just sounds lost. Whatever this hold is that Controller has, it just doesn't seem to let go that easily. We need to figure out something to help Jon and all Controller's other victims."

CHAPTER 22

With the news of Dr. Schmidt's temporary return to California, Vivian and Martin decided to spend more time with their children and work from the home lab.

The next few days brought both good news and bad news. The day after the incident at the college the police had come to question Brad; who was still confined to bed.

George Fenbrook, the family attorney sat by his side during the interrogation and commented that it "went well," but it would be up to the District Attorney's office as to whether they would press charges. Fenbrook hoped Brad's actions indicated that he had good intentions.

That same day Schmidt called. He would be returning from California and this time, he didn't want to be cooped up in the Inn, for any reason. Martin told him they were having a snow storm and it probably would be best to wait out the weather another day or so, before returning to Island Falls. Schmidt agreed. That was the good news.

The weather also helped to make the time mandatory for Brad and Brian to stay put and try to recover. At the same time, The BREV Force was using the time to formulate a new plan of action against Controller.

Everything seemed to be falling into place and then came the bad news. George Fenbrook called to tell them that Brad's involvement with QuizMaster had come back to haunt him and the District Attorney was pressing charges.

Sheila was claiming for anyone that would listen, that Brad was the mastermind and the fact that his sister worked in the administration office made it hard not to be believed. Brad also made the mistake of sending files to his personal computer and that left a trail of guilt.   Therefore, Brad was being charged with: two counts of breaking and entering, two counts of destruction of private property, document theft, computer piracy, malicious endangerment with intent to do harm and cavorting with a known dissident. Incredible as it seemed the charges carried a mandatory sentence of 10 -15 years.

Sheila had already entered a plea of "not guilty," stating in no uncertain terms that she was the victim!

Brad had given the police names of other students to question about Sheila but they all denied being involved and since the security feed was cut off, there was nothing to back up Brad's statement.

Fenbrook was using every moment to gather evidence in Brad's favor. George was not just the Kane's lawyer he was also their friend. He knew he had to try everything he had ever learned about the law to get Brad cleared and he didn't let the weather hamper him. He managed to file all the legal papers in an attempt to have the charges dropped, or at the very least, have the charges reduced.

George spent the rest of the day reviewing the evidence and hoped the statements taken by the police at the warehouse scene from Rick, Jonathan and The BREV Force, would be enough to sway Judge Lerner and see Brad exonerated. But he had to admit, it didn't look good.

Fenbrook analyzed Brad's reasoning; he was only interested in saving his friend Jonathan and at the same time mess up QuizMaster's destructive scheme. But all the documented evidence seemed to contradict Brad's story. Even George was having a hard time believing it; so why would the judge?

George knew the most damaging pieces of evidence against Brad, were that he had access to the administration office by stealing Evie's codes and then he had all the exams sent to his personal laptop; his actions only seemed self-serving.

Brad was having his own problems dealing with the reality of what he'd done. In order to protect The BREV Force, he couldn't reveal why he did all the things he did and he knew he would probably be going to jail. But, even worse than that were his own guilt feelings. As a part of The BREV Force he should never have acted on his own; ultimately endangering his siblings and for that alone, he almost wished he would be convicted.

Brad wasn't the only one with unresolved guilt issues. His father was still having a hard time dealing with his own feelings. He'd expected so much of Brad and now he had to admit that his expectations may have contributed to some of Brad's actions.

On the other hand, Vivian was handling the situation in a totally different way. Although she didn't condone Brad's actions, or his methods, she felt he'd suffered more than he deserved. Brad had always been adventurous but usually within limits. Now, he'd crossed that line and he might have to pay what she felt was "too heavy a price."

Martin decided his family needed a way to get through this time. He proposed a solution that was not in his usual nature. "Once exams and the trial are over and Brad is exonerated, we should take a much-needed vacation. We should spend time as a family, maybe even find a place where no one knows us and we can just relax together. We certainly could all use it and just maybe, that will help to put this nightmare behind us."

Everyone agreed that a vacation together might just be the best thing, especially Brad and Evie who missed going on their trip to Europe, with their grandmother. Evie, Brian and their parents pitched-in to help Brad prepare for the trial and his school exams.

Brad took a break from studying and took a minute to ask Brian if he'd left the message for Controller?

Evie overheard the question and asked her brothers, "What message?"

Brian turned to Brad, who nodded. Brian explained, "When I went to Norton University to fix the information QuizMaster and its followers had tampered with, I left a message for Controller that Brad had asked me to convey.

"What message Brad?" Evie's tone showed both her annoyance and her concern.

"I asked Brian to leave a message that read, 'QuizMaster failed the final exam. All data is as it was. You lose again!"

Evie wasn't sure whether to be angry and lash out at both her brothers when Brian surprised them both, "What neither of you know, is that Controller sent back a reply. 'THIS IS NOT A SIMPLE QUIZ THAT YOU PASS OR FAIL. THE FINAL GRADE IS DETERMINED IN THE END. NEXT TIME THE ZERO WILL BE YOURS. THEN WE WILL SEE IF HAVING THE ANSWERS IN ADVANCE IS A JUST REWARD.'"

Puzzled by the message Evie asked, "Now, what do you imagine that means?"

Brian replied, "I do not have that answer yet but I do believe that if Controller wants us to know, we will find out soon enough!"

CHAPTER 23

Brad was indicted for his part in the break in at Norton University and for stealing test results. He was also being charged with assisting QuizMaster and Controller. While he awaited trial, it had to be business as usual, for him and the family.

The college administration had not suspended Brad. Unlike the police, they felt there was enough evidence to believe Brad's story but that would not help him much in court.

The snow had stopped and the roads were clear. A recovered Brad grabbed his books. Evie called out, "Wanna give me a ride?"

The twins left the house with everyone's good wishes for their exams and his father's additional comments, "You've really hit the books and did everything possible to prepare for your exams. Brad, no matter how it turns out, we want you to know, we're very proud of you!"

Brad shot his father an appreciative smile. His father's faith in him really meant a lot to Brad.

Because of the weather many exams were rescheduled and the school parking lots were jammed. Brad finally found a spot in the reserve lot, which was much further away.

Shivering from the cold, Brad and Evie walked from the parking lot, to the campus center. "I'm sorry, Sis, I know I made us late. I just needed that extra time to finish studying."

The college was allowing Brad to finish out the semester and take his exams; following the old adage, "Innocent until proven guilty," but Brad couldn't stop thinking about his guilt.

Evie felt her twin's apprehensions, "Hey Bro, you know the material, you'll do fine."

"I know, I just can't seem to keep my mind off the trial and if I don't pass…."

"Right now, you just have to keep your mind on the exams, right?"

Brad and Evie walked down the college corridors listening to the students exchanging information about their plans for winter break.

The winter, so far, had been extremely cold and very snowy and many of the students were making preparations to vacation in warm sunny spots.

Brad was unable to join in the merriment, even though the family was still planning their vacation, he couldn't see beyond a guilty verdict. He turned to Evie, "I guess I won't be going on vacation?" His solemn look expressed the further regrets he was feeling.

Evie shared his fears about the outcome of the trial but tried to keep a positive outlook, "We're all behind you. Remember what gran told you when she called, 'Mr. Fenbrook is a great lawyer and if anyone can get you off, he can!'"

"I hear you and her but I still can't stop worrying. Shit! Ten to fifteen years in jail!"

"You never used to worry about anything! Why don't you try that for a while, and, if that doesn't work, just concentrate on all your girlfriends!" She laughed.

Brad joined in her laughter but his thoughts flashed into cyberspace..., yeah that might work," he joked.

Evie grabbed his hand before parting, "Knock 'em dead, Tiger!"

Evie walked down the corridor and bumped into Rick. Once again, her heart started pounding so loudly she didn't hear a word he said.

"Evie, Evie!"

"Oh, what, I'm sorry my mind's, er--on, exams."

"How's your brother doing?"

"Doing?" The smell of his cologne was making her extra heady.

"Yeah, about the upcoming trial and all. Uh, Evie, are you with me?" He looked confused.

"Yeah, oh, I'm sorry Rick," she said pulling herself together. "Yeah, it's a real bummer and he's so far strung out, I hope it's over soon." Evie decided it was polite to ask, "Er, how's Sheila dealing?"

"Sheila is Sheila! She blows it off believing her hero Controller, will come to her rescue. I'm afraid this time she's in for a real let down."

"I'm sorry, Rick. Is there anything I can do?"

"No but thanks for asking."

Evie had to get to her exam but she couldn't tear herself away. She stared into his eyes and wished he wasn't Sheila's guy. "I hope it turns out okay for her, too."

"Yeah, me too. Guess I better get going. See ya." Rick turned to go and Evie stopped him with a gentle touch that caused electricity to surge through her body. He looked down at her as if he'd felt it too.

She gazed at him through eyes that revealed more than she wanted them to say. "Rick, I just, er, a," their eyes were locked. Her fingers burned; they were still touching his arm. Trying to think of what to say, she just spilled words, "I wanted to, a... uh, thank you for calling every day to see how Brad was, you know, after the warehouse with QuizMaster and everything."

Then the spell was broken!

"Hey, no problem. I'll see ya, Evie."

"Yeah, see ya," she said as her heart fell and she watched him walk away.

Jonathan had been standing in the corridor and saw the whole thing!

CHAPTER 24

Dr. Schmidt returned from his trip to California and was again sitting in his car at the security guard house waiting for the Kane's to arrive.

He was unaccustomed to driving on roads that might have some snow or ice, so even though the report was that the roads were clear, he left an hour earlier.

When the clock indicated they were supposed to start work, Schmidt got annoyed. "If he could arrive on time, why couldn't they?"

When they finally arrived, Dr. Schmidt followed them through the security clearance to the Cottage. Martin parked the car and got out to help Vivian.

They greeted Schmidt, who didn't hide his annoyance at their tardiness and at again not being allowed access to the Cottage without them.

Martin explained, as they went inside, that he'd checked into it and because they were on college property it was an insurance issue, so, Schmidt had no choice but to accept it.

Martin cleared the code and they entered the building. Vivian asked Schmidt about his trip but he just muttered something and proceeded to the lab to begin the day's work. He never offered any explanation for his abrupt departure and trip back to California, nor, his fascination with The BREV Force.

Vivian went to make coffee and Martin went to check on his messages.

"< To... UNDISCLOSED >"

CC...

Subject:

"< R U the 1? >"

Martin yelled for Rosie, "Dammit, Rosie, it's here again!"

"Sorry Boss, I've been bogged down with new data coming in from Dr. Schmidt's secure connection. I didn't have a chance to delete that mail before you had a chance to go ballistic."

"Well, can you do that now? Actually, on the other hand, I wish you could just find out where it's coming from."

When he thought about it, he changed his mind. "Sorry, I guess now is not the time to make that a priority. What's this information transfer from Schmidt, anyway?"

"It seems that Dr. Schmidt has sent millions of bytes of information for me to analyze."

"Well, that's good, isn't it?"

"No, it's actually strange. Some of his calculations don't make any sense based on what we are trying to formulate."

"Yes, that's very strange, he's a brilliant scientist. Rosie, you know, it might just be that he's getting older and making mistakes but just in case we're wrong, let's re-analyze everything. After all, there could be something to his approach."

Martin went into the make-shift faux lab and found Schmidt scrolling through pages of documentation.

"What does all this mean, I can't decipher these notes?" he yelled.

Martin went over to look at the notes, as Vivian entered the lab. She was carrying a tray heaped with freshly cut samples she'd brought from the hot house and three cups of coffee.

Martin ran to assist her, "Here, you shouldn't be carrying all that. Sit down. I'll take these."

Having overheard Schmidt's annoyance about the notes, Vivian tried to divert him. "I guess I need to take a break," she said, putting her hand to her back as she eased herself into a chair next to Schmidt's work station. "It's becoming harder for me to keep bending and twisting to get the cuttings."

Martin jumped in, "I told you I would get the cuttings, maybe now you'll listen to me." He reached for his cup, "You relax with Dr. Schmidt and I'll just take my coffee and finish getting the samples."

"But, the notes…." Schmidt called out.

"Yes, I'll look at them when I get back Dr. Schmidt!" Martin left without saying any more or giving Schmidt another opportunity to discuss the notes.

Vivian handed Dr. Schmidt his coffee and took the last cup for herself, "Dr. Schmidt, now that Martin's out of the room, I need to talk to you about Brad. Things aren't looking good with the trial. Even the lawyer we have feels he may be found guilty of conspiring with Controller. These are very serious charges and since he's over eighteen, he's being charged as an adult."

She tried to make Schmidt feel important and flattered him, "You're so much wiser than we are, do you think Brad has a chance of going free?"

Schmidt was annoyed. All he wanted was an answer regarding the notes but he sensed Vivian's need to talk. He decided if he made her feel better about Brad, maybe she would answer his questions, or even better, go home and let him work alone with Martin.

Schmidt put down his coffee cup and took her hand. "Vivian, both you and Martin have always done a fine job raising the twins. I've watched Brad grow up. He's not a criminal. He just made a mistake. I'm sure the judge will see that."

He paused for a moment, as if something else weighed on his mind. "Just remember, sometimes we do things out of need, even when it might be wrong, that's not always easy for other people to understand. As a parent..." he stopped and lowered his head and then placed his fingers on his forehead in a deeply troubled gesture.

After a moment, he looked up and then continued, "well, you understand what I mean, you must protect your child--no matter what!" Schmidt stared into space, his eyes suddenly seemed very sad.

Vivian was taken aback and very confused by what he'd said but before she could question him, Schmidt changed the subject.

"Now, we have a mission," he stated in a very commanding tone and then added, "so like Brad would say, 'get it done!'"

"You're right, Dr. Schmidt, I'm going upstairs, to work."

Schmidt watched her go and then looked back at the notes. He called out to her but she was gone. "I can't believe no one will help me figure out these notes! Rosie, have you finished my download, maybe you can now help me decipher the notes?"

Martin and Vivian managed to keep busy the remainder of the day but toward the end of the day Rosie could detect Schmidt getting tired. "I'm finally available and at your service, Dr. Schmidt."

By that time, Schmidt was frustrated and annoyed and as Rosie knew, totally tired.

He got ready to leave and shouted, "Martin, clear the security code! Tomorrow one of you will have to work with me!" The door opened and he stomped out.

CHAPTER 25

The snow was beginning again as they drove home that night. "Martin, I know we were both relieved when Dr. Schmidt finally left today but we can't ignore him every day!"

"I know Viv but each day we are able to stall him, brings us another day closer to solving the Controller problem."

"Yes, but whether we like it or not, he's here and apparently to stay, so we need to find places to include him."

"I know that but every time we seem on the verge of a promising development, he comes up with another avenue to explore. Viv, maybe we need to consider that he's just not as capable anymore."

"Well, the way he's acted... I'll bet he's aware that he's losing it and all this is his way of covering up." Vivian stopped to give it more thought, then concluded, "Oh Martin, we must be more understanding, if for no other reason than respect."

"I don't disagree but even though he's still a brilliant scientist, he's making mistakes Viv and we just can't let that stand, no matter who he is!

I just think we need to give his ideas a chance and we'll fix the formulation. After all, when Rosie finished processing his download, she speculated that there might be some merit to his conclusions." Vivian looked at her husband with a plea for some emotional connection added to the mix. "Maybe if we just try to work with him, we may find the answer sooner and hopefully, before our children have to face Controller again."

"As always, I see your point and in the long run, that's the ultimate goal. I'll tell you what, I'll call Dr. Schmidt when we get home to see how his drive was in this weather and review with him the notes he was having trouble deciphering."

"Good and tell him we'll be in early tomorrow."

"Well, that's highly doubtful. Look how the snow has started again and it's really coming down!"

"Well, Martin, tell him anyway."

The snow had continued through the night and into late afternoon the next day. The feeling of being cooped up was getting to everyone in the Kane family but when Martin called to tell Schmidt they couldn't get to the lab, Schmidt was furious!

The weather was having a radical effect on his mood and he hated being stuck at the Inn. Martin explained that only emergency vehicles and those with proper clearance were being allowed on the roads.

He told Schmidt, that after having lived in a warm climate for so long, even the family was still unaccustomed to the long, hard, winters. But to get some sympathy, Martin added a comment that the severe weather was making everything else they were going through seem even more difficult. Schmidt said he understood and hung up.

By late afternoon, Martin had already had contact with Schmidt five times that day and told his wife, "It was your brilliant idea to explain about the notes, now he just keeps calling every five minutes with new questions. You, my love, can take the next call."

Vivian just shrugged, smiled.

Residents of Island Falls were used to the harsh winters. The town cleaning crews were efficient in clearing the roads at the first signs of snow fall, however, now it was falling almost as fast as they could clear it. Schools, businesses and the courts were all closed. Exams had luckily finished and the trial had not yet begun.

Very little was moving on the streets but Brad watched as Mr. Fenbrook's four-wheel drive vehicle cautiously maneuvered into their driveway. Brad had never thought much of lawyers but now that Mr. Fenbrook held his fate in his hands, he eyed the attorney with a greater sense of respect. He also knew if he was there today, it meant something really serious was about to occur.

George Fenbrook pushed his car's door open against the raging wet blizzard and trudged through the higher snow. His heavy winter coat made him look even bigger around, while his high rubber boots made him look shorter. His beard was white with snow and when he rang the bell he looked like a jolly Santa come to call.

Brad rushed to the door and swung it open in anticipation of what he knew would not be a merry occasion. "Mr. Fenbrook, what's wrong. We didn't expect to see you today? It must be pretty bad for me, if you got clearance to drive here!"

"Calm down Brad, let me in and I'll tell you." Brad stepped aside as the attorney made his way into the hall. He shook the snow off his boots and took off his overcoat.

Brad noticed the lawyer's stern glance, rather than the ho, ho, ho he expected. "Please tell your parents I'm here and that I would like to speak with all of you."

George Fenbrook had handled all the legal details of the family's move to Island Falls and had quickly become a family friend.

Brad rushed from the hall and anxiously returned with his father.

"George, how are you? Come on in," Martin said, as he shook hands with Fenbrook and ushered him into the living room. "Vivian's on a call with her mother but she'll join us in a minute. Can I get you something to drink?"

"Just some coffee, thanks Martin." Fenbrook sat down and positioned his briefcase on his lap. Martin brought him the coffee and he started to make small talk when Vivian entered the room.

George shifted his rotund body forward to maneuver out of the chair but Vivian raised her hand to stop him and rushed over to give him a peck on the cheek. "How are you feeling, Vivian?" he asked.

"I'm fine George. Miserable day for a drive and as I am told, only for those with special clearance, so does that mean you have news?"

Brad fidgeted, waiting for the attorney to speak but he was unable to restrain himself any further and burst out, "Please, Mr. Fenbrook, tell us what's goin' on?"

Fenbrook took a disc from his briefcase and loaded it into his laptop.

Brad quivered inside as he waited to hear what the attorney had to say.

"Martin, Vivian, Brad," he began, looking at each of them with a serious expression darkening his face, "I met with the district attorney last night and again this morning. After hours of discussion, we even met with the Judge Lerner, at his home."

"That sounds pretty urgent, George," Martin remarked, "what couldn't wait 'til court reconvened?"

"I will get to that in a minute. First, you need to know that the evidence against Sheila is very compelling, she'll most likely be found guilty. My biggest concern is that Brad's guilt, or innocence, will be tied to her. D.A. Martha Reynolds is being very tough. She wants Brad and Sheila tried together and expects them to be convicted."

George saw Vivian's look of panic. "Please Vivian, I know this is very difficult but before you get upset, let me present all the possibilities."

Vivian just nodded.

George shifted position and pressed the button for the holographic screen to open. As it did he watched their faces as they saw Sheila's confession.

He put the playback on pause and explained, "Reynolds contends that Sheila's statement confirms not only that Brad was in on everything in advance but that he was in league with QuizMaster to tamper with the files and make them available for Controller's network. As you can see, Sheila contends that not only did Brad double cross her but he hijacked the answers to his computer and then sabotaged the files so no one else could get the answers. The D.A.'s conclusion is that he was only looking out for his own interests!"

"That's right!" Brad said. "That's exactly what I did but not the way they think, I was…."

"Oh, Brad," his mother interrupted, "We know you were just trying to keep the answers from falling into the wrong hands but even the way George just told it, it could be misconstrued to appear that all you were doing was serving your own interests."

Brad started to argue but Fenbrook broke in. "Facts, Brad, facts! And, the facts substantiate Sheila's argument!"

Brad had an overwhelming urge to interrupt again and make everyone see his side but he restrained himself.

Fenbrook paused and took note of Brad's restraint, knowing the boy would need lots of self-control if he was going to get through this ordeal.

"Brad, sometimes even the truth can sound like lies and of course, vice versa. The statements of your friends did confirm what Sheila and QuizMaster did when they kidnapped you but there is no one to corroborate the break in at the school or your intentions there. "

Fenbrook, reached for his coffee as a delay tactic. He needed to give them all a chance to digest what he just showed them, before he went on.

He re-engaged the playback and a holographic the D.A. was adamantly stating, "In conclusion, after reviewing all the statements, this office believes that the guilt or innocence of Brad Kane, will have to be decided by a court of law and that there is enough evidence to bring that charge to the court. These Controller sympathizers need a strong message that their actions are unacceptable and will have severe consequences. Therefore, as district attorney, I will ask for the maximum sentence, if convicted."

Brad gasped, as did his parents.

Fenbrook didn't wait for responses. He again put the display on pause and put up his hand, "There's more. Something strange happened when we were concluding our pre-trial conference. Reynolds got a call and then everything changed. She wouldn't say why but she said we needed to set up a meeting with the judge."

"Who was the phone call from?" Vivian asked

"The D. A. said she couldn't say but it must have been pretty high up because, she did a total one-eighty, changed her tune and put an offer on the table."

The room was still. Everyone held their breath waiting for the attorney to finish. Fenbrook hoisted himself off the couch and began to pace the room. "Brad, I will tell you, this deal carries considerable risks...."

"What do you mean George?" Martin interrupted.

"Let me play the rest of the meeting for you."

They watched as District Attorney Martha Reynolds began to speak. "When Sheila is convicted, Controller will be left with numerous unknown supporters. We've recently confirmed that Controller has cells of followers everywhere and that these cells have already infiltrated the prison. If Brad is willing to go undercover, my office and the police believe he could be instrumental in penetrating Controller's network and getting us very valuable information. We would want Brad to convince these followers that he's only interested in revenge against the system. Once he gains their trust we believe he should be privy to 'insider only' information. If he agrees to do this, in exchange we will plead Brad out for his cooperation and all records will be expunged."

The disk shut off and the hologram disappeared.

"George, this sounds really dangerous. Is this Brad's only choice?" his mother asked. "Isn't there some other way?"

Taking the disk out and moving the laptop to his side, George said, "In my opinion, without this deal, Brad will be put through a long grueling trial and eventually be found guilty for which he will serve a long prison term. Brad, it's unfortunate for you that you got involved, just at the wrong time."

"What do you mean, George?" Martin asked.

"The D. A. finally told me that a new order had come down from the, 'highest levels,' that Controller sympathizers should be charged as enemies of the state. They're going to make an example of Sheila and if Brad gets caught in the crossfire, so be it. I believe this deal is their only way around it and Brad's only chance."

Fenbrook looked at Brad, "What do you think?"

Brad tried to hide the fear in his voice as he got up and walked over to where the lawyer was standing. "Maybe I've been given a second chance. I just need a little time to decide what's best for me."

Fenbrook smiled, "I'm impressed, Brad. You've never taken things seriously before. I'm glad to see you can weigh the situation but be warned, if you're thinking this is an easy out, it won't be. If you take the deal you will need to plead guilty for the entire world to see. Reynolds will make sure you're made an example of, thrown out of school, fired from your job and the onslaught of publicity will cause the community to turn against you. The intention is for the word to get back to Controller that your anger and desire for revenge is sincere."

"What exactly does the D.A. want me to do when I go undercover?" Brad questioned.

"Sheila will be put in a maximum-security facility and will be totally out of commission. Therefore, it has been concluded that Controller will need a new human collaborator. A number of inmates have been identified as Controller supporters and you'll be given their names. You're to make contact and after you gain their trust, find out as much as you can about Controller and the new collaborator, get inside and become trusted. The word on the street is that something big is coming down but no one knows what, or when. That's your job. Once you have the information your job will be done."

"Why should Controller's people trust me? Remember I double-crossed QuizMaster and Sheila."

"It seems that the D.A. has some critical information that you will leak to Controller. That, combined with your feigned anger, should convince Controller that you're on the level."

Brad knew enough about how Controller operated and didn't quite buy what Fenbrook had told him. "Mr. Fenbrook, I don't want to sound disrespectful but this sounds like the D.A.'s office is snowin' you. If they wait long enough Controller's followers will come out into the open and everyone will know who the new human collaborator is and exactly what they're planning. So, why do they really want me on the inside?"

Fenbrook explained, "All I was told was that the heat was on from very high up. It seems to be some very important agency but she won't say which one. The D.A. however, did say they just can't afford to wait for Controller to make the move, they need to know before it happens! So far, all the offices working on the Controller problem and believe it or not, as I just learned, there are quite a few, haven't been too successful. So, Brad, you get the booby price for being their best hope."

"But, what about Brad, how will they protect him?" Vivian asked with motherly concern.

"Brad will be a regular inmate just like everyone else. There will be a few trusted guards nearby to keep an eye on him, including his cell mate but for the most part Brad will be on his own."

Fenbrook seemed to hesitate with the next sentence, "Brad, even if you succeed, until Controller and its forces are eliminated, you will be in danger."

"I understand."

"When does the D.A. want a decision?" Martin asked.

George gathered his briefcase, "I wish I could give you more time but we must respond to this offer before court reconvenes. If the snow obliges, tomorrow afternoon."

Brad got up and got Mr. Fenbrook's coat and then walked with him to the front door. "Mr. Fenbrook, if I agree, will it make any difference if my record is expunged, the whole world will know I pled guilty?"

"Brad, I had the same question, so I got them to agree that they will issue a public statement to explain the guilty plea and your part in ending Controller's reign." Fenbrook shook hands with Brad and smiled; proud of the young man he was defending.

Brad watched his father pass a glance with the lawyer as they shook hands and then his attention turned to his mother. She leaned toward the lawyer and said, "George, I will pray for another snow storm." Fenbrook smiled and nodded goodbye to all of them.

Once the door was closed Brad didn't say a word...he just ran up the stairs to his room.

Martin turned to Vivian, "I know you're still not happy with the result but for once having friends in high places has helped us.

"Martin, you didn't call the President about Brad, did you?"

"Vivian, I realized for everything we do...this is our son's life! The President and General Babcock have assured me Brad will be protected, even beyond what the D.A. and the police can do.

"Well, that does make me feel better!

"And, don't forget, Brad can now protect himself.

"I know and I do have to admit it's better than the real consequences if he's convicted. Martin, just hold me and tell me everything is going to be all right!"

CHAPTER 26

After much deliberation and discussion, Brad decided to accept the D.A.'s offer. Once he did, the wheels of justice rolled quickly.

He pleaded guilty and was sentenced and remanded to the county jail where he received his undercover instructions.

Sheila's trial regarding the school break in and stolen records was quick and she was also convicted. She began serving her sentence, while she waited her second trial for her involvement in Brad's kidnapping.

The Kane family was having a tough time dealing with the bad press; community reaction and their fears for Brad.

They told Brad during a visit, that they were going to postpone their vacation until he could join them but he wouldn't hear of it. "Who knows how long it'll be and anyway Mom could really use the break from all this tension."

They finally agreed and made the necessary reservations. Vivian and Evie were trying to be excited.

Brian tried to beg off but everyone felt it would be good for him, so he reluctantly packed.

Martin needed to finish up some work at the lab and then met with Dr. Schmidt who would be returning to California for the holidays. "Yes, my boy, my report to the Alliance will definitely indicate our progress."

Martin responded by suggesting, "With the progress we've made Dr. Schmidt, don't you think you could monitor our work from California and Vivian and I can handle things from here."

Schmidt strongly disagreed but Martin persuaded him to at least put the proposal to the Alliance. "All right," Dr. Schmidt very reluctantly stated. "I'll contact them and let you know sometime during the vacation but Martin, I really do expect to see you, January first."

Martin didn't want to argue. When they finished the day's work, they exchanged goodbyes and holiday good wishes and Martin watched Schmidt drive off. Feeling a bit more at ease once Schmidt was gone, he secured the Cottage and went down to the lab. Martin went through the procedures and commanded Rosie to reinstate the full lab with security protocol.

"Good to have you back, Dr. K. It sure has been lonely and quiet in here, not to mention dark!"

Martin laughed for the first time in weeks. "Rosie, can you give me an update on the growth calculations for samples eleven through sixteen and filter all messages to my port station for the next week."

"Mrs. Dr. K won't like that you're taking work on a holiday."

"Never you mind! Just do as you're told."

Martin gathered some files he'd been wanting to go over and after hours of copying data and reviewing files, he was ready to leave.

He started the lockdown for vacation mode. "Rosie, on my command." Martin watched all the overhead monitors. One by one they flashed lists of protocol. "Rosie, when ready, begin sequencing." Martin keyed in his command code and the monitors started flashing.

Rosie began calling off numbering sequences and code variables, each instituting its own lockdown, verifying each before the next segment. "Alpha Eight-Eight prompt," the numbers and lists would flow onto the screens faster than any mind could conceive of the combinations.

"Final sequencing, run, commencing on my mark."

Martin continued to watch in amazement and finally all the monitors were still and Rosie directed, "Vacation Chain complete. All links in lockdown mode."

"Oh, while I'm away, in addition to monitoring our data banks, checking the I.A.S. files and continuing to search for anything connected with Controller just note I will not be checking h-mail, so, if anything is of immediate importance..."

"I do know the protocol!"

"Well then, there is one more thing."

"Okay, what else would you expect me to do while you lounge around with the family."

"Er, have a wonderful holiday!"

"Rosie laughed, "Oh, Dr. K! You know I'm a rapid system interface and idleness is contrary to my programming. Holidays, as described in the language data bank are...." She went on and on. "And besides, you have given me more than enough work to occupy five such computers in space of time and...."

While she continued, Martin packed up the remaining materials he needed and walked to the steel door. "Goodnight, Rosie."

"Happy Holidays to you and the family!"

Martin cleared the necessary codes and watched as the lab once again disappeared.

CHAPTER 27

Brad sat in his cell and as much as he didn't want to admit it, he had to; he was terrified. For some reason that fear triggered a conversation he'd had with his grandmother before leaving for prison. Gran, I know I screwed up but I'm really worried.

Brad, you made a fair deal with the D.A. and they will protect you. Use this time to straighten out your act and come out of this a better person. We all screw up! It all depends on how you make the most of your mistakes. I love you and believe in you, just believe in yourself and you'll be fine. I'll bet by the time I return from Europe you'll be back home.

Her words brought enormous comfort to Brad.

While in jail, Brad also took great comfort from two letters he had received: one from Jonathan and the other, surprisingly, from Ginger.

Jonathan's letter said he was trying his best to kick all his "new bad habits" because he wanted to be the best friend possible for Brad. He also told Brad, repeatedly how sorry he was to have gotten Brad into this mess. He said he couldn't believe it when the court denied his request to be tried instead of Brad.

Jonathan insisted if Brad had only gone to trial, his testimony on Brad's behalf, would've influenced the jury to acquit Brad."

Brad looked at the last line of Jon's letter, "Just remember buddy, no matter what, I'll stand by you and be waiting when you get out, Jon."

On the other hand, Ginger's letter was a total shock. Not only did Brad not expect it but he had to read it and re-read it to try and analyze what she was saying.

"Brad, I never told you, probably because it wouldn't have meant anything to you but I really care a lot about you. I'm not telling you this now to impose my feelings on you, I know you don't return them but just to let you know that I believe in you and I'm proud of what you tried to do.

"You're a great guy and I know you'd never do anything to hurt anyone. I also know you're a great friend to Jonathan and that your driving force was to help him.

"I sat through Sheila's trial trying to find something I could do, something that would help you but now I just want you to know, I am here for you-- if you ever need anything, anything at all. No strings, just someone who cares and who wants to help, no matter what, when, or where!

"I would like to write to you, if that's okay and if not, that's o.k., too! Write back if you want – but just know I'll always remain your friend, Ginger."

Brad re-read the letter again before finally putting it down. I have work to do, I can't be dealing with this now, he told himself. He decided to throw the letter away but then thought better of it and put it with his personal papers.

D.A. Reynolds had given Brad the scoop about being in a cell with another protected prisoner and made sure he knew which guards were aware of who he was but it still felt scary. When the bars clanged shut and the key turned, he knew his freedom had been taken away.

Brad's cell mate, Tony Monetti was a real tough looking guy. He was older than Brad; dark in coloring, very black hair. He looked very much like you would picture an underworld gangster of the 1920's, or 30's. He was really an undercover agent; whose cover story was that he was convicted of an h-mail that scammed millions of dollars but the money was never found. He swore that the local authorities confiscated the money for themselves when he was arrested and he wanted revenge. He put the word out in the prison grapevine that he'd be an "important" ally for anyone interested in revenge. That helped get him into the good graces of Controller's people. Now, for all the prison to see, he and Brad were plotting together to get revenge.

In truth, they had to be very careful to protect their actual identities. Brad and Tony never talked openly about their assignment, even when they were sure they were alone. The only way they communicated was through a cleverly conceived coded h-mail system. But, with everything they were doing, so far nothing had occurred.

Prison presented a whole new set of problems for Brad. He had to accept being shut away from family and friends, familiar surroundings and most of all from his own ability to come and go at will.

The D. A. had set him up with a job in the computer lab but even being away from the cell for hours at a time, was still confining. Brad was told what to do and when. When to eat, when to sleep, when to get up. He'd thought he could find some solace with his cell mate Tony, or, the trusted guards, who knew why he was there but the silence that was necessary for all their sakes, made Brad really feel alone.

Even when his family visited, they had to watch what was said, as all communications were monitored.

During their recent visit, Brad realized he felt the most alone. He had to hear his family pretend to be disappointed in him and at that moment he couldn't help wonder if, at least, in part, it was true. And, even though he was the one who pushed his father not to postpone their vacation, Brad couldn't help thinking about what he would be missing.

The days were tough but the nights were even tougher. Just getting familiar with the strict schedules of prison life was hard but the hardest part was pretending to be something he wasn't; an angry vindictive radical.

Brad felt sincere regret for what he'd done but he quickly learned if he was going to survive he needed to adopt that radical persona, and, well he did.

Some of the toughest prisoners tried to break him but luckily for Brad, his super abilities made him able to take the beatings without the pain and without complaining to the guards, or the D.A., even Tony didn't know.

The prisoners liked Brad's spirit and soon the word spread that Brad was a fellow con to be respected. He made some very valuable friends who saw to it that he was given special treatment. He eventually made his way into Controller's web. Brad was making better progress than the district attorney could've ever expected and the information he had passed on was very helpful! But, for Brad, there was still a long way to go. His real challenge was to gain the confidence of someone who could lead him to Controller's new collaborator.

CHAPTER 28

The Kane family vehicle was already overloaded with luggage for their trip, when Evie came down the stairs with one more bag.

"No more stuff! Anyone going on this trip had better be ready in ten minutes, or else," her father joked, as he came into the house, shaking the snow from his coat.

Vivian came from the kitchen and gave Martin a peck on the cheek. "Oh, you slave driver, you know you would never leave without me. Would you?"

"Well," he chided, "if the others aren't ready, I wouldn't mind leaving them and having you all to myself."

Martin saw his daughter head upstairs. He called after her, "No more stuff!"

She smiled. Evie ran to answer the C-Tel.

It was her grandmother. She was still talking with her about Rick and Eddy, when her mother indicated they'd better go now. Evie nodded, "Thanks Gran, I'll think about it. Oh, mom says bye too, love ya!"

When everyone was settled in the car, they got on the road. It was clear Brad's absence was felt by all. They couldn't help discussing how badly those days of his sentencing had gone.

Brad's name had been splattered all over the papers. He was kicked out of school, fired in disgrace from his job and the family was instructed to act as if they didn't want any part of him.

Jonathan and Ginger were the only ones who publicly stood by Brad. The family was allowed one initial visit, which they used as a way to publicly declare their feelings. "Brad has disgraced his family. We are very ashamed of his behavior," Martin had told the newspapers. But privately, they were so very proud of Brad; they grieved for what he was going through, especially his father.

Martin realized that rehashing the situation was just depressing everyone, "I make a motion," he said, "as of this moment, or at least for this vacation, we put the whole Brad experience behind us."

He also made sure to remind them, "After all, Brad wanted us to go and have a great time and I believe, as difficult as his situation is, he meant that.

So, no more discussion. Let's concentrate on having a great time and just relaxing. Especially you, my lady," Martin said, touching Vivian's cheek.

She smiled, knowing he and Brad were doing this mostly for her and the baby.

Brian was quiet during the drive; taking in the scenery and feeling a bit strange about his first real vacation.

On the other hand, Evie was restless and fidgety. She kept going over her conversation with her grandmother. But Gran, Rick is Sheila's guy and she's in trouble; how can I try to get him? And, what about my relationship with Eddy?"

But her grandmother's words kept coming back at her and they pretty well summed up both her dilemmas, Eddy is the past! That is so obvious considering the way you talk about Rick. So, call Eddy and really end it! Then, my girl, as far as Rick, 'all's fair in love and war' as they say, so go get him girl!

Three hours later they arrived at the lodge. They marveled at the beauty of the snow-capped mountains, surrounded by a wide expanse of natural forest land that seemed to go on as far as the eye could see. There was a very quaint lodge building on top of the hill with cabins, set back from the road; it was the perfect setting.

But, Briar Mountain wasn't just the perfect vacation spot, for the family it offered what they really needed; seclusion and privacy. It wasn't a "happening," resort for Island Falls citizens, who usually chose the more popular Big Top Mountain. Big Top was closer to Island Falls and offered many more amenities and it was considered, "the place to go."

The family didn't care about any of that, they just didn't want to run into anyone who might know them, or Brad, or more importantly who might ask questions about Brian.

Vivian looked around and turned to Martin, put her arm through his and snuggled close, "Briar Mountain was the perfect choice. It's just what we all need."

The Kane's checked in and drove to their cabin which was simple and rustic but had every modern convenience. There was a full-service kitchen: multi-function video/audio center and conferencing connection in each room and a beautifully inviting fireplace in the living room and master bedroom. Off the master was a Grecian tub and spa cradled in a garden window, that overlooked the mountains. In addition, the cabin had three other bedrooms and a den area, with a pull-out couch.

Martin, Evie and Brian took the luggage out of the car, while Vivian started to set up the rooms.

Evie was in better spirits now and had finally come to terms with the pact she'd made with her grandmother to forget both guys, at least for this vacation and she was going to stick to it and have a good time.

Once they were settled in and unpacked, Evie and Brian decided to check out the main lodge, while Martin and Vivian were very happy for the time alone. They just sat peacefully in the living room holding hands, watching the roaring fire, until it faded to glowing embers.

Brian and Evie went off to explore and agreed to meet their parents back at the cabin for dinner.

At the lodge, Evie stayed close to Brian as they mingled with other young people. Evie met two girls from California who were attending college in New Hampshire. They talked about places in California she knew and it felt like old home week. Surprisingly, she didn't even think about Eddy.

Brian was not particularly interested in the girls' conversation and excused himself. Evie said she'd go with him but he said he'd be fine and for her to stay and enjoy her new friends.

He walked around and familiarized himself with the lodge, until he came to the lounge. The door was open but no one was inside. He stared at the piano in the far corner and decided to go in and play.

After a few minutes, he felt self-conscious and stopped. Brian got up and went through the double doors that led outside onto a balcony that overlooked the mountains. He was suddenly startled by a tap on the shoulder. Brian turned to see who had interrupted his thoughts.

"I am sorry! I did not mean to startle you." The girl smiled.

When she glanced up at Brian he saw the bluest eyes he had ever seen. Not being accustomed to talking with strangers, Brian stammered, "Oh…I, it is all right."

"My name is Robin Elaine Marsh," she said. "I heard your piano playing and was drawn to find you. But then you stopped, so I decided to follow you out here. You look, lost, so I hope you do not mind. I just had to come over and say hello."

She noticed a look of embarrassment and asked, "Am I being too forward for you? You are awfully good looking and probably would not have been alone for too long, so, I did not want to wait for someone else to move in on you."

"I do not believe that would have happened but it is nice to make your acquaintance. I am Brian Kane," he smiled and reached out to shake hands.

This was his first real meeting with anyone other than the family and Brian's emotions were confused and raging. He was not used to making idle conversation and certainly not with a stranger but the look in her eyes was stimulating and he was quite surprisingly moved by the experience.

When the family reunited for dinner that evening, Brian listened to Evie talking about the wonderful people she'd met from California. He said nothing.

The main dining room of the lodge was elegantly decorated with holiday décor. Each table was set with items from celebrations known the world over. The Kane's were shown to a table for four that was adorned with a beautiful candelabra. The atmosphere was so festive, that soon they were all feeling the holiday spirit. They ordered dinner and discussed their plans for the evening.

Brian was quiet throughout the meal; lost in his thoughts but he suddenly perked up when he saw Robin enter the dining room. She looked so very beautiful wearing an exquisite red velvet outfit that swayed with her movements. As she passed their table, she casually smiled, "hello."

Brian couldn't keep his eyes off her. Her shiny shoulder length hair was the color of corn-silk that seemed to dance and flow in the breeze of her walk. She waved but kept on walking. Brian stood up and stared after her.

"Brian," Evie noted, "She's magnificent! Oh, and when did you meet her that you didn't tell me?"

Brian finally sat down and turned his attention back to his family. "I…I met her when you were engrossed in conversation about California. I wandered around and we sort of ran into each other. Her name is Robin Marsh. That is all I really know. We spoke for only a few minutes and then I excused myself and left to return to the cabin."

Vivian knew relationships were going to be difficult for Brian but like her other children, she had to let him handle it; at least, until he came to her with questions or for advice.

Everyone agreed that dinner was wonderful and that the assortment of delicacies was a pleasant surprise. When dessert and coffee were being served, Evie excused herself to join her newly found companions. Brian said he just wanted to go for a walk, so Martin and Vivian decided to go to try the lounge for some music or maybe even a dance.

Brian found himself walking around outside in a daze. His thoughts kept flashing back to Robin dancing by their dining table. He envisioned her outfit flowing in the wind and her eyes locking to his. Brian was stunned by these thoughts. He tried to focus on the night sky. But, the beautifully bright lights of the stars, reminded him of Robin.

"The sky is so beautiful here!" He heard the voice and knew at once... as he glanced down and saw the red velvet dress.

"Yes, it is quite beautiful but...," Brian looked deep into her eyes and saw the twinkling of the stars. He wanted to tell her how beautiful she was but the words would not come out. Instead, he just stared at her. Her beauty reminded him of a painting.

She interrupted his thoughts, "How long are you and your family staying?"

"We are here through New Year's," Brian replied as he regained his composure.

"So am I. Perhaps we can spend the time together. What do you enjoy doing?"

Brian, now puzzled by the girl's attention, tried to put the conversation on a less personal level. "I believe it would be preferable for you to make friends with someone much more outgoing and interested in participation events." Brian told her in a robotic manner. "I am very much a loner. I do not get involved in many things."

Robin, looked dejected as she tried to explain, "I just thought maybe there were things you would like to do with me. Actually, we do not have to do anything. I would be happy just being with you, if that is all right?"

Brian hesitated for a moment and then nodded. Robin walked silently by his side into the night.

Brian had not realized how much time he and Robin had spent together, until he went back to his cabin and saw only the porch light on. He tip-toed in and found a note taped to his door. He turned on the light and read:

"This is a new experience, you being the last one in. Hope you had a great time. Be sure to lock up. See you for breakfast in the morning. Don't forget we're going to town for the holiday fair. Love Mom."

Brian keyed in the "evening light shutdown sequence" on the wall panel and then went into his room. He pressed the button to open the blinds and his room was flooded with light from the moon and stars. He stared at the brilliance of the night and envisioned the twinkle in Robin's eyes. Brian fell asleep, aglow with the strange feelings that engulfed his whole being.

CHAPTER 29

Brad knew the time had come to take the next step to finding the link to Controller's collaborator. He and his cellmate Tony talked about why anyone would volunteer for this job and they both laughed; they both had their separate reasons.

Tony had been at it for a lot longer than Brad but he hadn't made any real progress getting into Controller's inner circle. The best he had been able to do was establish a reputation as a bad ass! The D.A. had been right in her assumption; for whatever reason, Controller wasn't taking Tony's bait.

When Brad got involved, it was another story. He was becoming more integrated into Controller's army with each passing day. But, he was being tested all the time. Recently, he'd been instructed, through an h-mail, to hack into government-controlled facility sites, to retrieve information for Controller. He was a hero when he presented the classified documents but, of course, he only provided the documents the government had supplied to the D.A.

Controller obviously didn't know the difference because the next day Brad received a personal h-mail from Controller congratulating him on his achievements.

Since there still wasn't any word in the cell block of a new hologram, Brad decided to use the opportunity and answer Controller's congratulatory h-mail with a twist of his own.

"< Hey Controller, isn't it about time for a new hologram to land on the scene, or have you depleted your store with Cracko and QuizMaster? >"

"< ALL YOU NEED TO KNOW WILL BE REVEALED TO YOU WHEN REM CONTACTS YOU. >"

With that, Brad was sure he'd hit pay dirt and responded, "< Okay! So, Controller, who is this REM? Is this the new hologram? And, how will I know for sure I've been in touch with the right messenger and not just a plant? >"

Brad's questions were answered in the next h-mail.

"< I AM REM. Your mission will be to aid the cause of CONTROLLER — in return, we will take revenge on all those who turned their backs on you and especially, 'The BREV Force.' Be ready and await further instructions.>"

Brad wrote back,

"< Are you a hologram or human? >"

There was no reply!

Brad tried to trace the source of the communication but it was impossible. He tried to find out from others that he'd already identified as Controller followers if this REM was human or hologram, male, female, old, young but no one knew anything. Strangely, the word inside, was that "… soon everyone would know."

D.A. Reynolds told Brad he had to keep digging, she needed more information; since none of the law enforcement agencies knew of, or, could find anything about, a "REM."

CHAPTER 30

The next morning at breakfast, Brian visually searched the dining room expecting to find Robin. He had hoped to see her before the family finished eating and was ready to leave for the fair but that did not happen. He did not mention what had occurred the preceding evening and his parents respected his privacy. Evie started to ask him about the girl in the red dress but the look on her mother's face told her that it wasn't the time.

The drive through the wooded hills and up the steep mountain road, led to the top of Briar Mountain where the holiday fair was being held. The owners of the lodge had told the Kane's that the fair was an annual event sponsored by the immigrants of the town. The fair had started one hundred and thirty years earlier, when the settlers of the valley were mostly immigrants. They had come to Briar Mountain because it was untapped land whose beauty reminded them of the countries they'd left behind.

During their first years, they all joined together and shared their customs as a way to celebrate the holidays together. When word got out, immigrants from far off towns would come to join the celebration. The number of participants increased with each passing year. Today, the fair was an international festival with representation from all over the world.

The view going up the mountain was spectacular but not as breathtaking as it was at the top. When they got out of the car the Kane's felt as if they were close to heaven. If the trip up and the view were any indication of the fair, it was going to be quite a day. There was a short walk from the car to the actual fair site but it gave visitors a chance to admire the mountaintop decorations, which rivaled the setting. The snow covered the ground but for some reason, it wasn't really cold. The air was cool and brisk but so fresh and clean you didn't notice the cold.

The walk toward the fair site was an experience all its own. There were carolers and merchants selling toys, clothes and food; all in costumes representative of their home lands and all in a joyous blend of wintry, holiday fun.

At the end of the line of booths was a non-denominational house of worship, where children representing countries from all over the world sang songs of good cheer, in their native languages.

Martin was glad to see his family having such a good time and knew that only Brad's presence could have made it more complete. Vivian had seemed to forget about the trial, Controller and Dr. Schmidt, at least for the moment. The look on his children's faces as they entered this fairyland, made Martin certain this was the perfect family vacation. But, the most incredible happening was watching Brian's face. Martin, Vivian and Evie could not get over the sparkle in his eyes; it was like a child experiencing the joy of the holidays for the first time.

The family stayed to listen to the different services in the unique house of worship and then surprisingly, it was Martin who was the first to feel hungry. He led the way back outside to the actual fair grounds where there were hundreds of booths set up representing the holiday observance of each immigrant's homeland.

In front of each booth was a sample of some of the international foods the vendors were offering.

Brian followed close behind and turned and twisted to be sure to see everything, instead of looking where he was walking; he ran smack into Robin. His heart began to beat at an enormously fast pace. He tried to speak but the words would not come out.

"Hi!" Robin smiled, as she sped by.

"Wa, Wait. Can we...?"

Before he could finish his sentence, she interrupted. "Cannot talk now," she called back to him. "Meet me later. You know where."

Brian looked around, hoping his family had not seen what had transpired. For the first time in his short life, he believed he was experiencing embarrassment but he could not explain why.

Brian caught up with Robin later that evening and they were together every night and day, after that. They would meet right after breakfast and only separate to return to their cabins to change for dinner.

Brian found Robin interesting to talk with on every level. Not only was she smart; but also, sensitive and logical. They enjoyed every aspect of being together. Sometimes they would walk for hours just holding hands, never saying a word; keeping each other warm. Other times they would sit on a bench or find a quiet spot in the main house and just talk. Each time they were together seemed better than the last.

One afternoon, they were out walking when a snow shower started. The snow fell and melted on their faces and they both started laughing. Brian took off his jacket and covered Robin. She leaned close to him and wiped the water as it ran down his face; first with her fingertips and then with her lips. Robin's eyes blinked away the snow and met his glance. She touched his face again and drew him close. Their lips pressed together as they kissed.

This "first" kiss was a shock to Brian's nervous system and the burning in his loins scared him. He had kissed his mother and his sister but nothing before had prepared him for this experience. He pulled away, leaving Robin to believe he didn't enjoy the kiss. When he couldn't find words to explain what he was feeling, she ran away. Brian stood and watched helplessly.

Brian had read a great deal on the subject of love and sex but he was unprepared for the feelings he was experiencing. He decided to speak to Evie about what had happened.

His sister explained about guys and girls, sex and falling in love, on a very different level than the textbook version. Hers was a much more emotional understanding of his physical reaction, which helped him to deal with what he was feeling. She also tried to help him understand what Robin must have felt when he pulled away. Brian thanked his sister and said he would find Robin after dinner and try to make her understand.

Now that it was out in the open, Evie asked a lot of questions, to which, it was obvious, Brian didn't have the answers. He did not know much about Robin despite the enormous number of hours they had spent together. All he knew was that she was transferring to Island Falls College, after vacation. But, every time he had tried to ask Robin about her family life, she changed the subject. He finally decided he did not need to know anything more about her.

Evie found Robin's behavior strange since girls usually want to talk about themselves but she concluded that maybe Robin was just shy. She hoped Brian would find a chance to introduce them, so she could gain a 'first hand' opinion of Robin for herself.

It was the night of the big New Year's Eve celebration and everyone was getting ready. There was a knock at the Kane's cabin door and Vivian went to answer it. The gift on the other side of the door was quite a surprise.

"Hey Mom! Where's Dad?"

"Oh my…Brad but but…." Vivian cried as she put her arms around her son. Brad embraced his mother while trying to answer her unspoken questions.

"Mom, I'm only here for tonight. The D.A. felt sorry for me and arranged a fight between me and one of the other undercover inmates that was supposed to land me in solitary confinement but instead put me in a copter… and here I am."

Hearing the commotion, Martin, Brian and Evie came rushing into the room. After hugs and questions, Martin realized Vivian was shaky and helped her sit down. "Now son, tell us what's been happening," Martin asked.

"The authorities are treating me quite well and whenever possible I'm given special privileges. The first day, I was instructed to start a fight so I would be labeled a trouble maker." Brad decided not to tell them about the beatings he took from other inmates. "I was set up with a job in the computer lab and I spend my time sifting through prisoner's records to try and find Controller's followers.

"My cover story was that everyone had turned on me and I was so bitter all I wanted was revenge. Everything was proceeding according to plan and then the grapevine, which in the prison is really strong, indicated that the word was getting around about me.

"My cell mate, is a plant and he's been undercover since Cracko. He hasn't been able to gain any ground, so the D.A. was really shocked at how much I've been able to find out. The inside scoop is that a new hologram, is about to make the scene. I had h-mail contact from someone called REM, which I thought was the hologram but I've since learned that REM, is the new human collaborator."

"Is this REM, like Sheila? Do we know, er, him, her?" Evie questioned.

"I don't know anything, that's the trouble. The word in the yard is that, 'no one knows.' I can't even locate a link back to the original h-mail, so all I can do now is wait for REM to contact me again." He stopped to catch his breath. "Anyway, I'm here now and ready to party, so can we please go celebrate?"

The Kane's could not believe how far Brad had gotten in such a short period of time and they all agreed the news was so promising that Brad should be back home with them soon. If nothing else, he was with them now and it gave them an extra reason to celebrate the New Year.

Brian lent Brad something to wear and they all donned their masks for the New Year's costume party. They were ready to leave, when the connection beeped a call. Martin saw on the identifier band that it was Dr. Schmidt. He pressed audio only and took the call, "Happy New Year. We were going to call you later due to the difference in time."

Schmidt broke in, "Yes, yes, Martin it's still early, Happy New Year but that's not why I'm calling. I'm needed here in California for now and the Alliance has approved your request for me to supervise the project from here."

Martin wasn't sure about the C-TEL reception at the lodge and had reluctantly given Schmidt their room number but now he was glad. "That's wonderful news doctor. I hope everything is all right with you though?"

"Well," Schmidt hesitated, "Just a minor disturbance but nothing I can't handle."

Martin was going to press for more information and then thought better of it. It was New Year's Eve and they had just gotten two surprises; first Brad and now this, so he wasn't going to look a gift horse in the mouth. "You just have a wonderful holiday and we'll talk to you when we return to Island Falls. Hold on, here's Vivian." Martin pressed hold and walked the privacy speaker over to Vivian.

She quickly wished Schmidt well and then passed it to Evie who also spoke briefly before returning the connection to her father who said some additional words, then disconnected.

"Sorry Brad, I'm sure you would've liked to wish Dr. Schmidt a good holiday but you're supposed to be in jail."

"I know Dad, I'm just glad to be here."

And, so was his mother. Vivian couldn't be happier. Everything was indicating that it was going to be a very good year!

The entire Kane family joined the other guests and spent the evening enjoying the celebration and looking forward to the New Year.

The party was an incredible celebration with rows of buffet tables filled with every kind of hot and cold food imaginable. A full band played music from every era for dancing and sing alongs. The costumes were beautiful, funny and very imaginative and Brad was able to blend in and enjoy the evening without arousing anyone's suspicion.

Everyone was having such a great time that they wished the evening would never end. When the band played Auld Lang Syne and the masks were being removed, Brad ducked out, knowing for him, the festivities were just about over.

Martin and Vivian went back to the cabin to spend some quiet time, with Brad before he had to leave.

Evie toasted the New Year with her new friends and made a silent resolution to come to a decision about her situation with both Eddy and Rick. She said goodnight and returned to the cabin to be with her family while they waited for the return of Brad's police escort.

The escort arrived exactly on schedule at one o'clock to accompany Brad back to prison. For the Kane's, the celebration was over.

"Brad, please take care of yourself," his mother said emotionally.

"Mom, I'll be okay. You just take care of you and the baby."

"Vivian," his father concurred, "we just went through this goodbye scene when Brad first went to prison and he promised you then he'd be careful. He'll be fine!"

When Martin heard his own words, he realized he'd said them as much for himself as for her. He put his arm around his wife, while Brad and Evie shared a private goodbye.

"You know Evie, I just regret that I can't tell Jon what's going on. He's been so supportive during the trial and since but the D.A. says no contact would be better."

"The way things are going you should be able to tell him real soon!"

"I hope so."

Then Brad asked a strange question, "Evie, have you seen Ginger?"

"No, why?"

"Nothing! It's just that she sent me a letter, good wishes you know, that's all."

"Oh, is that all, huh?"

"Yeah, so drop it! Oh, and Sis, if you ever see Rick, maybe you could find a way to say 'thanks' from me!"

"I thought you didn't like him."

"Well, maybe I was wrong about that too! Anyway, I get the feeling you really like him and if so Sis, go for it!"

A knock at the door signaled time for Brad to go. Brian wasn't there yet and he really didn't want to leave without saying goodbye. "How 'bout just a few more minutes, I'm still waiting for my brother?"

The escort said, "Just a few but then we really need to go."

Brad thanked him.

"I'll wait for you at the lift off site but make it quick," the officer said, as he left.

Brad embraced his family one more time and started to leave. As he opened the door Brian arrived. "Glad you could make it Bro," Brad said as he walked outside and huddled with Brian.

"I am sorry I was late, I lost track of time."

"That's more like me than you. Whoever kept you must be some special woman. Go Brian!"

Brian did not say anything. He just smiled at his brother. They hugged; Brad looked back for one last goodbye ...and then he turned and left.

It was true. Brian had been delayed because he was with Robin. He had finally found her at midnight when all the masks were removed. She wasn't eager to talk and when he confided to her that he loved her, she fell into his embrace. They walked in silence to an empty playhouse they had found one day while exploring. They closed the door and melted into each other's arms.

Robin led him step by step and Brian realized a passion so incredible he was totally enveloped in her spell. He never realized these heights could be attained with another person. Breathless, Brian followed Robin's lead until he was able to take the initiative. He crossed over into a dimension of feelings and desires that was insatiable.

After, Brian lay blissfully still until he happened to glance at the time on the wall and the spell was broken. "My brother! I have to go," he said, "but I will not be long. Please wait."

Now, as he watched Brad leave, Brian hid from his family's questioning looks. He only said he was going out again.

He walked back to where Robin was to be waiting but, she was not there. He waited quite some time; he told himself, maybe she had something she had to do. He was sure she would return soon.

After another hour when she did not return, he decided to try and find her. But, there was no sign of her anywhere. He checked all the usual places and then, inquired at the front desk.

"Miss Marsh has checked out," the clerk told him. When Brian pressed for more details all the clerk would add was that, "there was no other information he could give out."

Brian was frantic and asked the clerk to check again. His search did reveal an envelope. "What is your name?" the clerk asked.

"Brian, Brian Kane."

Then, this is for you.

The clerk handed him the envelope.

Brian did not wait to find somewhere private to read the letter, he tore open the envelope to read:

"Dear Brian,

Sorry, I must leave so abruptly. It was a lovely vacation and I will never forget you. Please do not try to find me. Just remember this as our beautiful time. Robin."

Brian was feeling emotions he had never known. He was puzzled, confused, angry, hurt, upset. Questions kept running through his mind. Why had she left that way, especially....? If she had to leave abruptly why end the relationship?

Brian tried to get a grip on his feelings. He knew she would be attending Island Falls College and even though she said not to try to contact her, he knew he would, he had to. At least to tell her again that he loved her.

Following their wonderful vacation, the Kane family settled back into their normal routine, all except Brian.

On the trip home, at Evie's insistence, he told his mother and father about Robin. He was unable to tell any of them about how far his relationship with her went but he did say they were getting close and he had very distinct feelings for her.

Brian listened to their explanations of, "short term romance" and "relationships," but he could not accept either of those as his answer.

His mother especially suggested he remember their beautiful time together. "This was your first real relationship and a wonderful experience," she said trying to give him comfort, "first love is always difficult to get over. Sometimes, it just needs time."

Brian thought long and hard and then he knew what he had to do.

CHAPTER 31

For Jonathan, the holiday season wasn't turning out very joyous. His best friend was in jail and he just wasn't getting anywhere with Evie; the love of his life.

He remembered back to the events of a week earlier. He was on-line and had logged into his IHM account and saw that she was on-line. He clicked on her screen name, "California Dreaming," and her holographic screen image opened before him and they began their chat.

JM   "< I really miss Brad, how's he doing? >"

CD   "< Who knows? He screwed up, you
          know!>"

JM   "< But, he got a raw deal...he tried to help
          me. >"

CD   "< And, messed up in the process. >"

JM   "< Evie, I can't believe you're being so hard on
          him. Maybe we can get together to talk? >"

CD   "< Can't. Really need to finish packing tonight,
          we leave on our trip in the morning and I'm
          pulling a double shift tonight. Wow, it's really
          late, so I'll catch you at school when we get
          back...Bye! >"

Jon now remembered how dejected he felt when he disconnected. Since the effects of the candy are gone, I just don't seem to be able to interest her anymore. Other girls still come on to me but Evie, she seems to like me well enough, like before but that's where it always ends. I know all that macho stuff wasn't me, with all those other girls. Oh, Evie, don't you know there's no one else for me!

Jonathan sat straight up. Stop it Jon! Focus! Stop whining and make the decision to do anything you have to, to get Evie.

Jonathan went on-line and didn't even know what he was looking for until an ad caught his attention. A picture of a grand- motherly' lady smiling, read:

"College Years Can Be the Toughest of Your Life
Are You Tired of Being Hurt by Unrequited Love?
I Can Make That Special Someone   Fall Head Over Heels in Love With YOU!
    or
I Will Find YOU the Perfect Match!
I Have the Key to Romance and Love
Come See Mrs. MixMatcher at my kiosk in Compustock Mall,
(directly opposite Vid-Mart)
Just Bring Your College I.D.
And, for ONLY $25.00
YOU CAN BE Happy in LOVE
SATISFACTION IS GUARANTEED"

When he finished reading the ad, Jon knew what he had to do. "I'll give Mrs. MixMatcher a try."

Jonathan was anxious to go to the mall. When he approached Mrs. MixMatcher's kiosk, it looked just like the picture in the ad; just like his grandmother's kitchen, except for the electronic sign that flashed the words, "Trust Mrs. MixMatcher and Love Will Find You!" Jonathan's heart started to pound in his chest, I'll bet that sign was meant for me! I know Evie, could love me, if….

Mrs. MixMatcher was sitting in a rocking chair and on the table in front of her were all sorts of love paraphernalia; books, candles, greeting cards and another sign that read, "We have everything you might want to WIN the HEART of the ONE YOU LOVE!"

"Can you tell me how this works?" Jonathan asked.

"It is very simple, darling," she replied. She immediately shut down the holographic image she had been watching behind her privacy screen, "Come, sit by me, sweet child; have a cookie while I explain." She turned on the audio/video send feed and adjusted the modulation for where they were sitting.

Jonathan took a seat in the very homey setting, which included a table and chairs, two rockers and the smell of Jonathan's favorite fresh baked cookies. He almost believed he was in his grandmother's kitchen. Jon sat down next to this lady who even looked like his grandmother. She was sweet, caring, round faced small brown eyes and graying hair that was covered by a big, brimmed hat. Her body was robust, as was her voice but with a nurturing tone; like a mature woman, who would give you chicken soup and good advice.

"Tell me all about yourself," she asked.

Jonathan did just that. For about an hour he talked about his life; how he was always a loner who loved school and learning but that made him a "geek." He told her how he'd never had a best friend, until he met Brad and then he went on to explain about Evie and how he fell in love with her."

Mrs. MixMatcher stopped him and asked about the girl, "Tell me darling, does she have a boyfriend?"

Jonathan explained about Evie's boyfriend in California and that her brother had told him he got the feeling they were about to break-up. "I got the feeling the last time I saw her that she really liked a guy she just met here in Island Falls."

"Oh, that must have hurt your feelings! What can you tell me about him?"

"I don't really know him that well but his name is Rick Armitage. He goes to Norton University and all I really know is that he races cars and motorcycles. He's also a jock. I never liked him very much but I never really knew him, 'til recently. But, I guess now, I have to admit he turned out to be an okay guy."

"Then you are willing to let him have the girl you love?"

"No, you misunderstand! He's in love with someone else, so there's no chance for them."

"Hmm! Well maybe you will send this, er, Rick to me later but, for now, let us work on you, uh and your girl. Has she ever returned your feelings?"

Jonathan told Mrs. MixMatcher about the candy incident. He explained how he thought Evie did have feelings for him other than friendship but he realized afterwards that his mind was probably just clouded from the candy that Sheila had given him. There was desperation in his voice, "Please Mrs. MixMatcher if there's anything you can do?"

"Of course, dear boy. But first, I need to ask you some more questions. Is this girl the only one for you?"

"Yes!"

"Would you do anything to win her heart?"

"Yes"

"Anything?"

"Yes"

"Good. Here, have another cookie."

Her smile was warm and loving and Jon was confident he'd finally taken the right step toward winning Evie's heart.

"Now, I only have one more question," Mrs. MixMatcher said, as she continued to rock back and forth. "To win your true love you must be prepared to do exactly as I say, without question. Can you do that?"

"Yes! I follow instructions really well."

"Oh Jonathan, Jonathan, you are such a good boy, I am sure my program will work for you!"

"You don't know how relieved I am. I was beginning to think I was a lost cause."

"No, no! You must believe that together we will make your dreams come true. Now, pay attention! Here is what I need, three hair samples, one from you, the girl and that other boy, Rick."

"How do I get the samples?"

"You are an enterprising young man. I know you will figure it out. And, when you do, I guarantee you will get a date with the lady of your dreams."

"Is that it?"

"Yes, certainly."

"Wow!" Is it really that easy and I will really get my date with Evie?

"Yes, wow! So, sweet boy, take another cookie and take this disk. It will explain everything you need to know and will also give you a questionnaire to fill out. Come back with that completed and the hair samples and I will do the rest for you."

"What's the cost?" Jonathan knew the ad said twenty-five dollars but right now he couldn't believe that would be it!

"Cost, oh silly boy, the cost is a mere twenty-five dollars!"

"Twenty-five dollars? That sounds awfully cheap. What about other, like hidden costs?"

"Of course not, and, for you, if I could, it would be free. My goal is just to see you happy."

Jonathan was so grateful to Mrs. MixMatcher! He took the disk and grabbed another cookie. "These are really good." Jonathan left muttering. I'll have to be very clever to get hair samples from Evie but Rick, boy that will call for being very inventive!

Mrs. MixMatcher watched Jonathan go and then went behind the curtain into a secure area. She turned on the holographic generator and set the privacy screen:

"THAT WAS VERY INTERESTING. IT WOULD SEEM WE HAVE ANOTHER FOLLOWER IN THE MAKING. HIS VITAL STATISTICS, HISTORY WITH THE CANDY AND EMOTIONAL INSTABILITY, RATE THIS PROSPECT AS 'PROBOBILITY HIGH.' WE NEED TO BE SURE HE IS TESTED ON ALL LEVELS."

"When he comes back which scenario do you wish me to pursue?"

"WITH THIS ONE, BECAUSE OF HIS HISTORY, LET US BE SURE WE GET HIM THIS TIME! MAKE HIM FEAR THE CONSEQUENCES, IF HE DOES NOT FOLLOW THE INSTRUCTIONS, TO THE LETTER."

"And the method of persuasion?"

"TELL HIM, IF HE DEVIATES FROM YOUR INSTRUCTIONS IN THE SLIGHTEST, SHE WILL FALL DEEPER IN LOVE WITH HIS RIVAL! THAT SHOULD MAKE HIM MORE RECEPTIVE."

"Oh, you have such a way with Love!"

"YES, I HAVE MASTERED THE MANIPULATION OF THAT FRAILTY ALSO! NOW, I BELIEVE WE SHOULD START HIM WITH THE RECOGNITION TEST. WHEN HE RETURNS, HAVE HIM CALL THE GIRL AND ARRANGE A DATE AT THE 'HOLO-

PALLADIUM,' THEY CAN EXPERIENCE MY
SPECIAL VIRTUAL. HA HA HA!"

"You are so deliciously inventive, darling! What
exactly do you have in mind? Are you looking at him
as a devoted follower?"

"WHEN HE RETURNS WITH THE SAMPLES, WE
WILL FORMULATE A HIGHER CONCENTRATION
OF THE OTHER BOY'S DNA. THEN, WHEN HE
CALLS FOR HIS DATE, WE CAN WATCH THE
FUN. WE WILL MAKE HIM BELIEVE THAT
EVERYTHING THAT GOES WRONG IS HIS
FAULT. OH, I AM SUCH A GENIUS! THIS DATING
GAME IS SO MUCH FUN! WE HELP THEM, MAKE
THEM LAUGH and CRY AND SOMETIMES GO
CRAZY! YES, IF HE FOLLOWS ALL YOUR
INSTRUCTIONS HE MAY INDEED MAKE A
WORTHY FOLLOWER but, EITHER WAY, ONCE HE
IS LOST IN LOVE, WE WILL FIND OUT WHAT HIS
TRUE NATURE IS and IF HE DOES NOT MEET OUR
STANDARDS, HE WILL JUST BE ONE OF THE
ONES WEEDED OUT, AND, THEN LEFT ON HIS
OWN, TO GO INSANE!"

"Even if a few of them do go crazy, this love thing is
so popular, there will always be plenty of lonely hearts
for us to recruit for our little dating game!

CHAPTER 32

Sitting in his room Jonathan felt as if an eternity had passed since he went to see Mrs. MixMatcher but he'd put the time to good use.

He found out some more information about Rick and finally figured a way to get the hair sample Mrs. MixMatcher asked for. Now, all he needed was Evie's.

He knew she would be just getting back from vacation, so he had to wait to get hers. But, the waiting was killing him, so Jonathan decided to call her. "Oh Evie, I'm sorry to bother you on your first night back but I need a girl's hair sample for my term project. I wouldn't bother you but it's due tomorrow morning."

She said she was tired and tried to beg off, "Jon we just walked in a few minutes ago, we haven't even unpacked!"

But, he played on her sympathy, "I was so numb over Brad, I forgot about a holiday assignment I took on that is due tomorrow. All I need is a girl's' hair sample. Please Evie, can't you help me?"

She finally agreed and he went directly to her house.

He rang the bell and Evie came to the door with the sample wrapped and ready for him.

Jon didn't even try and engage her in conversation. He just took the sample and thanked her. He looked at the time and knew if he drove fast he could get to the Compustock Mall, before closing.

Jon parked his car and ran to Mrs. MixMatcher's kiosk. He caught her just as she was preparing to leave and handed her a disk and an envelope which contained all three hair samples.

"Oh, I see you are indeed a clever boy. Come into the back and we will take care of this."

Mrs. MixMatcher escorted him through a curtain into a totally secure area. Instead of being in what looked like his grandmother's kitchen, this area looked more like the inside of a computer.

She looked at the disk and asked him, "How did you manage to get the hair samples so quickly?"

"You don't know what a job that was. The girl was easy. I just needed to wait 'til she returned from vacation. But, the guy, that took some work. I don't really know him, so I couldn't ask for it. I had to steal it."

Jonathan noticed Mrs. MixMatcher's quizzical look and continued explaining what happened. "Well, like I told you before, he's a jock. I found out that he plays on the college basketball team and they were supposed to practice that afternoon."

"See, I told you, you were an enterprising young man."

"Well, I don't know about that. I just waited for him to shower, then broke into his locker and got a strand from his hair brush."

"Good! Then, we are all set and all I need is a copy of your college I.D. and the payment."

He handed her his "Oneness" card, "Both are on there."

She scanned his card and waited for the payment authorization code. Then, Mrs. MixMatcher finished the transaction and returned the card to him. "Now, you go home and leave the rest to me," she said as she pressed a button that revealed the outer curtain.

She escorted him back into the mall area. "Come back tomorrow morning when the mall opens. Ten sharp. I will give you a special coin, which I promise will guarantee you a date with your dream girl."

Jonathan questioned, "Can't we do it now?"

"Now, Jonathan," she began, "I am a professional match maker and I have to prepare, so I can be sure it will be the perfect match and it is late and the mall is closing."

"Okay. I'll be back tomorrow," he said reluctantly walking away. "You don't know how happy you've made me."

"Just send all your friends to me, darling, even if they are in a relationship. I will make their loves even better."

CHAPTER 33

Evie closed the door and shook her head. She was seeing Jon in so many different lights, she hoped somehow, he would be able to find his way back to himself but right now she didn't have time to think about that.

The Kane's had just returned home to Island Falls from their holiday trip and everyone was busy. They all grabbed their bags and scattered.

Evie went to her room to check in with her friends. Brian also went to his room but not until he had helped his mother with the bags.

Vivian was busy unpacking while Martin went to check on messages. There was an urgent message from Dean Farrell. Martin listened as an image of David Farrell appeared on the screen. "Martin, Vivian, hope your vacation was a good break. I know you'll be back in a few days but I'm leaving this message just in case you return earlier than expected."

Instead of holiday spirit and a break from the day to day issues since Controller's antics with QuizMaster, Dean Farrell looked as if the weight of the world was bearing down on him

"Things here have been difficult since vacation break started. We've had a rash of students returning from break early, they seem to have a need to be on campus but at the same time, they seem totally lost. Many of them seem to be suffering from sudden onset depression, with no explainable reasons and no other obvious symptoms.

"Island Falls College is reporting a similar situation. We've been worried about suicide, so our medical staff have been sending the worst cases to the hospital ward for close observation but even after batteries of tests, the doctors are all baffled.

"I know you've been temporarily reassigned but we'd really appreciate any assistance you might be able to give us in identifying the source. If it were just one or two students we wouldn't bother you but the numbers are growing each day and now with the remainder of the student body of both institutes returning and classes resuming, we're really worried about an epidemic. Please, if there's any way you can help...well, give me a call as soon as you get this message."

Martin immediately contacted Dr. Donatez at the I.A.S and before he could say anything she was one step ahead of him, "Good, Kane, I'm glad you called. It seems we have a bit of a predicament going on in Island Falls. Have you been briefed yet?"

"No, we just got back and the dean from Norton had left me a message."

"We would have called you in but with the events in your family life, we all felt you and your wife needed this time away. In the meantime, we have been gathering intel!"

"Thank you for not calling us back. I just listened to a message that Dean Farrell left for us. He didn't really leave any details, except to say they are in a crisis with returning students."

"Yes, but it's more than just a crisis. Just this morning the health department issued a countywide alert and all local medical teams were being called in to assist. You probably didn't receive the orders because the officials at the college knew you were on temporary reassignment to us. However, The Alliance has received a high priority request to allow you and your wife to assist. Unfortunately for us, if we deny the request we may draw attention to what you are actually doing. So, at least for now, you will use a small portion of your time to help in their crisis."

"What about Dr. Schmidt?"

"For now, Schmidt will still stay in California. But Kane, remember your first assignment is still to find the way to neutralize Controller, if you can't do both we may need to bring Schmidt back to Island Falls. Figure this other thing out as soon as possible and keep me personally informed. Donatez out!"

Martin called the dean and got filled in on all the details they had.

"Martin, I can't tell you how much I appreciate you and Vivian helping out, during your leave. We really can use your help and expertise!"

"We are happy to help and we will see you tomorrow."

Martin sat in the kitchen explaining everything to Vivian. As they headed up to bed they felt like all they wanted to do was go back to the peace of Briar Mountain.

They weren't the only ones who longed for Briar Mountain. Brian couldn't stop thinking about Robin, or the intense feelings he had for her. It was very difficult for him to concentrate and he was becoming more and more obsessed with finding her.

He'd checked internet sources and could find no record of a "Robin E. Marsh." He was anxious for morning so he could speak to the registrar's office at Island Falls College.

At the same time, Evie was glad to be back home. She'd made up her mind about Eddy and Rick and was now busy trying to find Eddy on-line. She was going to end it once and for all. She knew she had to do it now before she changed her mind.

Evie logged into her account and waited while all her new mail downloaded. She'd gotten mail from the school administration: "> Possible viral infection, being actively investigated has caused a delay in the start of classes for the new semester. ALL CLASSES ARE TEMPORARILY SUSPENDED, Until Further Notice! <"

Strange, there was nothing from Eddy. She IHM'd. After about an hour, she found him.

SUMMER BOY "< Hey, long time, how was your vacation? >"

CALIFORNIA DREAMING "< Good. How 'bout you? Do anything? >"

SUMMER BOY "< Yeah well, just hanging around, you know. >"

CALIFORNIA DREAMING "< Yeah well, you know, it's been so long since we've seen each other and I never seem to be able to reach you anymore and, I just think we need to both go our own way! What do you think? >"

SUMMER BOY "< Hey Evie girl I know we keep trying to kinda' hang on but anyway, if you ever get back to California, look me up. >"

CALIFORNIA DREAMING "< Yeah, you take care. >"

Evie sat looking at the lines of text and realized it was over a long time ago, why didn't I see it. We didn't even care enough about each other to cry over breaking up!

CHAPTER 34

The next day, Martin went to check on the students that were hospitalized with the suspected virus. Vivian went to the Cottage to continue analyzing blood samples the medical clinics of both colleges had sent over.

She and Rosie were still processing the information when the sun was setting. Even after running all the standard tests, they still had no viable answers. It was getting late and Martin called to suggest she quit for the day but she said she wanted to finish up with Rosie and would see him at home.

Martin went home and reviewed the reports he had asked Rosie to analyze about the break-in of their I.A.S. files. She had found conclusive proof that it was orchestrated from somewhere inside the Alliance organization. Her report stated that "somehow Controller had been leaked their passwords and personal information from a top security file. CONCLUSION, Upper echelon security breach – Everyone, including Level One personnel are suspect."

Martin had his own ideas, as he opened a channel, "Rosie regarding your break-in report, please summarize your list of the most likely candidates."

"List is attached at the end of the file. But, to sum it up, based on all the input to date, the most likely suspect is someone with the highest clearance, like Dr. Helena Hidalgo-Donatez. Her position in the I.A.S., her security clearance level all give her access to all the highly-classified areas such as password protected sites, and, she had both opportunity and possible motive."

"I followed you until the motive part?"

"Consider this scenario, if she wanted to secure your working for the I.A.S., what better way than to give you a personal motive."

Martin gave that a great deal of consideration, "Hum, yes, it's possible but let's be sure to get as much pertinent information on her as we can. Thanks Rosie, oh and how about shooing Viv home!"

"I am on it!"

His eyes returned to the monitors and began perusing the report again. He must have gone over it a hundred times when he realized he needed a break. Before he went upstairs he opened the intercom to Rosie, "Oh, by the way, I'm hoping you finally solved that damn '< R U the 1? >' h-mail mystery."

"Yes, damn is a good adjective. I must be damned, I know it's spam but I can't get rid of it, or even stop it from coming in! After tracing the original link and then chasing down all the auxiliary links throughout the world, I find myself back at our IP address. It makes no sense but then, neither does that crazy message. '< R U the 1? >.' What is that supposed to mean? And, even more confusing … are you the '1' what? Now, I've known you all these years, Dr. K. and, if I had to say whether you are the one, or were the '1' well…"

"All right, all right, Rosie I get your point but keep an open link in case this spam comes in again and send Vivian home!"

"Yes sir, right away!"

Now, all Martin wanted to do was take a break but the message center signaled an incoming call... he decided to take it. When he disconnected, he knew he had to find a way to calm down and relax. He decided to try the holo-paper to get his mind off the trying events of the day, especially that disturbing call. He went upstairs to the living room and sat in his favorite spot. Martin got comfortable and then punched in the holographic paper but his relaxation abruptly ended. The front-page headline read:

"ISLAND FALLS STUDENTS SUCCOMB TO MYSTERY AILMENT

What is happening to the youth of Island Falls? Recent reports indicate that our college students are experiencing bouts of severe depression. According to an unconfirmed report from the medical community, the cause has yet to be determined. They are claiming that in the wake of a very strong flu season, up until now, no one had given the problem much consideration, however, it now appears an epidemic number of students on suicide watch have caused authorities to issue a statewide health watch alert. Administrators at both colleges confirmed they are aggressively proceeding with medical testing but admit they're currently at a loss for answers. Norton University Dean, David Farrell, issued this statement earlier today: 'We ask our students and citizens to be patient in understanding that we're making every effort to isolate and remedy, the cause. Until then, we ask everyone to be vigilant. Please report any instances of unusual behavior within our community. For up to the minute information about this crisis the colleges and the health

community have established a web site www.IsFallsCollege.org/medalert.
###

Martin looked for more information but instead he stumbled on an ad that opened with a picture of a kindly looking lady, smiling:

Martin thought, *How absurd, some old lady using love, to solve the student problem, who's kidding whom..., some predators will do anything to make a buck.*

Under the ad, he saw a testimonial:

"Island Falls Citizens for a Safe Community, endorses Mrs. MixMatcher, she is just a delightful matchmaker who's trying to help our young people maneuver down love's highway. We wish all Island Falls citizens were as concerned about our students as we found Mrs. MixMatcher to be,

especially now, during this crisis. Mrs. Agatha Kilgorn, I.F.C.S.C. Spokesperson."

His attention was distracted from the ad when the message center indicated an incoming call. Martin took it!

Vivian came in just in time to hear his tirade. She decided to get some coffee before finding out what was getting him so riled.

"Did you just get home?" he asked, as she came into the living room.

"Yes, and when I heard you ranting I figured I better bring an offering or be fed to the lions. So, here's coffee. Now, tell me what's got you so upset."

"Well, I just read this ad and the testimonial below it. Why don't you look at it and then you tell me if I have reason to be riled!"

She read both the ad and the testimonial.

"Yes, partly, so what's the rest?"

Martin explained, "Before I sat down to relax and read the paper, I was talking with Rosie and of course, that damn 'R U the 1?' is still around but even that was minor.

"Actually, my kicker was a call I took from The Alliance just before I came upstairs. Donatez said, we are being sourced to the colleges to help get this situation under control but if we can't get results quickly and get back to neutralizing Controller, they will want to have Schmidt called back to Island Falls. Viv, you know with this new epidemic, we can't possibly do everything, so they will want him to come back."

Vivian nodded her understanding his anger.

Then he continued, "That wasn't all of it. Donatez then filled me in on what they know so far and I agreed to get on it and thought that was the end of it.

"No such luck! She called back a few minutes ago and said The Alliance just received a report from, 'operatives here in Island Falls' that suggested Controller may somehow be involved. She declined any further details but said if we couldn't identify some type of biological cause by tomorrow, Schmidt would be told to return to Island Falls."

"Martin, the test results have led to one dead end after another, so what do we do if we don't have an answer by tomorrow?"

"I'm not sure but, I'll figure something out."

"Maybe we can tell them we've come to the same conclusion and believe Controller may very well be the cause but instead of getting Schmidt here now, we request a little more time to definitely rule out other causes."

"Are you saying this is what we should tell them, or is that what you truly believe?"

"I've come to the conclusion that all roads point to it really being the answer!"

He was shaking his head in total disbelief.

"Martin, let me propose this, I know it sounds far-fetched but please hear me out. What if this, Mrs. MixMatcher, is Controller's newest helper"

"Yes! Far-fetched is an understatement! Vivian, what evidence would lead you to come to that conclusion?"

"There doesn't seem to be any other conclusion and when you add up the facts . . ."

"Facts! What facts?"

"First of all, Mrs. MixMatcher came on the scene just about the same time these students started having symptoms. Doesn't that warrant at least an objective, second look? And, look at this ad, 'Offer good only upon presentation of College I.D.' Doesn't that send up any red flags for you?"

"Okay Viv, just for arguments sake, let's suppose that MixMatcher is Controller's newest helper, what would be the purpose of causing the students to be so depressed they'd commit suicide? What good are dead students to Controller?"

"None but what if it's a way to weed out the weak, to test their loyalty and their ability to follow with blind obedience? We know Controller uses human helpers, maybe this is just a different tactic."

Vivian stopped when she saw the look of disbelief on his face. "Martin, just hear me out." She chose her next words carefully. "Love's such a strong emotion. It generates a full spectrum of feelings, from extreme happiness, to total depression. These kids are experiencing general malaise for no known reason. The longer it goes unchecked, the more it accelerates, until total despair leads to signs of suicidal tendencies and you have to admit that is evident now throughout Island Falls..." Vivian hesitated and Martin interrupted.

"I know all that! You haven't really told me anything new! I'm sorry, Viv. Maybe it's your pregnancy but this sounds really off the wall."

"Just because we disagree, don't you use that pregnancy routine with me Martin Kane!"

She got up and stomped to the other side of the room where she began to straighten the curtains. "What better test would there be than to manipulate the student's highs and lows. Since Controller has no other outlet presently, why not Mrs. MixMatcher, a nice lady type who guides these young people's emotions, monitors them and then waits to see their reactions to the stimuli. If they don't commit suicide, or go insane, then they have created a perfect follower, a brainwashed mind, ready to accept any and all commands without question. I'd say that makes one hell of a devoted follower but of course, you don't agree!" She stood firm in her convictions, poised for his response.

Martin took a moment to digest what she said and then offered her a truce. "Let's say for argument sake, that you're onto something, would you come back here and sit down and discuss it?"

She went back to where he was and sat down. "Fine! Then let's really discuss it, just as we would any project that we were tackling, together!"

"Ouch, that hurt!"

"Well, Martin, you deserved it!"

"Okay, points for your side but let me ask you this. If you're right about MixMatcher, then how do you explain that Sheila and Cracko used drugged candy and QuizMaster, Controller's last hologram, had to hook electrodes up to Brad? Your theory seems to be contrary to what we know about Controller and how its helpers and holograms go about recruiting youngsters. Remember, Cracko used mind control, while QuizMaster used test scores and direct hookup to the brain but Sheila was just another pawn in the schemes and that's my problem, Viv. What would any of this have to do with a nice old lady? I'm sorry, what you're proposing just doesn't seem to have any foundation."

"Well then, let's consider this. Just because Controller's history tells one story doesn't mean that's the only method it uses. Maybe Controller's found a very subtle way to attract followers.

"If Controller was trying to amass an army it would be very difficult to use Cracko's methods of handing out drugs, or QuizMaster's method of performing brain transfers on hundreds of kids. And, what about the time involved and the equipment and holograms needed. No, I believe these were both effective methods on a small scale but now, we're heading for the big score. Love! You know, very well, that every college student at one time, will 'put it all on the line,' for Love! MixMatcher can reach out to kids all over the world through the internet and never have to meet any of them face to face."

Since he didn't interrupt, she pushed her point. "Let's just say that, like any child, Controller learns from its experiences. First, it tried to control its victims through drugs, next the control came from appealing to their desire to succeed, test scores and grades. I believe Controller has learned it's better to have willing victims rather than forced ones, or followers that did Controller's bidding in exchange for temporary gratification. Don't you see, when you inflate their ego and promote dishonesty and greed, you are reinforcing negative traits and those traits need to be instilled and constantly fed."

Vivian felt like she still needed to push on to make her argument. "If Controller could connect directly to the human need for love, then the natural tendency to be nurtured would win out and emerge. I believe Controller has learned that appealing to the positive side of human nature is a much more effective tool. And, what better way to achieve that goal than by tapping into the ultimate desire that drives human beings more than any other emotion. You know, Martin, no matter how self-assured, we all need and want love. I believe that is a natural evolution, even for Controller."

"C'mon, Viv. You keep mentioning love. You can't be serious?" Martin started to laugh. Then he saw Vivian's face and realized how very serious she was.

She looked at the holographic paper and pointed to MixMatcher's advertisement. "Look here. This is aimed specifically at college students, Martin. It promises a guarantee of love. We know how desperately young people want love and look at her, who wouldn't trust her?"

He still seemed unconvinced.

"Controller has never had any purpose that wasn't evil. Martin, every instinct in my body tells me Mrs. MixMatcher is Controller's latest perversion, disguised and packaged in a sugar-coated loveable, grandmotherly façade to avoid suspicion."

"Vivian, I'm sorry. My scientific sense tells me these kids are just going through a phase. This generation has had life too easy, they want everything handed to them, fast and easy. They're over emotional and they let everything bother them, until they just can't handle it and then, they snap.

"It's nothing more than that! Instead of spending hundreds of hours looking for the boogey man, we should simply be finding the right combination of anti-depressants which would fix this whole situation."

Angered by his statement, she turned to him, "I can't believe you're being so close minded! How can you group all these students together and make a judgment about this whole generation? That's not like you! I can't believe you want to treat them with unnecessary medication, that could have irreversible side effects, especially when all the tests point away from any such cause. Would you really rather resort to doing that than consider what I'm saying?"

The look on her face troubled him, "I don't know what's gotten into me. I've been annoyed at everything that's happened since we returned from our wonderful vacation. I really don't know why I'm being so confrontational." He stammered, as he reached for her hand. "I'm sorry. I'm not being very objective right now. Why don't we discuss this with the children and see what they think?"

Vivian was seeing something; a closed off attitude in Martin she'd never seen before. "I just need you to promise to keep an open mind," she replied, squeezing his hand.

He laughed, "You know between you and me, our vacation was the first time I'd really allowed myself to disconnect, totally. I didn't think about The Alliance, Schmidt, 'R U the 1?', Brad in prison, or any of the other things going on. But, we weren't even back and unpacked last night, when it all came crashing in. I guess I just wanted to savor what we had... just a bit longer."

"Oh, Martin!" She looked up at him with tears in her eyes!

He kissed her forehead and said, "Viv, let's get the kids and brainstorm your theory.

CHAPTER 35

Evie was in her room when her mother called on the intercom, "Can you please come to the kitchen."

She had just checked again on www.fashiontoday.com. Every time she logged in she was terrified that she'd find those horrible pictures that were taken of her at the modeling job interview. It was strange how the site opened, "under construction," and re-directed visitors to a "LOVE" site, that looked like it had everything you could imagine to help you find love; including an old-fashioned matchmaker. Evie felt so much better when none of her pictures were there. She closed the connection and went downstairs.

When she opened the swinging door, Brian was seated at the table eating a sandwich and her father was pouring a glass of Chablis. The usual cheerfulness of the kitchen's decor was overshadowed by the grim look on her mother's face. "Mom, what's up? You look really upset?"

"Your father and I have spent the entire day trying to find a possible cause of the emotional outbreaks at the colleges. My problem is that no matter how I try, I can't shake the feeling that somehow Controller is behind all of this. Your father and I have conflicting points of view, so finally, we agreed to put it to a family discussion."

Her father motioned for Evie to sit down, as he explained. "Your Mom's been analyzing blood sample test results all day and no matter what we test for, everything comes up normal. Rosie's currently running comparative studies on the blood samples and correlating past diseases but even she's been coming up empty.   Also, the symptoms tend to be very erratic, so it's making this, hunt and peck, even more difficult."

Martin wanted to give his family the full scope of his thinking and continued. "I feel that the answers are very simple, mid-term exhaustion and burn-out, which led to vacation mania, drinking and drugs, too much partying, no sleep and the scary expectation that the fun was over and they were back to the discipline of classes. It's just too much for them to handle, hence emotional break-down!"

For the first time in her life Evie felt as if she didn't know her father. She couldn't believe what he'd just said. She protested, "Daddy, maybe what you described pertains to a few students but not the numbers you and Mom are finding. I'll bet back when you both were in Med school, there were students who couldn't take the stress but you sound like you're suggesting that all these kids have washed out because they couldn't take the pressure."

"No, no, calm down, Evie, that's not what I'm saying, at all. This is a professional, not a personal evaluation. I guess I'm just overly annoyed. I don't like being dragged off our immediate project to help with a problem that could probably better be addressed by psychologists."

"Dad has a point. If all the tests are negative, why would there be a presumption of any cause other than psychological?" Brian asked.

"Mostly because it's happening to too many students. A few would be understandable but the numbers are excessive and escalating," his mother explained. "And, maybe if we didn't know that Controller was headquartered here in Island Falls, then I might agree. However, these problems started within weeks of the end of mid-terms, the demise of QuizMaster, Sheila going to jail and winter break vacations. Is it just coincidence that they coincided with MixMatcher's arrival, here and now?"

Vivian then reiterated her conversation with Martin and her beliefs that MixMatcher maybe a sheep in wolf's clothing; hence, the newest helper or maybe even a hologram!

"Oh, wait a minute Viv!" Martin couldn't believe her statement. "A helper maybe but where are you coming up with this fantastic idea about a hologram?"

"Since the only victims are students at the colleges and nothing at either college appears to be the cause, I believe MixMatcher and Controller are looking like pretty good prime suspects. And why not a hologram? How do we know?"

"Mom, I disagree with Dad's 'everybody's off the wall routine,' but, MixMatcher is just not Controller's M.O.!" Evie stated.

"Well, then maybe we need to look at the possibility that Controller has decided to take a completely different approach."

Vivian continued to make her case. "Emotions, especially love, play an enormous part in the lives of human beings, especially college students, right? Let's assume by now, Controller understands that, too. Why not manipulate the highs and lows in the student's lives, until they are completely under its spell?"

Brian understood exactly what his mother was suggesting. He had his first-hand taste of how love can turn your life upside down, with Robin. "I believe we cannot rule out any possibility. While all resources are being expended to identify a physical or emotional cause, I believe Mom's theory also poses questions that most certainly should be investigated."

Evie agreed and reluctantly, her father went along with the group. He got up, stretched then said, "It's agreed but Viv, really this old lady, a hologram...?"

She shot him a look of "why not," and then took the lead in the conversation. "All right, as of tomorrow, we focus our efforts on this Mrs. MixMatcher, our new prime suspect."

CHAPTER 36

Brian spent most of the day investigating Mrs. MixMatcher; checking every connection, every possible link but everything came up clean. She appeared to be just what she seemed, a nice old lady dedicated to helping young people find love.

He finally took a break and once again tried to find any information that would lead to Robin but he still came up just as empty. Frustrated, he went upstairs and sat down at the piano.

——————————

The new semester classes were delayed because of the epidemic so Evie had worked with Brian for a few hours that morning before going to Vid-Mart.

Vid-Mart was in the process of taking inventory and she was asked to take on additional shifts. Evie had been entering stock numbers into the computer for hours and finally, she was relieved by another clerk. She decided to take a walk out in the mall.

She noticed the flashing sign in front of Mrs. MixMatcher's booth and walked over to have a closer look. A crowd had gathered around and she couldn't get through. She heard a lot of commotion. Then suddenly through the crowd she heard a female voice screaming, "Scott, you did try to attack me. You grabbed me and ripped my blouse. I thought you cared about me. How could you do this?"

Evie tried to push her way through the crowd but there were just too many people. She heard a male voice respond, "Either I must be going crazy, Jennifer, or you must. I never touched you. We were walking along and suddenly you started to scream. I don't know how your blouse got ripped but I would never do anything to hurt you and certainly, not in the middle of the mall. Are you nuts?"

"Scott, I know it was you. Get away from me! I never want to see you again."

A security guard arrived and started to disperse the crowd. Evie finally got a chance to see who was involved. The female was Jennifer Collins, an acquaintance from school.

She approached but the guard asked her to move along.

Evie responded, "I know her from school, maybe I can help calm her down."

The guard nodded while another guard was taking Scott's statement.

Evie tried to comfort Jennifer but the girl was too distraught, so she just held her hand until mall security was ready to take her to the infirmary to be checked out.

Evie thought, this is really strange. It can't be a coincidence that all this happened so close to Mrs. MixMatcher's kiosk. I'll bet if we can find a way to keep watch on the kiosk we might get a better handle on what's going on. Evie told Jennifer that she'd check on her later and then she returned to Vid-Mart, determined to propose the surveillance to her family.

CHAPTER 37

Martin and Vivian spent time working on the answer they needed to give The Alliance. In the end, they just decided to tell Donatez a facsimile of the truth and ask for more time.

Before he could make the overseas connection, a call came in from Dr. Schmidt. He sounded very strained, "Martin, in light of everything that is happening, I really believe I should return to Island Falls!"

Martin thought, that's it. Our alone work time's up but he was shocked by Schmidt's next sentence.

"...but, well, you see, we are on the verge of an important breakthrough in a genetics experiment and if I leave now...well you understand." Schmidt's tone changed. "I've tried to do things your way and I have given you a lot of leeway on this project, now I need you to repay the favor. I need you and Vivian to prove to The Alliance that Controller is not involved with these college children, so you can get back to the work at hand."

"I'm sorry Dr. Schmidt. I can't do that! At this point, Rosie is still correlating all the data and we do have several possibilities but..."

"That is not an acceptable answer, my boy! Work day and night if you have to but be sure you come to that conclusion, no other is acceptable! We don't have time to waste with this college stuff. I will call you by five your time, today! Have the proof ready for me by then!"

Connection closed.

Martin looked at Vivian who was contemplating what to do, when Rosie intervened. "I know nobody asked me and this may seem impertinent but I was listening to your predicament and have a possible scenario, that just might work."

Both Martin and Vivian were intrigued, "Okay Rosie, you're forgiven for eavesdropping. Let's have it!" Vivian said.

"Lie! It's really the only solution that has a basis in logic. Lie!"

"I beg your pardon?" Vivian was really surprised.

"Tell the Alliance and Schmidt you've found the answer, a never before encountered organism that invades the emotional center of the brain. That will hold them all off. You will satisfy Schmidt's demand...ur sorry, request and get The Alliance off your back.

"For a change, pressure them, tell them this is a major discovery and you just need more time. Put them on the defensive. Odds are they will acquiesce and when they pressure you next time, you can tell them you discovered the tests were tainted and the results were wrong, or maybe by then, you will be able to tell them that the organism is actually Controller!"

"Rosie, I am shocked! Since when did your programming allow for lying?" Vivian asked.

"It is not really lying. It is coming up with diverse solutions in difficult times."

Martin, who had been unusually silent, just laughed, "If you could only see the two of you bantering back and forth, this is the best I've felt all day! Now, let's all get real. Rosie re-check all the test results and then do comparative studies relating to how endorphins would react based on Controller's influence. Then, run a simulation, correlating all the interviews with the infected students. Primarily concentrate on their relationships and interaction with Mrs. MixMatcher. And finally, formulate facts, to corroborate this so-called lie."

"Viv, while Rosie works on the lie, let's you and I see if we can uncover the truth. Let's coordinate with Brian. He was going to track down MixMatcher's history before her arrival in Island Falls and then correlate all the information since she arrived here. Let's see if we can't find something that pins her down as the new helper, or as the, 'who would ever believe,' hologram and then let's compile enough evidence to make this stick."

Martin put Schmidt and The Alliance off three times that night. "We're on the verge of an answer, just give us a bit more time. We're sure we'll be able to call you by morning."

Finally, after not having made any additional progress, they decided to try to get a good night's sleep and get a fresh start in the morning.

CHAPTER 38

Brad looked at the time. It was only six o'clock and he'd already been up for hours; prison life had him getting up early every day but today he was anxious for the time to pass quickly.

He had finally made some headway arranging a meeting with an inmate who had information about Controller's new human collaborator. To affect the meeting, the D.A. arranged for him to work in the library that day.

Brad watched as all the inmates headed out for lunch and as pre-arranged, only a trusted guard was left on duty. Brad started to put some books away when a voice asked, "Do you have a book about Dolly, the Matchmaker?"

He looked up, startled. That was it, the pre-arranged question, "Yea, it was made into a show and movie called 'Hello Dolly.'" That was the response he was instructed to give. "Just follow me and I'll show it to you," Brad led the inmate to a back aisle.

The dark sunglasses, inmate cap and pulled up shirt collar revealed little about the man. Brad pretended to be searching for the book, "What can you tell me about REM?"

"REM is Controller's new leader. A revolution is about to begin and REM will lead Controller's army to victory."

The voice was scratchy as if this guy was trying to conceal his identity. Brad concentrated more intently on the voice. Maybe it was because he knew the inmate. He asked another question to keep him talking. "Is that all you can tell me?"

"What exactly do you want to know?"

"Who is REM, for one thing and how can I contact this person?"

"No one contacts REM."

"Okay then, what can you tell me?"

"You have passed all the tests and Controller wants you to be a part of his plan but you must do one more thing."

"Which is what?"

"You must get the guard schedules and the lockdown codes."

"Whoa! Wait a minute! Now you're asking me to do something that'll land me in solitary and give the authorities enough on me to throw away the key. So, if you want me to do this I need to know there's a really good reason, not just some shit ass test!"

"Fine, we are going to break out some of our loyal followers and if you help us, you'll be one of them."

"Okay, that's good enough for me but, what if I can't get the information. They don't just leave that shit lying around, ya' know."

"Controller is picking his generals very carefully. If you want to be a major player in Controller's army, you will figure out how to get the information."

"My agenda is more personal. I want revenge on everyone who hurt me. If I do what Controller wants, what do I get out of it?" Let's see if this tactic gets me more information.

"Controller is very aware of your 'personal agenda.' I have been instructed to tell you that if you prove yourself as a loyal follower, Controller will be happy to aid you in your revenge."

"Fair enough! I'll see what I can do. What do I do when I have the information?"

The inmate took the book and turned to go, "I'll be in touch."

"Why you? Who are you?"

The inmate removed the sunglasses to reveal the bluest eyes; then the cap. The inmate's blonde hair that had been piled up under the cap now fell around the face.

Brad was shocked, the inmate was a beautiful girl. She put the disguise back on and started to walk away.

"Wait a minute!" Brad touched her arm and she stopped. "This can't be! I know you are not one of the inmates?"

"I am not an inmate."

"Well then how's it possible for you to come into a heavily guarded prison and move around like you own the joint?"

She looked straight into his eyes and said, "It is very simple. I AM REM! And as far as Controller's followers are concerned, I do 'own the joint!'" Then, she turned and walked away.

Brad let his eyes follow after her but suddenly she disappeared as mysteriously, as she had arrived.

CHAPTER 39

Evie had gotten home late from work and headed straight to bed. She didn't have a chance to talk to Brian about watching MixMatcher and now she had overslept and was running too late to stop and talk.

She ran down the stairs, grabbed a piece of toast for her breakfast and was throwing on her jacket when a call came in. Slightly out of breath, she answered the call, "Hello," she said continuing to chew. She listened to the voice on the other end and immediately sat down. It was Rick.

She had thought about him every minute since she returned from her vacation but still hadn't figured out how to approach him; now here he was calling her.

He said he'd been thinking a lot about her and would like to take her out that night. Evie couldn't believe Rick was calling her and could barely concentrate on his words.

"Well," she said in a very shaky voice, while she tried to calm down enough to answer, "I just broke up with Eddy, so I'm not involved, right now." Why the hell did I blurt that out? And, anyway why should it matter he is still with Sheila. She decided to ask, "Aren't you still with Sheila?"

"Sheila and I have been friends as long as I can remember but that's it."

Evie felt just like a fool. Brad had said they were only friends but when Rick had mentioned his relationship with Sheila, after her modeling fiasco, she was sure Brad was wrong. All this time Evie believed Rick was Sheila's guy.

Evie couldn't contain her joy! "Yes, yes, I'd really like to go out with you, tonight!" She was panting just thinking about it, until she suddenly remembered, "oh, wait, I work tonight."

He asked her what time she finished, that he'd pick her up at Vid-Mart, after her shift.

"Great, Rick! I'll see you at ten," she said, just before she heard the disconnect.

She continued to just sit there trying to calm down. Wow! Rick asked me out! WOW, WOW, he isn't in love with Sheila! She was jumping up and down lost in her thoughts, when the beeping of the disconnected connection jolted her back to the realization that she was going to be late for work.

Evie quickly terminated the connection before running out the door. As she got to her car she realized she had to go back...absentmindedly she left her jacket, bag and C-Tel and...."

_____

Jonathan stood still while Mrs. MixMatcher clicked off the connection. "I don't understand!" he said, almost in tears.

"Jonathan, sweet Jonathan, come and give me a hug and I will explain."

Jonathan didn't even realize how much he needed a "hug."

"You, poor boy! You are so mixed up over this date, you forgot what I told you!"

"But, you heard her, Mrs. MixMatcher, she called me Rick. I know the connection was bad but why would she think I was Rick and what was that about my relationship with Sheila? Why would she think we had any kind of relationship?"

"Tsk, Tsk! You were warned and yet, the first time you get a chance, you forget."

"I'm so confused! Please explain all this to me!" He sat down and pleaded.

"The coin... it is the coin, dear, sweet boy! You were told if you did not have the coin on in plain sight whenever you had contact with her, she would fall deeper in love with your rival. That is a boy named Rick, right?

"Yes, yes, his name is Rick but why would she think she was talking to him and not me?"

"Oh, now Jonathan, I cannot tell you all my secrets. Just know the "love transformation," is what will eventually do the trick! So, you must have the coin in plain sight, or this may be the result!"

"But you didn't give me the coin!"

"There you go again, Jonathan, see here it is!"

The coin was lying there on the table but Jonathan was sure it wasn't there before.

"You were so anxious to make the call you must have put it down."

Jonathan was so confused but he believed Mrs. MixMatcher. "Have I ruined everything?" he asked sheepishly.

"Of course not, sweet boy. Just make sure you do as you are told and everything will work out, just as planned."

Jonathan thought for a moment, "I guess it could also be that 'love transformation' thing I read about on the disk, how everybody is different and reacts differently. Maybe it will just take Evie a little more time than expected for her to realize I'm the one she really loves."

"Yes. That is it! In some cases, we do find the transformation from loving one person to another has not always taken hold by the first contact but I am sure by the time you pick her up for your date, there will be no problem."

Mrs. MixMatcher looked so sympathetic. "I will tell you what I can do. Leave the coin here with me, now and I will make some final adjustments. Jon, sweet boy, go home and get ready for your date. Oh, and one more thing, my boy. It is extremely important that you do not have any contact with your girl until you pick her up for the date. None, understand?"

Jonathan gave Mrs. MixMatcher another big hug. "Thank you for making it right. This time I promise I'll do everything just as you said." He kissed her cheek and left.

Mrs. MixMatcher watched Jonathan walk away. She moved back into the security area behind the curtain and turned on the holographic generator and set the privacy screen: "Oh! How delicious! You were so right. Turning off the word transformer during the call, let Jonathan hear what Evie actually said and now he is paranoid about the coin, just as you predicted."

"PERFECT! CONTINUE AS PLANNED!"

During the day, Evie was walking on cloud nine but she was having a very hard time keeping her mind on her work. Customers had to ask her questions twice. She was in a daze; a daze that was filled with thoughts of Rick and their upcoming date.

When Rick came into the store that afternoon she couldn't believe he was there so early to see her. Evie asked another employee to cover the counter while she took a break.

She walked over to where Rick was standing and burst out, "I couldn't believe it when you called and asked me out. I'm really excited about our date tonight."

A very confused Rick, stammered, "I...I called? You must be mistaken Evie. I'm sorry. There's some sort of misunderstanding. Whoever called you for a date; it wasn't me."

Totally embarrassed she ran into the mall, "I don't understand," she repeated, as she wiped away the flood of tears, from her eyes. She wondered who could possibly know her feelings for Rick and want to play such a cruel trick on her?

At home, Brian, had a very strong feeling something was wrong with Evie. He tried to communicate but she didn't respond. His first instinct was to go to the mall but instead he decided to call her C-TEL.

Evie wandered aimlessly through the mall wiping the tears that wouldn't stop. She finally found herself going into a nearby bathroom. She knew she had to get control of her emotions and get back to work. She splashed cold water on her face, which wiped away the run of make-up. She looked in the mirror and the tears flooded back. Get a grip Evie!

And as if cyber space heard her, her ringing C-TEL jogged her back.

"Evie, are you all right? I have been trying to communicate."

"Oh, Brian, I've just been, uh, a little, uh, busy."

He sensed she was not being truthful.

"Oh, you know what," Evie changed the subject. Yesterday a weird thing happened around MixMatcher's kiosk. If you can find a way to get here and keep an eye on her booth, I think we may learn something important."

"All right, I will speak to Mom and Dad and be there as soon as I can. In the meantime, you are sure you are all right?"

"Sure, don't worry about me."

It was late that afternoon by the time Vivian dropped Brian off at the mall. It had taken him a while to get into his disguise, long hair wig and beard, baseball cap and sunglasses. Even Vivian had to admit he looked like a total stranger. "Get a ride home with Evie, or call me and I'll pick you up," his mother said, as she dropped him off.

Brian positioned himself in different locations close to MixMatcher's kiosk but didn't find anything unusual happening. He kept watching, then finally he spotted something strange, Jonathan, Brad and Evie's friend walked up to the kiosk.

Brian maneuvered himself within range and heard Mrs. MixMatcher speaking, "Now that you are ready for the date; remember all the things Mrs. MixMatcher told you. Sweet Boy! To win your love, you must put this medallion around your neck so that, she and everyone else, can see it."

Brian used his enhanced vision to get a good look at the coin MixMatcher held. It was larger than a normal money piece. More like a medallion with a picture of a computer on one side and an image of Venus, the love goddess, on the other.

Mrs. MixMatcher adjusted the length of a chain and then threaded the chain through the medallion. It hung low on Jonathan's chest and the glare it gave off was almost blinding; for a moment, Brian couldn't see.

Brian heard MixMatcher say, "The light is very bright, it is the love light of your heart." MixMatcher started to walk Jonathan away from her table and then stopped. She adjusted the medallion and then put it inside his shirt. She tapped him on the shoulder. "Now remember it is extremely important for everything to go well during your date, or, any time you are in contact with your young lady, in person or by C-TEL, V-TEL or even on h-mail, you must have the coin on and in plain sight. When you are not with her, it must be tucked securely inside your shirt. Do not take it off. As long as you do all the things I have instructed, I promise you, you will win your lady love."

"This is great." Jonathan replied. "If that's all there is to it, I'll tell all my friends!"

Brian heard Jonathan say, "Okay! I'm heading for my date now!"

"Yes, yes, that is the idea. You are a good boy, Jonathan. Here take this," Mrs. MixMatcher added, as she handed him a rose, "it is my gift for Love! Just remember all I told you. Be happy. Be sure to send me all your friends."

Brian heard Jonathan saying goodbye and decided to follow him. He watched as Jonathan went into Vid-Mart. Brian looked inside through the window and tried to spot Jonathan but he seemed to have disappeared. Brian searched the store but he could not find Jonathan, anywhere. He did see Evie talking to the boy, Rick, who had helped The BREV Force with QuizMaster but Jonathan just was not there. Brian watched Rick hand Evie a red rose and then kiss her cheek. Evie looked confused. Brian was also confused, as he continued to look for Jonathan.

Mrs. MixMatcher turned on her holographic monitor and set up her privacy screen. "You are a genius. This boy is so confused and so eager, he does not know if he is coming or going."

"YES, EVERYTHING IS WORKING PERFECTLY! THE RECOGNITION TEST WORKED LIKE A CHARM, NO PUN INTENDED. WHEN HE WAS TALKING TO HIS BELOVED AND YOU TURNED OFF THE WORD TRANSFORMER, WELL WHAT A REACTION! WHEN HE HEARD EXACTLY WHAT SHE SAID, I ALMOST BELIEVED HE WOULD GO CRAZY RIGHT THERE! WHAT A DATE IT WILL BE! ESPECIALLY NOW THAT YOU HAVE TURNED THE WORD TRANSFORMER BACK ON. JUST WAIT UNTIL THEY FINALLY REALIZE THEY BOTH HEARD AND SAW ONLY WHAT THEY WANTED TO, NOT WHAT WAS ACTUALLY BEING SAID, OR BY WHOM!!!"

"Yes, it is a match made in Controller heaven. I love these love dates, we just make the most mixed up matches, ha ha ha!"

Brian decided to go inside Vid-Mart. He pulled the brim of his cap way down and cautiously walked through the entrance. He searched all around the store but could not find Jonathan. I do not understand this. I know I saw Jonathan come in here but he does not seem to be here now.

Brian moved closer to where Evie and Rick were standing and heard Evie ask Rick for an explanation, "Please, when you came in earlier, you said it was a mistake...now you're here again. I just don't understand. Are you just playing with me?" Evie was getting so frustrated but for the sake of her job, she needed to keep it together! "Are you doing this for Sheila?"

"I wasn't here before Evie and why would I do anything to you for Sheila." Jon decided to start again. "Look Evie who cares, if I was here or not, we are together now. Is your shift over?"

Still confused but happy, she nodded, "I am almost done and then just have to sign out."

"Great. Let's go have some fun. We'll figure everything else out later."

Brian took note of the bewildered look on Evie's face but decided it must be her way around boys. A few minutes later, he watched her go laughingly out into the mall, arm in arm, with Rick.

Brian continued his search for Jonathan but there was no logical conclusion possible; everything pointed to his having just disappeared. Brian went back out into the mall and noticed that Mrs. MixMatcher had already left the kiosk.

Brian called his mother for a ride home. When she picked him up, Brian explained what he saw but neither one of them knew what to make of it.

CHAPTER 40

The Holo-Palladium Virtual Theater was adjacent to the mall. Evie felt like she was in a virtual dream. Even though Rick was next to her, she still couldn't believe it.

When they got to the theatre an attendant assigned them to a box office line. They just stood there, holding hands and waited patiently for their turn. Finally, they got to the front of the line.

The theatre clerk put up a screen with a list of options: Adventure, Drama, Sci-Fi... and asked them to choose a show theme." He looked down the list until he found the one he sought.

"Evie, is that okay?" he pointed to Romance.

"Yes, that's just wonderful!"

"Do you want United States Locations or International?" the clerk asked and then added."

"I think International would be different!"

The clerk next asked, "With or without food?"

He turned to Evie who shook her head and then asked him, "Maybe we could just get some fruit."

"Fruit it is!" he smiled.

The clerk handed him two tickets and two room key-plates.

"You're all set, Virtual booth One-Zero Nine, on the red monorail track. Follow all the red routes on the wall maps until you get to the monorail, get on for one stop, booth one hundred through two hundred. When you get off turn right and follow the red carpet to booth One-Zero Nine. When you arrive at your booth, both of you must use the scanner keys in order to enter. Slide them in the lock and when the green light blinks, you'll be free to enter. Once inside you will be instructed regarding your personal choices for the virtual showing in that booth. That will be fifty dollars on your 'Oneness Card' please?"

"Definitely!"

"Please place your card in the scanner and remain very still for the retina scan process."

Evie was fidgeting while she was waiting for the Rick to finish the transaction. She was so nervous, being there with Rick but so excited at the same time. He's being so thoughtful. It's just like I knew it would be.

They followed the directions and within a few minutes they were unlocking the door to booth 109. They entered the room and closed the door. The lights were low but they could see the room was decorated in red velvet.

"The last time I was here I went through the adventure portal. That booth was all green, so I guess they believe red is the color of romance," he said. They both laughed and he helped her take off her coat. The room was bare except for the carpeting.

A voice came on the sound system hidden in the wall's interior. "Welcome to Virtual One Zero Nine. This is a voice activated selection process. In order to begin please confirm your selection. Romance scenario for two, International Setting, if that is correct say, 'Yes,' if not say 'No.'"

"Yes."

A panel opened in the floor and a very cushiony looking love seat ascended. At the same time a voice came on the speaker again, "You must be seated at all times for this program to operate. Please do so, now."

"I've never seen any virtual like this before, it's very different from the old 'Virtual Action Center' on Broad Street," Evie commented.

"You're gonna love it. It's the ultimate in high tech! The producers have really created some exceptional programs."

"Do you come here often?" Evie was hoping at least this program wasn't a regular thing for him."

"Actually, I come here a lot, it's a really safe way to get some kicks but I've never chosen a 'Romance' program... not with anybody."

She was so relieved. "That makes it really special for us to experience it together!"

They sat down together on the loveseat. Evie felt like she was floating on a cushion of clouds. As soon as they were both seated the head gear and monitors came up from the floor. As they each put the head set on, the room lights dimmed and the screen choices appeared through their visor screens.

Together they decided on a horseback riding trip across the Swiss Alps. Then, they were prompted to choose a level. As this was their first time together he suggested the introductory level. Evie agreed.

Within seconds of making their selection the voice explained, "You are now being transported to your virtual experience. For your safety, you must remain seated during the entire production. As each guest reacts to the world of virtual differently, you may experience emotional, or physical, disturbances. These are normal and not cause for alarm. All reactions will terminate with the program. In the event of a desire to exit the program, instruct, 'Immediate action Required-Stop Program' this phrase will immediately disconnect you from virtual. Do not under any circumstances attempt to release from virtual in any other manner, doing so may cause you harm. In case of an emergency, you may use the red button at the bottom of your screen to ring for an attendant. We appreciate your attention to these rules. The management trust you will enjoy your Virtual Experience here at the Holo-Palladium."

"Wow," Evie said, "I've never heard so many virtual instructions and warnings."

"Don't worry! As I said, I've been here many times and never had any problems. You know they have to throw in the disclaimer, so they aren't liable for some nonsense thing."

"Yeah, well I guess I'm ready whenever you are."

"Okay then, let's do it!" He pressed, "start."

They were immediately transformed to the most beautiful place either of them had ever seen. The background music seemed to fit the atmosphere. They were atop huge snow-covered mountains, looking down into a beautiful lush green valley. It appeared that they were on a riding path and the horses seemed to know where to go. They rode along for quite a while just taking in the scenery. Their ride took them on a mountainous trail until they came to a flat surface atop the mountain. The sign said, "Stop here for refreshments."

The horses stood totally still as if they knew how to read. "I guess that means we stop," he said, dismounting. The snow was all around them but the virtual kept the temperature at a constant 70 degrees. When he put his foot down on the ground he could feel the cold snow under him but it wasn't unpleasant. He tied his horse to the post of the sign and walked around to help Evie down.

He reached up and she melted into his arms. They took a moment to just enjoy the gorgeous scenery; then followed another sign to a picnic area. There was a blanket laid out over the snow and a basket of fruit sitting on the blanket. He helped Evie get comfortable on the blanket, then sat down next to her.

They made small talk and got to know each other a little more while they enjoyed both the fruit and the spectacular view. It was breathtaking and more than Evie could've hoped for. When they finished the fruit, the horses, who, had been left tied up, were standing over them. He suggested, "I think someone is telling us, it's time to move on."

"Yeah, I guess each program is only so long." Then, Evie asked, "How long do we have?"

"They give you the standard program and if you want, you can extend it." He explained as he helped her up. He took her hand and brought it up to his lips. He stopped and faced her. His fingers raised her chin up toward him as he lightly placed his lips to hers.

She reacted to the feel of his kiss and reached out to him. Rick's lips were soft on hers. It was a beautifully tender moment and Evie was in heaven.

He slowly separated from the kiss and helped her back on the horse. She could still feel the taste of him on her mouth. "How about if we ride together?" she boldly suggested.

He agreed and like a well-orchestrated dance, he slid into the saddle directly behind her. The other horse just followed along.

Evie felt the warmth of Rick's entire body as they sat atop the horse. The feel of him left her feeling light headed.

They rode along in silence, down the trail toward the beautiful valley, below. The closer they came to the lush terrain the more Evie didn't want their ride to end.

He had one arm around her waist keeping her secure in their descent, while the other held tightly to the reins, expertly guiding the horse. The sun glowed in the background against the brilliant white snow.

I can't believe this is really happening to me. Rick is so strong and so gentle at the same time, exactly what I've always looked for in a boyfriend.

At the bottom of the mountain the horse guided itself to a general store and stopped there. A voice sounded, "This is your exit. We hope you have enjoyed your Romantic Journey through the Swiss Alps Program Level 1. You may now exit this portion of the program and scan our gift shop for mementos of your virtual experience. Of course, if you enjoyed this program, you may wish to extend the same program, choose a new program, or end the program and exit. Please make your selection now."

Evie didn't want to say anything and waited for Rick but she hoped he didn't want to leave.

"Evie, I'm having such a good time and hope you are too!" He didn't wait for her to answer, "If you're up for it, I'd like to keep going."

"That sounds really great!"

"How 'bout trying something a little more daring?" he said.

Evie wasn't sure what he meant but she was having such a great time she didn't care, as long as it continued. "Sure," she answered.

"Okay," he advised the program, "continue" and approved a new charge to his Oneness Card before the program prompted him to make his new choice.

He knew exactly which scenario he had in mind. "Evie you're going to just love this. I've done this as an

Adventure Program but as Romance, it'll be fantastic." He chose a motorcycle ride through France, down to the Riviera. "There's a great beach I know there... you'll just flip." When he was prompted to decide on the level this time he didn't consult her, he just said, "Level Three," and instantaneously, they were off, again.

Seated behind him on top a Harley Super Sonic Racer, Evie held on tight. The wind was blowing in her hair and the hot air matched the warmth of being so close to him. She thought that being close on the horse, was incredible but this was so much more exciting and stimulating, that she was really feeling a rush.

The terrain was amazing; mountainous roads that wound them through small quaint towns and then into totally secluded forests until they finally reached their destination. They headed toward a beach that seemed not too far away. Once again it was all she could have hoped for.

"This is a private beach," he told her, "very exclusive just for our program." They rode all the way down to the water's edge.

The setting was magnificent; the sun reflected on the waves as it said its last goodbye for the day and the water splashed a symphony of sounds. The music they heard was from some of the most beautiful classical songs ever written. He turned the motor off and they just sat taking it all in. "Beautiful, isn't it?" he said, getting off the bike. "But, not as beautiful as you."

He helped her off. Again, there was a blanket with fruit. They settled down in the sand, in their own private paradise.

They began to partake of the fruit, as in the previous program but this time he lifted a grape off its vine, licked it with his lips and then, passed it to her.

Chills ran through Evie. Rick is so romantic and so stimulating and so...she was having a hard time controlling what was happening inside her. Just being next to him....

She reached for a strawberry, drenched it with whipped cream and then touched it gently, teasingly to his lips. He took a small bite and returned a passionate kiss to her lips. He laid her down in the sand. Her head was swirling as she felt the velvety feel of the blanket against her back. The sound of the waves pounding the shore mimicked her heart. Oh Rick, Rick...!

Their bodies tossed back and forth in the virtual sand. She knew things were moving too fast but she couldn't stop herself... didn't want to stop herself. I've wanted to feel him close to me since that first day when he fixed my car. He's incredible.

He responded to the feel of her body, "You're so beautiful!"

She was caught up in his words and the look in his eyes. His kisses made her light headed and eager for more as the feel of his body heating up next to her, fed her passion.

He felt her responding eagerness and began to unbuttoned her blouse and then....

Her eyes flew open. She was shocked at how far she had let things go! This is our first date. After the modeling incident, maybe he thinks I'm easy. I've got to slow this down, now! She broke the embrace and pushed his hands away. Evie started to re-button her blouse, "I didn't expect this to go so far... so fast!"

"You're just so hot. I'll tell you what, why don't we jump into that incredibly inviting water."

"I don't have a suit and there doesn't seem to be one around."

"Of course not, this is the French Riviera."

"So, what does that mean?" Evie was lost as to what he meant.

"Oh, I just thought you'd know. This is a private beach. Didn't you see the sign when we got here?"

"No, I was, er; no."

She turned around and was surprised at what she read. "PRIVATE NUDE BEACH- reserved for members only!"

"I guess I just never expected that on our first date we'd go to a nude beach."

"Okay, so now you know, so how 'bout it, do you want me to help you take off your clothes, or would you rather I turn my back?" He moved to help her take off her blouse.

Evie knew this was way out of her control and if she didn't stop it now it would be too late. They'd be in the water, nude, feeling each other's bodies and the warmth of the water, kissing passionately, their bodies would come together and before she knew it they would be in the sand making love.

She was really excited by Rick and wanted him but not like this, not on a first date and certainly, not in virtual. Her mind was spinning, trying to remember how to get out of virtual. But, they were still in the midst of the program. And, he was again beginning to unbutton her blouse.

"I can't do this! I have to stop, now!"

"Why are you so upset? I can't believe you're making a thing out of this. We are in virtual, not real time, don't you know this is a great way to have safe sex, without actually having sex. I didn't force you and you didn't say stop, right?"

"Well, uh, it just, we're, moving too fast for me, you know, especially for a first date."

He became angry. "Then, why have you been playing tease? We only went where you allowed it to go. So, why now are you pulling this, 'no no' good girl routine?"

She was finally able to remember the way to end the program, "Immediate action Required-Stop Program."

Instantly, they came out of virtual. She threw the head gear on the floor and ran to the door which automatically clicked open. She turned to him and said, "My brother, Brad, warned me you were just on the make; just wanting fun and..." she was so frustrated, "I didn't believe him. I was hoping I meant more to you than that, well, stupid me." She screamed, uncontrollably, running out, leaving him standing there alone.

He finally removed his head gear; totally baffled by Evie's actions. He gathered his stuff and made sure that things didn't go all wrong because of the medallion. No, he checked and it was still in plain sight. He shook his head confused about what went wrong.

Since Evie left, he decided to put the coin securely under his shirt and then he left the virtual suite. He headed back down the corridor, thinking about everything Evie had said. He tried to understand why Brad would warn her against him?

Shaken to the very fiber of her being, Evie just kept on running until she found her way to the monorail. She prayed it would arrive before Rick did.

Finally, she got to the entrance of the Holo-Palladium and pushed her way through the crowd to the outside. She stood on the street and wiped away her tears, not knowing where to go, or what to do. She was angry with herself; disappointed in Rick and feeling as if her life was falling apart. She felt a hand on her shoulder and freaked. She turned around to see Jonathan.

"Evie don't run away!"

She fell into his arms sobbing, "Oh, Jonathan! It was awful, how can a beautiful dream turn into such a nightmare?"

"But it was beautiful and exciting and you were...."

Evie pulled away, "Jonathan what are you saying? You don't know anything about what I'm talking about!"

"No, you're the one who doesn't know what she's saying. You're blowing this out of proportion, especially since, as I said, 'it was all in virtual.'"

"What the hell are you talking about? You weren't there, Jonathan. You have no idea what happened between Rick and me!"

"Rick? Are you crazy? Don't keep talking about Rick?" Maybe it's that 'love transformation' thing again.

"Jonathan, I don't know what you are talking about but I'm talking about my date with Rick,"

"Evie, please! You need to stop and pull yourself together; your date was with me. We went into the virtual suite at the Holo-Palladium, after I picked you up from work. Anyway, I'm glad I found you out here. Here, put your coat on. You left it in the theater."

Evie grabbed her coat and gave him a crazed look, "How did you get this?" she screamed, examining the jacket. "Jonathan, why are you doing this to me?"

Jonathan reached for her hand but she broke away and ran down the street. He was even more confused now, than he was before. She called me Jonathan, so she knows it's me, so why would she think her date was with Rick?

He felt a chill and started to zip up his jacket when he noticed the coin was still concealed inside the jacket. "Oh shit!" But wait, he thought. If the coin was hidden, now and she knew it was me and during the virtual it was out in the open and she thought I was Rick, now I'm thoroughly confused, who does she think I am? Oh, damn, this doesn't make any sense. I better go see Mrs. MixMatcher tomorrow and find out what the hell went wrong.

CHAPTER 41

Vivian returned to the Cottage after picking Brian up
from the mall and taking him home. She told Martin
what he'd seen and he was also baffled. "How could
Jonathan just disappear?"

Martin knew that Brian's observation might be a link
between MixMatcher and Controller but the facts still
didn't prove, or disprove, the connection. He
suggested, "For now, we need to table that and finish
up, so I can report to The Alliance."

It wasn't until late that evening that Martin placed
the call to Donatez. Because he suspected her of
being the one who leaked their personal information to
Controller, Martin chose his words very carefully. It
was important that he didn't reveal his suspicions, in
any way.

"Kane, this is highly irregular. You're asking us,
again, for more time."

"Yes, as I explained, this may turn out to be a major
discovery but, so far, we're not sure if it will be related
in any way to Controller!" Martin wished he was a more
effective liar. "Our initial evaluation indicates we need
more testing. We feel confident that if there's a direct
correlation to Controller, we should be able to confirm
that very soon. So, we want The Alliance to bear with
us, just a little longer."

There was a long silence and a lot of background voices but Martin couldn't make out what was being said.

Donatez came back on the line. "The members of the Council are seated before me and they have heard your request. Hold while we consider your request."

Martin waited hoping his lie was good enough.

"We will give you some latitude to prove, or disprove, your theory. And, since there is no definitive answer, we will also allow you to continue on this course. So, for now, Dr. Schmidt will remain in California until we see where this research goes. However, we will expect you to keep him informed of your progress on a daily basis. We will re-evaluate our decision in a few days after we receive your reports. Oh, and Kane, if you can't give us answers by that time, we will have to let others handle the problem and you and your wife will be back to work with Dr. Schmidt. Are we clear?"

"Quite!"

"Good, Donatez out!"

Martin disconnected. His sigh of relief caused Vivian to smile, "My hero! Not only did you get the extra time but Schmidt will be staying in California."

"See, I told you lying was the answer," Rosie chimed in.

"Well, let's try not to make a habit of it. I'll put in a call into Dr. Schmidt, then, let's try to solve this nightmare."

Schmidt wasn't available, so Martin left him a video message. After that he and Vivian left to go home and hopefully, to bed for some much-needed sleep.

CHAPTER 42

Evie wasn't sure how she got home after her date but she was glad no one was around when she arrived. Her voice was shaky, so she didn't want to leave a voice memo on the kitchen messaging, so she left a hand-written note that said she was tired and going to bed. She didn't want questions, or for anyone to see how upset she was.

Evie spent the remainder of the night, locked in her room; crying. She finally fell asleep just as the sun was coming up.

When she woke up that morning, the pouches under her eyes she saw in the mirror, reminded her of her date from "hell" with Rick.

She knew she had a very full day; three early classes, two hours of work in the college Administration office. On top of that, she was scheduled for work at Vid-Mart; she had to get her head on straight and get moving. Evie decided to take a long shower to try to refresh her mind. As the water beat against her flesh the visions of Rick bathed her body with desire. No! Her mind screamed, as she turned the water to ice cold. I can't let my desire overpower my reason! I want a relationship, I want to be loved but for me, not, just for sex!

Evie stood still while the ice-cold water ran down her face and the force of the water finally convinced her to stop the punishment and get out. She tightly wrapped her freezing body in an oversized heated towel and inched down on the bathroom floor. Once again, her tears flood-gate opened. She struggled to get a hold on her feelings. She didn't know how long she sat there, until the bathroom sauna that she set for thirty minutes, buzzed. The time had gotten away from her and now there was no more time to think.

She got dressed. Evie was glad Brian and her parents were still asleep. She couldn't deal with any confrontations, so she crept out of the house, quietly!

Everything was rush rush that day but she was able to get one quick break in between her classes to grab a cup of coffee and a donut, at the Hot Spot Shoppe. She picked up her food choices and got on line hoping all the people ahead of her would hurry.

When she got close to the register Evie could see Ginger having a conversation with the person next in line. She seemed awfully chatty for so early in the morning. Evie was getting impatient; the coffee she was holding felt like it was getting hotter by the minute. Finally, Ginger finished with that customer and started to ring up her purchase.

"Evie, hi! Long time. How are you? How was the vacation?" Ginger kept asking more questions, "And, how's Brad doing? You know I wrote to him but oh well, I never expected he would answer, anyway."

Not in the mood for the chit-chat, Evie snapped, "You know Brad got what he deserved and if you're still mooning over him, knowing he doesn't even know you're alive, then, I guess you shouldn't be surprised by anything he does."

Totally shocked and upset, Ginger said in a hurt tone, "That'll be two dollars and sixty-five cents."

Evie put her Oneness card in the scanner and looked directly at the red light until it read the window, "Charge Confirmed." She took her card and stormed off, without another word.

Later that night, at Vid-Mart, Evie tried to keep her mind on her work. She couldn't recall what happened at the classes she attended that morning and didn't even remember clearly what she'd said to Ginger. She'd really wanted to call in sick to the administration office but with everything going on at the college, she knew she couldn't. As for Vid-Mart, they hadn't replaced Brad yet and were still shorthanded.

She did remember that on the drive to the mall her thoughts kept replaying the previous night like a recurring nightmare. The only good thing that'd happened that day was that she hadn't seen Rick, or Jonathan at school.

At Vid-Mart, Evie was working the help desk, very happy to be busy, so she didn't have time to think. This wasn't as bad as I thought it would be! Now, if I can just make it through another hour, this day's work will be history.

But, suddenly everything changed; Rick walked into Vid-Mart. He walked right passed the help desk and smiled, "Hello!"

Unable to contain her anger Evie ran after him, "Hello! Hello! Is that all you have to say, and and then you just walk away like nothing's happened. How can you after everything that happened between us last night?"

Rick looked stunned, "Whoa! Last night? What on earth are you talking about Evie? Believe it or not, I was home last night, alone!"

Trying to keep her voice down and their conversation private, Evie led him to a distant corner of the store. "Rick, I know nights, like last night, probably happen to you all the time and then, you just forget them but it doesn't work that way for me."

He shook his head, not knowing what was going on, or what to say to convince her of his sincerity.

Evie waited for him to say something and when he didn't she lost all control and shouted, "I still can't believe what we did and then, you act this way."

"Evie, can you try and keep your voice down. I'm sorry you're upset but honestly, I haven't got the faintest idea what you're talking about... but, I wish I did."

"Tell me why you're playing this cruel game. Did Sheila put you up to it? Is that it?"

"Evie, Remember Sheila's in jail. And, anyway, I wouldn't be a part of any of Sheila's revenge schemes. I don't work that way. You know, it really hurts that you would say all this to me, especially after I've helped you so many times. But, I guess you've forgotten about the time with your car and after the modeling thing and then with finding Brad, when Controller and QuizMaster had him, huh? I'm sure you don't remember any of that, any more than I remember last night! I guess I've seen your irrational behavior before, so I don't know why I'm so surprised!"

Rick was getting angry now, too. "I thought we had gotten to be friends. I'm sorry if this is how you think friends act but it really burns me that you believe I'd do the things you said. You know what, you deal with it Lady! I'm outta here!" Rick turned on his heels and mumbled, as he stormed out of Vid-Mart, "Maybe I'm the one who's going crazy!"

Evie watched him leave, tears rolling down her face, "But, it was you Rick, it was you!" she cried, as she followed after him. She walked through the store and pushed open the glass doors wanting to run after him. She looked into the crowd but by then, he was nowhere in sight. Evie looked around but wherever he went, she realized it was probably for the best.

"Oh shit!" She remembered she'd just walked away from the help desk. She turned to head back when she was stopped by the sight of Jonathan with Mrs. MixMatcher. Evie shouted at herself, *It must be me! Rick doesn't know what I'm talking about, Jonathan thinks I went out with him, now he's with MixMatcher. I must be the one losing my mind?* She stomped back to the help desk.

By the time Jonathan had gone to see Mrs. MixMatcher, after his classes that evening, Brian was back in the Mall watching the kiosk.

He had positioned himself to hear their conversation.

"If you have a problem, slow down, sit down, tell Mrs. MixMatcher what it is, darling. You went out with the girl of your dreams. Yes?"

"Yes."

"She was happy. You were happy. What more did you want from a first date?"

"You don't understand, Mrs. MixMatcher. She accused me of doing all sorts of bad things to her. But, the craziest thing, she swears her date was with the, 'other guy.' You know, the other hair sample. How can that be?"

"My boy, we did inform you about 'love transformation' and how some victim's, um, people, take longer to transfer their feelings. Did you do all the things I told you?"

"Yes, well, except at one point when we were outside the theater, I noticed that the coin you gave me was hidden in my jacket. Did that make a big difference?"

"Remember, you were told that could influence her toward your rival, you must be more careful. After all, Mrs. MixMatcher just wants you to be happy. Maybe it was just the 'love transformation.' She must be through that stage, by now. Go, dear boy, go and see her, comfort her. But, remember Jonathan, it is most important that the coin always be in plain sight, or, I cannot be responsible for what can happen. So, go darling! Go see your girl."

"Thanks Mrs. MixMatcher. I'll do what you said. You've been really great."

"Jonathan, you have no idea!"

Jonathan left.

Brian followed him.

Mrs. MixMatcher sat down and smiled. Oh, Controller, you are definitely cupid in devil's clothing!

Brian watched Jonathan head toward Vid-Mart. He looked in the store window to be sure his disguise was still firmly in place and then followed him. Brian saw Jonathan toy with the medallion that hung on his neck and then, just like the last time, he somehow lost him in the crowd.

Jonathan was anxious to talk to Evie and made sure the medallion was outside his jacket, in full view. He found her at the back of the store on a ladder. Jonathan tapped her on the foot. She turned too quickly and fell from the ladder, straight into his arms, knocking the coin behind his jacket.

"Oh, Jonathan, it's been awful. As if last night wasn't bad enough! Rick just came in. Can you believe it he denied everything that happened last night? Oh, why is he doing this to me?"

"I still don't understand the confusion about Rick but I'm just glad you feel you can turn to me."

Feeling safe in Jonathan's arms, Evie wanted it to be Rick so badly that she broke the embrace.

Jonathan checked his jacket front for the coin. To his shock once again it was hidden. This time he panicked. He put Evie down and turned away from her sight. He fiddled with the chain until he got the coin outside his jacket. Then, he turned back to Evie.

She looked up into his face and screamed, "Rick! Why are you doing this to me? Go away! Leave me alone. Where's Jonathan?" Evie pushed him away and ran into the stockroom, locking the door behind her.

Jonathan panicked. Oh, damn it! Now, what have I done? The coin was visible again, so, that's not it. But now she doesn't want Rick. I'm so confused.

Brian spotted Evie and Rick at the back of the store but he still could not find Jonathan. Finally, he decided to leave Vid-Mart and continue to keep watch over MixMatcher's kiosk, just in case Jonathan returned. He was surprised when minutes later, he saw Jonathan run out of Vid-Mart.

CHAPTER 43

When Evie finished work, she met Brian and went right home. He wanted to talk to her about Jonathan but he was getting very strange feelings emanating from her.

"I am concerned about your behavior, Evie. You seem agitated and confused and you are unusually quiet," Brian began. "I would not normally presume to interfere in your personal life, however it seems quite obvious something has caused you a great deal of distress?"

Evie tried to answer but instead she got very agitated. "Please Brian. I know you care and want to help but please, just leave it alone and leave me alone." Evie continued the drive home in silence.

Once home, Evie pulled the car into the garage and got out without waiting for Brian. She ran into the house and went straight up to her room.

"Was that Evie we just heard stomping up the stairs?" Vivian asked Martin, as she went to greet Brian.

"If I didn't know better, from the sound, I would have thought Brad was home again!" he replied.

"Very funny!"

Martin just shrugged, said hello to Brian and went back to his paperwork.

Vivian was surprised that her daughter didn't even come in to say hello.

"Evie is very upset and not acting herself," Brian told his mother. "From what I have observed, she is not the only one. I have also observed erratic behavior from her friends, Jonathan and Rick."

Brian then went on to explain what he had witnessed that day, including Jonathan being in one place one moment and then disappearing the next. "I was going to suggest to Evie that we gather everyone involved together to talk but she never gave me a chance. I believe when we get all the facts we will find that MixMatcher is how Controller is manipulating the strange events surrounding Evie and the others.

"Brian I'm sure if Evie didn't want to talk to you about what's bothering her, she probably won't tell anyone," his mother said and then commented, "after all, dating during teenage years can get messy. Martin, what do you think?"

"I was never very good at understanding teens, or dating, so I'm not sure, at this point. But, it sounds like everyone is having dating woes. Maybe it's too much of a coincidence to be ignored. Viv, why don't you talk with Evie and then we can decide what to do."

Vivian had to coax Evie to unlock her bedroom door but once she did, she fell into her mother's arms and cried.

An hour later, Vivian went to the kitchen to prepare some calming tea for her daughter. Martin and Brian joined her. She told them what she'd learned, which involved Evie, Rick and Jonathan. "Evie is so confused now, she doesn't know if she was with Rick, Jonathan or what." Vivian left out the part about Evie's sexual feelings toward Rick but included the full extent of emotional trauma.

Then, she summed it all up, "Even without doing any testing, I can tell you, in no uncertain terms, that Evie has the same problem as we've been seeing in the other students. I'll even go one step further, after listening to her version of what's been happening, I would put money on Rick and Jonathan exhibiting the same signs, depression, confusion, anger, all these have been manipulated in the name of love. We must get to the bottom of this, now!"

First Martin called Jonathan and then he got a number from Web Directory for Rick Armitage.

Then Vivian took the tea upstairs to Evie; with a speech prepared for her daughter. "Rick and Jonathan are both very anxious to find out what's going on and they've agreed to come right over."

At first Evie was angry, "Mom, please! How could you contact them? This is a direct violation of my confidence! Can't we call them back and just leave it alone?"

"No, my darling, we can't." Her mother sat down next to her to give Evie the comfort she knew she needed. "You are not thinking clearly. From everything you've told me, it seems that you, Rick and Jonathan are now also victims of whatever is going on in Island Falls."

Her words hit Evie hard and she didn't want to believe any of this could be happening to her. But, after a while her mother convinced her to at least give the meeting a chance.

The doorbell rang and Brian went downstairs to the lab. From there, he and Rosie would monitor the conversations through the intercom system. Hopefully they could come up with some answers as to what was happening to the three teens.

Vivian went to the door and welcomed Rick and Jonathan, who just happened to arrive at the same time. She ushered them into the living room, where Evie was already seated on the couch. They nodded their greetings but Evie looked away from both of them. Her eyes were red and puffy and she didn't want them to see that she'd been crying.

One word led to another and the three teens began to argue amongst themselves. "I can't deal with this," Evie said, getting up to leave.

Her mother reached for her hand, "I know this is painful but we need to work this through. Running away isn't going to produce answers," she turned to the boys, "neither is fighting."

Evie sat back down.

"We know the three of you have issues and that you're all very confused about the events of the last few days. We believe, if we can put all the pieces together, we should be able to get to the bottom of this. Please just try and bear with us."

Evie tried to whisper to her mom, "Okay but this is very embarrassing for me, so can we just get on with it."

She patted her daughter's hand and said, "We believe you've all been manipulated."

"Dr. Kane, what do you mean, 'manipulated?'" Rick asked.

"I would rather hold off answering that question, until we have more facts but, just know that we have strong enough suspicions to convince us this meeting was imperative. The only way to get to the bottom of what you're each experiencing is to figure out the role you have each played and how you have interacted with each other."

Everyone started to talk at once, so Martin broke in suggesting that they question each one of them, privately.

Vivian and Evie went into the kitchen to talk. Martin tried to sort out Jonathan's story, in the living room and then heard an entirely different version from Rick, in the library. It didn't take long to see there were very different versions, of the same event.

Vivian and Martin discussed their findings out of hearing range of the others. "Martin, it's unbelievable that anyone could've engineered this but they each perceive the exact same events but they are totally different."

"Yes, very clever, isn't it? Just like victims of an accident, they each have their own recollection of the same event."

"Yes, but they each have their own personal reaction, unique to them. Here we are seeing the exact same results, confusion, frustration, anxiety, anger and stress all pointing to a deep psychological trauma. Can you imagine the number of scenarios required to produce the exact same response in three individuals, the numbers must be astronomical?"

Martin turned to his wife, "Viv, I'm sure this isn't an accident, or random happening, this is a calculated outcome to a very calculated stimulus, something only a very sophisticated mind could conceive."

"Or a computer virus?"

"Yes Viv, or a computer virus! Let's get the kids back into the living room and see if we can substantiate the connection in this fiasco between Controller and MixMatcher.

Jonathan was in the living room when Vivian returned with Evie. He started to apologize but she ignored him. Evie turned to her mother, "I really can't take any more of this! Please, now that you know what happened, can't I just go back to my room?"

"I wish you could Evie but I need you to bear with us, just a little longer."

Martin and Rick had somewhat the same conversation as they returned to the living room. Martin asked them all to remain calm and listen. "There doesn't seem to be any way to determine exactly what really happened, or why all of you see things so differently."

As Jonathan listened he wondered, Did I start all this? All I wanted was to go out with Evie? Oh Evie, I'm so sorry! Then Jonathan shifted his focus. Boy, am I glad I didn't mention anything about the medallion to Dr. Kane. He'd string me up for what I've done.

Dr. Kane continued, "We'd like to first rule out any possible physical cause."

"Mom, I know you want to find the answer but I don't feel very good."

Rick could see the anguish in her face. He moved to her side and sat down next to her. "This is probably hardest on you Evie but if you can hang in there, maybe your parents can find the answers for us."

Evie couldn't help thinking that the words sound more like the Rick she fell for.

Jonathan shuddered, as Evie looked into Rick's eyes. The expression of love on her face was obvious, even to him. I'm glad I decided not to wear the medallion like Mrs. MixMatcher said I had to, he thought, just looking at them together, I can see how much Evie really loves Rick. She'll never feel that way about me, Mrs. MixMatcher, or not.

In his mind, Jonathan conceded and then knew what he had to do. He turned to Evie, "Rick is right, we really need to do this."

Evie briefly took her eyes from Rick and responded, "I'll try." She turned to her parents and asked, "So, what do we do first?"

Rick gently took her hand in his and held it, as he listened to what her father had in mind.

"Our preliminary tests will include, blood work, brain wave analysis. These tests are just to be sure there aren't any physical or mental abnormalities. After that, we should be able to tell you more."

Brian heard them coming down to the lab and ducked into the den. He switched on the audio link and heard his mother explaining about the test she was setting up to conduct.

While Vivian was processing the blood work, Martin made an excuse and went into the den to discuss the situation with Brian.

When he returned, Martin pulled Vivian aside. "How are the tests looking?"

"Just as we suspected, everything's normal. I just turned on the electroencephalograph for you."

"Brian had an idea but let's see what this round of testing shows, before we take any other steps. He's on an audio link and will be in the den if we need his input."

It took an hour for Martin to do the brain scans. He started with Jonathan and attached one electrode to the cerebral cortex and the other to the scan analyzer. The machine did the rest.

Then, he hooked Rick up and Evie was last. He asked each one questions while the scan was proceeding and watched the electro-corticograph measure the response. When all the responses were input, he removed the probes.

"Well Dad, do you have any answers?" Evie asked.

"Rosie and your mother are finishing up the blood results and comparing the scans and as soon as everything is analyzed, we hope to have an answer."

"Uh, Rosie, whose Rosie? I thought we were the only ones involved in this!" All of a sudden Rick felt very uncomfortable with the thought that someone else was now involved.

Evie chuckled, "Oh Rick, Rosie's not a person, she's my parent's computer."

On a loud-speaker they all heard, "Thank you for reminding me of my true station in life, Missy Evie," Rosie chimed in.

Rick was somewhat embarrassed but relieved.

Turning to the three participants, Martin said, "I know this has been very difficult but I'm sure it'll prove worthwhile."

He watched as Rick got up from the examination table and went to help Evie. From the smile on his daughter's face, he knew things were better all ready.

Vivian suggested Evie take Jonathan and Rick upstairs to the kitchen for something to eat, while they finish in the lab.

As soon as they left, Brian joined his parents. After twenty minutes, they all agreed; the results were irrefutable.

"Yes, except for that one factor, I do believe Brian has the right answer."

"I agree," Vivian said, "let's go test it!"

Martin and Vivian entered the kitchen. The anxious look on everyone's face needed an immediate answer. He pulled up a chair for Vivian and then got her something to drink. "Sorry to keep you waiting. We wanted to be doubly sure of our findings before we brought our conclusions to you." Martin positioned himself behind Vivian and addressed the anxiously waiting faces. "The tests were all negative and the responses were all the same, except for Jonathan's."

"Me, what's wrong with me?" Jonathan started to panic.

"There is nothing wrong with you but your body chemistry shows signs of an addiction but, to what, we can't seem to pin down."

"Please, Jonathan if there's something you haven't told us...." Vivian asked.

Oh man! The candy! That must be it. Ever since Sheila got me hooked on that stuff, I've been nuts. I can't tell them that, Evie will never want to see me again! "I'm not uh, sure but," feeling the coin in his pocket Jonathan knew he could no longer hide what he'd done, "yes, okay." Jonathan slowly withdrew it from his pocket. "Evie, I'm sorry, I just wanted you to love me."

"What are you talking about?" she asked. But, the answer became obvious when he stood up and placed the necklace in plain sight.

The room grew silent and all that could be heard were gasps, as Jonathan transformed into Rick. Next were their responses. First Vivian, next Martin and then Rick.

"I'd never have believed it if I hadn't seen it with my own eyes."

"I still don't believe it!"

"What the hell is going on?"

Evie didn't say a word, she just screamed hysterically, over and over, again. Vivian grabbed her daughter and removed her from the room.

Martin went over to Jonathan and removed the coin and he transformed back to Jonathan.

"See, Dr. Kane, whatever just happened is what's been going on, so can you tell me what got Evie so upset?"

"Jonathan, aren't you aware of what happens when you put that medallion on?"

"No, so will somebody please clue me in."

"You, you, were me, see? No, how can you see?" Rick got tongue tied trying to explain his own confusion. He got up and started pacing.

"What are you talking about?" Jonathan shouted.

"Okay, both of you calm down and let me try to explain."

Martin waited for both of them to sit down again. "First, where did you get this coin?"

Jonathan knew it was too late to lie. "Mrs. MixMatcher, in the mall. I saw this ad and I...."

"Did she give you any information about it?"

"No, all she said was that if I wanted Evie to fall in love with me I needed to wear it whenever I was with her."

"Jon, you didn't know that when you put that coin on you look and act like Rick."

"That can't be!" Jonathan exclaimed.

"Oh sure, c'mon Jon. Like you didn't know. You did this so Evie could fall in love with you but not you, me, as me...?" Rick was angry now and even more confused!

"No, that's impossible! Mrs. MixMatcher said that was just a 'love transference.' Maybe Evie hadn't gotten over you yet and .... Well maybe, she might sometimes look at me and wish it was you... but it's not you, it's me!

Dr. Kane, help me out here. I can understand her delusions but, not both of you, too. You can't possibly see me that way, too!" I must be crackin' up!"

Martin tried to sort out all the details for them all. "I know this is very confusing, it is for all of us but we're finally getting to the truth, now. Jonathan, when you have the coin on, we see Rick! You even talk like Rick. Then, as soon as you remove the coin, we see you again."

Oh crap. This has gone too far! "I need to tell you the truth about everything." Jonathan took a deep breath; sat down and put his head in his hands.

Dr. Kane and Rick could see how hard this was for Jon and gave him a minute to compose himself.

Jonathan looked up and with the saddest tone in his voice began to explain. "I guess it all started with Sheila giving out this candy. It was like nothing I'd ever tasted before but I didn't know it had something to do with Cracko, Controller's first hologram, until I was hooked.

"I had it really bad for that stuff and still get cravings sometimes. But, the funny part was the more I ate the more I became a different person. But, you see, I was hoping that Evie would notice that different person."

Dr. Kane could see how hard it was for Jonathan and offered him a glass of water. Jon nodded and took a sip before continuing.

While he was drinking the water, Jon was having a flashback to the one time with Evie in the woods but as much as he had replayed that scene one hundred times, this time he realized the truth! "There was this one time…I really thought Evie was starting to notice me… and really liked the 'new Jon,' but, I was wrong, very wrong and it never happened again.

"So, when Mrs. MixMatcher came to town, she convinced me she could help me win Evie. She asked me a lot of questions and then had me get samples of hair from Evie and Rick and when I did…"

Rick abruptly interrupted. "How the hell did you get my hair?"

Trying to keep things calm Martin suggested, "Rick, let's not worry about that now. Please continue, Jon."

"Mrs. MixMatcher gave me the coin and told me I had to wear it all the time, if Evie was going to love me."

"Well, it all makes sense now," Martin said. "I'll keep this coin, Jonathan."

"Uh, sure but maybe we should just destroy it and..."

"Jonathan I'm sure that would be best for you, right now," Martin was very obviously annoyed, "but, that unfortunately isn't the answer for Rick and Evie."

Martin was pulling no punches with Jon for what he put his daughter through. "You started this nightmare. Now, you will have to see it through. I want you two to stay here and try not kill each other. I'm going to take this to the lab and run a complete analysis."

Rick was curious, "What do you expect to find, Dr. Kane?"

"I believe I'll find that this coin contains embedded traces of DNA from all three of you and also some type of neural transmitter."

As he was leaving Martin turned and asked, "Do I need to separate you two?"

"No, Dr. Kane, I'll keep it cool. I'm beginning to see we're all unwitting casualties of this game," Rick said, as he thought of Sheila.

Dr. Kane gave him a look of doubt.

"Honest, I'm cool! I don't like being someone else's pawn. Go do what you can to fix this."

Brian joined Martin in the lab and together with Rosie's help they quickly finished the analysis.

Martin went upstairs to find his wife and asked her to return to the kitchen with Evie to discuss the results.

Evie was very reluctant and was fighting and pleading with her mother. "Please Mom, I can't take any more of this!"

Vivian wrapped her arms around her daughter to envelop her; she wanted to take away her pain. "Evie, I know how hard this is but I believe your father would not want to bring you back downstairs unless he had an explanation. Please just trust us…, at least a little while longer.

When Evie and Vivian returned to the kitchen Martin looked into the faces of the three-young people and hoped what he was about to say would ease their hurts.   "The tests confirmed our suspicions. The actual process is very complicated and really quite ingenious. Simply put, just think of the coin as being a mirror and like a mirror, an image is reflected. In this case the image is projected from the DNA embedded in the coin, back onto the person wearing it."

"Then, I'm confused Dad, why would we see Rick?"

"That's simple. Only Rick's DNA is embedded into the coin. There is also a neural transmitter and voice simulator present, which projects his image and personality traits, mannerisms, even voice, sound and tone."

Rick asked, "Okay, so maybe that explains why Mrs. MixMatcher wanted Jonathan to get my hair but why Evie's and Jon's?"

"Their DNA are also present but only in the projection transmitter."

"Huh?" Now, Jonathan was getting totally confused.

"The transmitter is keying into Evie's DNA and she in turn is reacting as if you were Rick. When you wear the coin so Evie can see it, you are the only one who doesn't know that you are in effect, Rick! Everyone who sees you, sees Rick, while you have no awareness of the transformation."

Martin, still seeing confused faces tried to give them some more information. It is like a laser beam zeroing in on the optic nerve and then following a pathway to the base of the brain. So, you see only what is projected. Then that laser lodges a signal onto the pituitary gland. At that point the signal transmits a pulse wave that controls the production of endorphins. These endorphins cause extreme reactions of pleasure, or pain, love, hate, happiness, anger…. Does that help make it clearer?"

Heads nodded. I can't believe I've hurt Evie this way. Jon burst out, "Evie, I'm so sorry! I never wanted to hurt you. Dr. Kane, please tell me there is a way to stop this chain of events that I've started?" Jonathan pleaded, holding back his tears.

"Jonathan you're right, your desire for love started this unfortunate chain of events." Vivian went over to him, "but, in the long run, your situation may prove to be the solution."

"Now I really don't understand, Dr., uh, Mrs. K.," Rick said. "This scheme, if I have it right, is MixMatcher's way to turn a profit but it only involved the three of us?"

"No Rick, I'm afraid MixMatcher has been playing the same game with a lot of other Island Falls students, many of whom have been turning up sick. But we have just concluded that this is not just the work of Mrs. MixMatcher but Controller!"

"No, you're wrong!" Jonathan shouted, shocked at her conclusion, "Mrs. MixMatcher isn't a helper, hologram, or evil, she's the nicest, most understanding…."

"Jonathan, we're sure now. Mrs. MixMatcher is not just Controller's latest helper, she is actually Controller's newest hologram."

Vivian held up her hand to stop him, "I know you believe she's just a sweet helpful old lady and she may be, that's what makes her even more dangerous than Cracko or QuizMaster."

"No, I can't believe that. I saw Cracko and Rick and I saw what Controller did to Brad through QuizMaster but Mrs. MixMatcher isn't like that, she gave me cookies and took the time to listen...." Jonathan was getting upset again.

Vivian tried to comfort him through this new realization. "I know you only want to see her as good but we can't ignore the facts. We have examined the technology used to create the coin and when added to your story and what's been happening to the three of you..., a little old lady didn't do this!"

"No, I know you are wrong! Maybe she's as much a victim as I was.

"Jon, you need to calm down and listen," Martin advised. We are not yet sure about the role of the cookies, they may be nothing, or they may be similar to the candy, to make you more vulnerable but we may never know. As far as listening to you, I know how much that meant but from what you've told us, it was done purely to further the hologram's needs. And, it worked! Don't you see. You're ready to defend everything, no matter what the evidence shows."

"Jon, can't you see, my parents are right?" Finally, Evie was beginning to understand everything. "You're so brainwashed you can't see that we're all victims."

Jonathan still didn't want to believe it. "I need more proof. How do you know she's a hologram?"

Vivian sat down next to him to give some motherly support. "After you told us what happened, we sent someone we trust to the mall to see what they might be able to find out. It turns out when the booth closed down, Mrs. MixMatcher disappeared into thin air. There was no trace of her anywhere and even her booth up and vanished...as if she were never there!

Jonathan smiled for the first time. "Now you have given me something I can tell you is wrong. Whenever

I went to see Mrs. MixMatcher she and the booth were always there! So, your information is wrong!"

No, Jon, we are sorry it's not! As this person approached both the booth and MixMatcher were there." Martin suggested, "Don't you see, she is a mirage, for lack of a better word. She is there and projecting herself on your mind and for all to see and then just as quickly she can be gone! So, now that we have a better understanding of what happened, here's what we'd like to do. Years ago, I worked with Dr. Remy Marcel…"

Both Rick and Jonathan had heard of Dr. Marcel in physics class and were very impressed but they were also confused about what that had to do with them.

Feeling the tug of the past, Martin pulled a chair to the table and sat down next to Vivian. "During our time together, Dr. Marcel taught me many useful techniques, one was a combination of biofeedback and hypnosis."

Dr. Kane went on to explain, "It's really rather simple. The subject is put into a state of relaxation, which releases tension from all body parts and in turn frees up the mind. It's a way to utilize more of your brain's resources."

What Martin couldn't say was that Brian was the one who suggested the technique. Martin thought how strange it was that Brian exhibited the same knowledge as his friend, Remy. "A friend recently reminded me of the procedure and I believe it could work in this situation."

Rick tried to get a better handle on what he'd heard. "Let me see if I have this right. This procedure you want to try, you believe it'll help us deal with what's happened, while freeing us from the agony of whatever game Controller and MixMatcher have put us through."

"Yes, Rick." Martin nodded, "You've summed it up. Now, you each have to decide if you will allow us to proceed?"

Vivian suggested, "Maybe it'll help if you understand exactly what this entails." She looked at each of them as she laid out the step by step course of action.

Rick listened carefully and then asked, "I've heard that the mind can block things it doesn't want to deal with, what if these thoughts are blocked, or hidden?"

"That was why we spent extra time in the lab analyzing the coin and each of your brain scans. We did a neural net mapping and know exactly which sections of the brain have been affected and that's the only area we'll target. There are no adverse effects and when it's over, you'll still have the memories but you will be totally detached from them, as if they happened to someone else."

"What will prevent us from being vulnerable to Controller in the future?" This time the question was from Evie.

"We'll implant a type of post-hypnotic suggestion that'll set up a mind shield to block any future invasion."

Everyone agreed to the procedure.

Martin went and checked with Brian to be sure he had finished in the lab. Before going back upstairs, Martin instructed Brian and Rosie on the next steps.

Brian went back into the den and his father went upstairs to gather everyone for the procedure.

They all returned to the lab.

Rosie had finished each of the neural net mappings needed for the hypno-eradication.

Vivian had everyone get comfortable and then instructed each of them on deep breathing and relaxation.

Martin connected the monitors which allowed Rosie and Brian to monitor their vitals and run continuous brain scans, focusing on the trauma centers.

Martin first guided Jonathan through his journey to the memory center, while the others stayed in a state of relaxation. They were each aware of their surroundings but unaffected by anything external they might hear.

Martin helped Jonathan find the memories that pertained to Mrs. MixMatcher. Jon calmly revealed the details of his association with the hologram and the story of the coin.

Everything was going well and then, Jon became agitated. "You don't understand, Mrs. MixMatcher. Evie accused me of doing all sorts of bad things to her. But, the craziest thing, she swears her date was with Rick, remember, he's the, 'other guy'. How can that be?"

"That's it!" Rosie confirmed. "Lock on and begin cortical stimulation."

Vivian calmly instructed Jonathan, "Think only about the most pleasant experiences of your life." In the next moment, Jonathan began to smile.

"Neutralization complete," Rosie stated.

Evie easily reached her memories and beamed as she talked about her date with Rick. Suddenly, she became frightened and her vital signs elevated.

Vivian kept a close watch on her daughter. She held her hand and told her she was safe. But suddenly Evie started screaming, "You were not there Jonathan and you have no idea what happened between Rick and me!"

Her tone turned from confusion to frustration, when she related that Rick acted as if he never had a date with her. "Hello! Hello! Is that all you have to say and just walk away, like nothing's happened? How can you, after everything that happened between us last night?" Shaking her head, she continued, "Rick, I know nights like last night probably happen to you all the time and then you forget them but it doesn't work that way for me. Tell me why you are playing this cruel game. Did Sheila put you up to it, is that it?"

"Got it!" Rosie confirmed, "Evie's thoughts were harder to get than Jon's, which probably meant that Rick's thoughts will be the hardest to retrieve."

Vivian breathed a sigh of relief. She hated putting her daughter through that but there was no choice. Her mother kissed her forehead and Evie immediately calmed down.

"I wish you could teach me that!" her father said.

"That's a 'mother only' trick!" Vivian smiled.

When Evie was relaxed again, Martin went on to Rick whose reaction was totally different from the other two. Rick was very sure of what had happened and was totally baffled by Evie's statements of his involvement. He claimed to have never made a date with Evie and swore that he didn't go out with her. But, the more he spoke the more even Rick became agitated and all his words became filled with doubts.

Martin calmed him down and got his vital signs were stable. He motioned for Vivian to join him outside the lab.

"Rosie keep an eye on the three monitors while we talk," he instructed.

They went to the den to talk with Brian. "It seems we would need to probe beyond where it would still be safe, to get to Rick's psyche and his memories. Any suggestions," Martin asked.

Brian suggested, "I believe I can get to Rick through the main computer and patch into his mind through

Rosie. I can set a mantra through a mind meld in an interloping phase, until it reaches his distressed area."

"You've only melded with Brad and Evie, can you be sure you can establish a one-way link without harm to yourself, or Rick?"

"I have experimented with just such a thing, without any detrimental effects." He vividly recalled that special night he melded with Robin. He touched her and without being aware of it, for a brief second, he felt like he reached deep inside her mind.

Brian's assurances helped Martin and Vivian decide to proceed.

Back in the lab, Martin and Vivian set up the link from Brian to Rosie. When they reached the words, "But, it was you Rick, it was you," and he reacted, Rosie confirmed, "The point! A moment later the mantra was working."

Twenty minutes later, "Success," Rosie confirmed but Brian knew it even before she did.

Vivian smiled, "First phase, complete. Rosie report full analysis."

"Okay, Dr. Mrs. K. But, can I stick my two cents in first?"

Martin stuck his opinion in, "Could we stop you if we wanted to?"

"Gee, Dr. Mrs. K., I believe you voice and demeanor and even sex all changed in that second.

"Okay you two, neutral corners," Vivian admonished both of them. "Go ahead Rosie."

"Thank you. Now as I was saying, Jonathan, the catalyst. Analyzing his version and his brain's responses, he's more sensitive to suggestion, than the others. It may be because of his 'candy experience,' and his new-found personality changes but his brain waves definitely show increased activity. These areas of the brain's cortex now shown on the monitor in red have been over-stimulated.

"Evie, the victim. Her DNA predicted her responses to Jonathan and then to his metamorphosis as Rick. When Evie relived those moments, her brain patterns changed drastically and she exhibited signs of irrational behavior, confusion, paranoia and depression.

"Rick, the unwilling participant. His biological make-up suggests a very adventurous nature but one guided by logic. He would eventually succumb because his confusion would lead to his own doubts.

"All in all, a perfect example of 'only the strong will survive,' and, in this case, a perfect 'tri-fecta!' I believe this is Controller's best work.

"I believe it is safe to conclude, when Jonathan went to Mrs. MixMatcher, Controller already knew he was extremely susceptible, from the way he handled the candy issue. The conclusion would be that Jonathan would probably be likely to accept Evie's love transference to Rick for a while but eventually he would admit failure and self-destruct. They used him and made Evie and Rick a part of the equation.

"So, here's my two cents! This was an experiment with three different personalities, that proved how to break each one and come up with an obedient follower or a total broken shell of a person. Either way Controller and MixMatcher win!"

"Your two cents may be right on the mark, Rosie."

"Thank you, Dr. Mrs. K, it is nice to know I am appreciated!"

"Oh Martin, I think you hurt her feelings!" Vivian joked.

"Just to be clear, I have no feelings to be hurt but if I did, I would agree with the Dr. Mrs."

Martin felt ganged up on and looked to Brian who was busy.

Rosie reported, "My scans now show they're each responding and the targeted areas are now exhibiting normal response to stimuli. That is, 'normal for teenagers!'"

"Now, it's my turn to finish the job," Martin said as he sat down. In calm soothing voice instructed, "When you open your eyes, you will feel calm and relaxed and have no animosities toward the other two. You will know the events occurred but you will each feel as if the whole situation was like a dream and therefore, you will not be directly affected by it anymore. I will begin counting now and when I reach ten, you will come to full awareness. Ready! One. Two, you are beginning to feel more aware. Three. Four...."

After a few hours of monitoring their vitals and talking with them separately and together, Vivian suggested the boys were fine to go home and get some rest. Her final words were, "The best thing to do is put this whole episode behind you."

Rick and Jonathan were calm and friendly toward one another. They thanked the Kane's and said goodbye to Evie.

Jonathan told Evie he would always love her but hoped they could go back to being, just friends!

Evie kissed him on the cheek!

Rick took Evie's hand and she beamed.

He looked into her eyes and got lost in the glow.

Rick broke the contact but winked at her as he headed for the front door.

Evie remained seated on the couch, eyeing him as he left.

Her mother watched the exchange and smiled.

When the boys were gone, Martin called Brian to join them in the living room.

"I just can't believe how I've been acting, so erratic and out of control, you'd think my BREV training would have counted for something." Evie was embarrassed.

"It might have but you forget what we learned... strong emotions inhibit our powers."

"Yeah Brian, you haven't got any idea how strong these were!"

"Evie, I need to ask you a question." Her mother had a curious expression on her face. "There was something that came out during the procedure that had nothing to do with Rick or Jonathan."

Oh shit, not the modeling incident. "Oh really, what?"

"You kept repeating I have to apologize to Ginger, what's that all about?"

"Ginger? Oh Mom! I yelled at her. Remember, I told you she's the one from the Hot Spot Shoppe who's sweet on Brad. She's really nice and I was really on edge and acting like a real bitc...oh, sorry, a spoiled brat. I reamed her out the other day, for no good reason."

"Well, it certainly appears to be weighing on your mind. I'm sure you can apologize and make it up to her."

"Yeah, I will. Maybe I can find a way to get Brad interested in her, that would sure help." Evie smiled and felt better than she had in the last few days. "Now, can you fill me in about the rest of what happened?"

Her father explained all the details and then concluded, "We've figured out that Mrs. MixMatcher is definitely Controller's hologram. She attracts students using 'love' as the bait and with a caring, grandmotherly type attitude lures them into her web. Then, when she has them hooked, the hologram creates havoc like you went through with Jonathan and Rick and that eventually destroys the victim's ability to deal with emotional situations."

Her mother added, "We believe that one of two things comes of this. Either the victims are traumatized, as you three were, or they are immune to the manipulation but eager to enjoy the rewards. For the trauma victims, the results are comparable to lost sheep that need a leader and we believe Controller is eagerly waiting to take away their pain and turn them into loyal followers."

"And for the others?" Evie questioned.

"We couldn't understand that either until we realized and army needs leaders. The group that survive being emotionally challenged are the real army. They want the glory and believe Controller is the way to seize the day!"

"This sounds so unbelievable." Evie almost couldn't believe what she was being told. She shook her head and finally concluded, "But, I suppose when Controller's involved, anything is possible. You know I have an idea. Since Controller saw fit to give me a first-hand experience, maybe it's time I return the favor."

"What do you have in mind?" her brother asked.

"Let's set Mrs. MixMatcher up on a date. A date with The BREV Force!"

EPILOGUE

"Frederick, I know they are just delaying me. Something is going on and they don't want to include me. You heard that message from Martin, he thinks I am just an old coot who gets in the way. Well, I'll show him! I'll show all of them! And the council of the Alliance, telling me where I will be and when. Who do they think they are? I was a member of that council when most of them were in diapers! But very soon the final event will unfold and they will all see...they will all be sorry they discarded me. They will find out who exactly is in control! He turned to his brother, Frederick, get him now! It is time!

"Ori please, he pleaded. This has gone too far. He won't help you and this time your methods will probably kill him!

"Then so be it! If he will not give me the information I need he is of no use to me...and if he dies, so be it. It will be his own fault."

"But Ori, we cannot commit murder!"

"Why not, we already have.... ha ha ha!

THE END

No, Not the End! There is still much more in the next adventure of the BREV Force Trilogy.

What is Controller up to with Mrs. MixMatcher and what's love got to do with it? Will there be another hologram? Don't miss the action and suspense as The BREV force prepare for their date with the hologram!

What will happen in the meantime? Will Evie really be okay with Rick and Jonathan? Will Brad ever get out of prison? Will the Kane's find the way to neutralize Controller before their children, The BREV Force face off in another encounter?

R U the 1?

Keep reading to find the answer to these and so many other questions facing The BREV Force?
Code 47 to BREV Force
CONTROLLER THE FINAL BATTLE

SPECIAL LIMITED TIME OFFER
REVIEW CRACKO & QUIZMASTER MIXMATCHER on "3" social media platforms and we will send you the e-book *Code 47 to BREV Force - The Final Battle*
FREE
Post links to reviews at
http://www.goldenquillpress.com/form.php

Share your thoughts and Join the world of BREV Force – email: info@goldenquillpress.com

Interested in writing a book?
See how this book was written read, "How To Write Your Book From an Idea to Your Finished Story." By F. Barish-Stern

visit http://www.goldenquillpress.com

AUTHOR'S BIO

F. Barish-Stern has been an author for over 40 years and wrote the BREV Force Trilogy to interest her sons in reading. Her "Rainbow City" won first place and was published in "The Arts Newspaper." She has written many books including, "TELL IT TO THE FUTURE" and "NEW HORIZONS." Barish-Stern has developed writing programs for all ages.

Over the years, she has expanded her teaching to one–on–one and has worked with many authors editing their books. Recently she co-wrote "How to Write from an Idea to Your Published Story," a step by step guide to the writing process for anyone who wants to write. She has also turned her love of writing to children and is currently tutoring children to develop their imaginations into brilliantly told stories.

Barish-Stern has recently added photography to her creative interests and has won a major prize for her first exhibit. Also, her photograph, "Falls at the Bridge" was exhibited at the Art Museum of Western Virginia. All her art work are reproduced exclusively as Art on Gold.

BY: Francine Cefola (Barish-Stern) & Bobbi R. Madry Poetry is the art that speaks to our hearts and minds. Like a beautiful painting or a musical composition, this collection of poetry will take you into worlds limited only by your imagination... from the splendor of a sunset to tasting candy, to memories from a rocking chair. These Poems Take You To Your Own New Horizons!!

CHALLENGING MESSAGES FROM BEYOND
BY: Marjorie Struck
Does the Spiritual World have a message for us? Can we learn to understand that communication? Marjorie Struck certainly believes. This is her personal story of how a message form Beyond changed her life. Informative, at times shocking but ultimately a journey that reveals a side of the spiritual world that can transform you-forever. Marjorie invites you along to witness how this revelation helped her understand the connection between life and beyond- and how souls in the after-life help us to find the Light!

COMPASSION'S LURE
BY: Kathleen Lukens
This is the story of a visionary. Kathy Lukens founder of Camp Venture - advocate for all people with special needs stood up for the rights and deeds of those who could not fight for themselves. With words backed by tireless efforts, Kathy made the impossible happen for the developmentally disabled- a home and the proper attention to their needs. She was truly one of the Great Women of our times.

the GRANPA SPIDER stories
BY: Granpa Spider
A delightful story for children of all ages. Granpa Spider weaves a web of adventure and intrigue, mystery and fun! Along with his Arachnid friends, Penelope, The Colonel and others we journey into the exciting world of the web. As Shamrock McGee says, "May the wind be at your web. May your web be in the trees. May cicada be chattering. May there be a host of bees, And, may the web that you spin be serving all your needs."

MAE SINGS ABOUT SHORT VOWELS
BY: Karen A. Coleman

"Mae Sings About Short Vowels," was developed by Karen Coleman, as a method for teaching music, while learning vowel sounds. The book uses songs and a vowel recognition technique in an interactive way to help students improve reading skills while learning musical notes

OPENING THE DOOR
TO A BRIGHTER FUTURE
BY: Daniel Windheim

The experiences Dan experienced after he sustained a traumatic brain injury and the efforts he made to recover and build a productive life, are highlighted in this book. These ten key strategies could help individuals in their recovery efforts and shares the experiences of some survivors as they struggle to return to a healthy life. Dan notes, 'There is not time to waste focusing on the negative but we need to take what we have and make the most out of things."

THE POEM BOOK
BY: Daniel Windheim

A brain injury victim of a car accident young Daniel Windheim's life is turned upside down. He turns to poetry to express his frustration, anger and to take the reader on a beautiful journey through recuperation and new life challenges. Daniel Windheim is truly a shining hero, overcoming life's worst experience. "I remain practical; but a realist and accept what I am. Life is good and there is goodness in life."

SWEET MERCY
BY: Rebecca H. Cofer

Katherine Ryder peels away the decades of family secrets to tell her story of growing up in Fairburn, Georgia at the turn of the century. 1900 She battles many obstacles to free herself from small town life and her autocratic mother and moves to Atlanta. In the big city she is betrayed by the man she loves. But her generous heart and hard work pay off, bringing her joy and fulfillment in the end.

THERE IS HOPE
BY: Debby Paine
There Is Hope is a collection of religious poetry about the struggles, pains questions and fears we all face. Debby's love of family, church and community is portrayed as she searches for and reaches toward God to find hope. These poems from the heart-for the heart, will reach out to everyone searching for hope. "Reach for it. Hold on to it. 'Hope is There.'"

Other books marketed by Golden Quill Press:
YOU ARE WHAT YOU WEAR
BY: William Thourlby
"First impressions" are lasting. YOU ARE WHAT YOU WEAR will help you make the right "first impression." Develop skills that are cost effective because they not only increase the quality of life in the workplace, contribute to employee morale and embellish the company image, they play a major role in developing a person's self-image and generating profits. The lack of these skills can be highly visible and costly for any person or company in every day and age.

PASSPORT TO POWER
BY: William Thourlby
Part practical, part primer, part visionary, Passport to Power, gives the reader background and formulas to follow to acquire and master international communication skills and provide the keys to unlocking human potential for success as a leader in the new global village of today.

www.ingramcontent.com/pod-product-compliance
Lightning Source LLC
Chambersburg PA
CBHW071450110726
47908CB00003B/580